CW00850609

Blood on the Cro

Book 1 in the

Struggle for a Crown Series

By

Griff Hosker

Contents

Blood on the Crown i
Prologue 1
Part One- Will son of Harry 3
Chapter 1 3
Chapter 2 14
Chapter 3 28
Chapter 4 37
Chapter 5 47
Chapter 6 56
Chapter 7 68
Chapter 8 80
Part Two- Harry of Lymm.. 89
Chapter 9 89
Chapter 10 96
Chapter 11 108
Chapter 12 129
Chapter 13 139
Chapter 14 148
Chapter 15 160
Chapter 16 169
Chapter 17 178
Chapter 18 192
Chapter 19 204
Epilogue 210
Glossary.. 211
Historical Notes... 212
Other books by Griff Hosker 214

Blood on the Crown

Published by Sword Books Ltd 2018

SWORD
BOOKS

Copyright ©Griff Hosker First Edition

Prologue

My father was not a cruel man. At least he said he was not being cruel when he beat me. He said that he was a hard man. When he punished me, he would say it was for my own good to make me as hard as him. He would beat me when he said I had made a mistake and that was often. He did it, he said, to make me a better man. Old Tom said when my father was drunk and unable to take a heavy leather belt, his baldric, to me, that my father was punishing me for the sins of my mother. She had run off when I had seen less than five summers and my father had been stuck with me. My mother was just a face which came to me in my dreams. She had been gone so long now that I could not remember her voice. Yet the smell of her hair still came to me. It was strange.

I had been with him and the Blue Company since the campaign which led to the Battle of Poitiers. I travelled around with the men of the Free Company. I did not wonder that my mother left my father. I remembered that before she had left he had often beaten her. He was too free with his hands, especially when he had had a drink, and that was too often for me. It never affected his ability to fight. He was one of Sir Hugh Calverley's men at arms, a member of the Blue Company. He was a mercenary, a sword for hire.

My name is Will son of Harry. My father says that I am useless baggage and he wished he was rid of me but the other men in the company seem to like me. For some reason, I have some skill with the horses and I am tall for my age and strong. The others do not think me useless for I was able to groom their horses, when they had them, and fetch them water. Old Tom commanded our men at arms and he liked me. Each time the company went to battle I prayed, not for my father to survive but Old Tom. If he lived then I might survive. I knew that was unusual. Most of the children born to men of the Blue Company barely survived birth. The handful of children who followed the company were little more than extra baggage but I worked. I did not fight, save to join the other boys with their slings, but I was there, with my dagger, if we were needed.

We had gone to Spain to help depose Peter the Cruel and we were led by Bertrand du Guesclin. He was a Breton. He knew his business and our forces succeeded in driving the Galician king from his throne and Henry of Trastámara, Peter the Cruel's brother was crowned King. It was a quick, almost bloodless victory and we were paid well. My father was happy. I was not beaten for three days for he was drunk and away from our camp for most of them. Our work done we camped and my father spent his money.

The battle resulted in Prince Edward being hired to retake Peter the Cruel's kingdom. As the free companies were made up of Englishmen and Gascons, we left Bertrand du Guesclin to take service with Prince Edward, the Black Prince. Sir Hugh said the free companies had to fight for Prince Edward for he was their natural lord. We marched from one camp and into the other. Such was the life of a sword for hire.

We followed the Black Prince. He led us to Portugal to reclaim the throne of the rightful ruler of that land. We heard that he had been promised gold and the crown of Galicia for Prince Edward's eldest son, Edward. To our company, it mattered not. So long as someone paid Sir Hugh then the men at arms and archers were happy enough. When pay was not forthcoming the Blue Company sought other paymasters. If they found none they became bandits. This was not England nor even Gascony. This was the hot lands of Northern Spain, Galicia and Castile. So long as I tended the horses and fetched and carried then I was useful and I would be retained. I could not wait to be a man so that I could stand up to my father. That would be some years away. I swore that, one day, I would be more than the boy who swept up the horse shit!

When we crossed into Spain and Portugal we entered a world I did not know. It was a world of heat and men who spoke a language I did not understand. The Prince had us fighting for someone else. My father seemed happy fighting there for the wine was cheap and plentiful. His face grew redder and the beatings more frequent. One day the beating was so bad that the men who had fought alongside my father had had enough. Old Tom took me from my father and appointed me to the company. I knew not why for I could not fight with the men; I was almost big enough but I did not think I had skills save that of looking after horses. I was, as my father, said, 'useless baggage.' That all changed that hot summer's evening, two days after the battle of Nájera when Old Tom swore me in as a member of the Blue Company. My father's former shield brothers took me and swore to train me as a warrior. My life changed in that instant. Had he not then I know I would not have attained the rank of gentleman. I would be lying dead in a ditch in Gascony.

Part One- Will son of Harry

Chapter 1

As we marched from Nájera to Burgos the army led by Prince Edward was in high spirits. I was in high spirits. I had recovered well from the last beating. I had eaten better and I was healing. My father lumbered at the rear of our column while I kept close to Old Tom. Old Tom was a gentleman and rode the best horse in the company. That was another reason he liked me. I had a way with horses. I understood them and his jet-black horse with the white blaze, Badger, responded well to me. When other horses had died in the heat Badger had flourished and Old Tom or, to give him his proper title, Captain Thomas of Lincoln kept me close to him for that reason. Whenever we stopped, he handed the reins to me knowing that when he returned to the saddle his horse would have been watered and had food. I often went without but his horse did not. I knew that my continued employment depended upon the horse. We had lost many horses in battle and in the heat of Spain.

We now sought horses whenever we stopped. We moved more quickly with horses.

I was employed now that I was of the Blue Company. I was not the ragged barefoot boy dressed in torn clothes which were neither changed nor washed. The Company had shared what they had. I was now warm and had sandals upon my feet. When I had been Harry of Lymm's son I was nothing. I ate the scraps my father left for me or I foraged for myself. I was a good forager. I knew how to steal food and how to hide it. I was like a squirrel. I collected all that I could and hid it. Some was hidden in the wagon we used to carry our weapons while I secreted such treasures as dried meat about my person. When I ate them, they might be pungent and sometimes mouldy but they were food. One of the most respected members of our company, Red Ralph, commented that had I had proper food then I would be a giant. I had begun to grow rapidly once I had the same food as the other men. Being employed meant that I had a share of the food and a share of the pay. The fact that the Prince had not paid us yet did not seem to bother the others. Prince Edward was known as a fair paymaster. When he was paid then we would be too. He had been hired by Peter the Cruel to retake his kingdom and, as it was rich, there was the promise of much gold and silver. The one exception was my father. He whinged, moaned and whined about the lack of pay. No pay meant no wine unless he could steal some. Old Tom shut him up and Harry of Lymm stared with hateful eyes at our Captain and the son who had deserted him.

I did fear for my life. My father bore grudges. There were few of the company who liked him. He had lost most of his friends either in battle or after he had changed. That had been when my mother left him. I learned more about my father as we marched. It came in snippets: a word here a phrase there, a look exchanged. I was clever and had quick wits. I learned more about my father in those months after I became a young would be warrior than in the preceding years.

As soon as I joined the company Old Tom gave me a short sword. We won more than we lost and when we won we took whatever the dead left. This had been a poor sword which was not worth selling but it would do for the boy who watched the horses, fetched the firewood and foraged for food. There was no scabbard and it was not a good blade but it was a weapon and better than the short knife I had. I slept with both close to me. I feared that my father would do me harm. Red Ralph also liked me. He had known my mother and had not liked it when my father had beaten her. Ralph told me that he would try to get me some boots and a leather jerkin when next we fought. The clothes I wore were thin and that did not matter in the heat of Spain but they were ragged. The men of the Blue Company were proud men. They all tried to wear the same. When they had first gone to war, they had all worn a blue plume fastened to their helmets. They had long gone but each wore a scarf of blue. It was useful. As we marched through Spain on the dusty roads the men used them to cover their mouths and faces. I now had one. It had belonged to One Eyed Stephen who had died at Nájera. His shield brothers had shared the rest of his goods amongst themselves but they agreed that I could have the blue scarf. Until I had a shield and skills then I would have no shield brothers. I would be the boy who ran errands for the Captain and senior sergeants.

The men I rode with had been the shield brothers of my father. That was no longer true. When my young, and, so the men told me, beautiful mother had left my father for a lord, Harry of Lymm had changed. He had always been a drinker. He had always been violent but my mother had been a good influence upon him. He was less violent but, as I grew older, he beat both of us. With her gone, I was beaten. He fought with other men and they gradually shunned him. His shield brothers sent him from their fires but retained me. They had known me since I had been born. They had liked my mother and I became part of their camp. I felt honoured. My father ended up at the camp fire of the worst of our company, the thieves and vagabonds.

The journey south was through hot lands and we stopped frequently. We had stopped at noon. It was too hot to travel too far in the heat. Men suffered and horses could die. Captain Tom slipped from the horse and handed me the reins. "Find him some shade, Will, and water."

"Aye Captain." That was another change. When I had been Harry of Lymm's boy I had called him master. Now he was my superior and I called him Captain.

"I will be with Sir Hugh. He wanted conference with me."

The village in which we had stopped was poor and I could not see a well. I had an important job and that was to look after Badger. I had to water the horse. When the men rode I would water theirs too but we had lost many and most of the men marched afoot. When we could we would take horses again for our strength lay in the speed of our movement and the combination of men at arms and the finest archers in the world. Taking Badger's reins, I led him between the buildings and down the slope. My days as a forager had taught me well. If there was water it would be lower down the slope and there would be a path which led to it. I stroked Badger's mane as I led the horse down the path. The path was well worn. I turned a corner and saw water bubbling from a rock. It was a spring. I cupped my hands and drank first to make certain that the water was safe for the horse. I knew my continued existence depended upon the horse. It tasted sweet and I filled my hands with the water and then allowed the horse to drink from them. I knew when he had had enough for he stopped and raised his head. His whinny was the sign that I could stop. I drank my fill and then filled the waterskin which hung from my belt. It took time.

I led Badger back up the path. He now needed food. Most of the villagers had fled at the arrival of our army. The ones who remained where the ones who saw an opportunity to ingratiate themselves with this Black Prince. They had gathered around him and the nobles to sell them whatever they could. I saw the door of an abandoned house swinging wide. Tying Badger to the door handle I slipped inside. I had not understood the language when first I had come. I had taken pains to learn as many words as I could. I seemed to have some skill with languages. My father could speak English and he understood Gascon. I could speak both French and Gascon as well as English.

I tried a Spanish word I had heard, "Hola." There was no answer and I slipped inside the dark, one roomed house. The people who had fled were poor but I spied some barley. That showed they were poor. They ground barley for bread. Some was already ground in the pestle. I took the small sack of barley and emptied the pestle into my cap. We could not bake with it for we had no oven but it might thicken a thin watery stew. I spied some cheese hanging in muslin. It was fresh and I took that. Then I found treasure. There was a cured ham. Most of the meat was gone but there was enough left on it to go with the cheese. The bone would make a stew. There was half a loaf of barley bread. I took that too. I put the ham bone, loaf and the cheese in my leather bag. I had taken that after the battle of Nájera. It had been on the body of a dead Portuguese. Everything else of value had been taken, even the cross from around his neck but to me the bag was treasure. The bone, when we had finished with it in the stew, would make boiled water into soup. I went out to Badger. I took handfuls of the barley out and allowed Badger to eat from my hands. He was very gentle. His teeth never once even touched my palms. I gave him half and put the small sack and my folded hat in my satchel. I led him up the path to the others.

My father had managed to get some wine. He and a couple of other men were playing dice. Whatever coin my father had had he would soon lose. Ralph had told me that it was a good job my father was such a fierce warrior. The men would have tired of him otherwise. When he fought he was unbeatable. I steered clear of him and took the horse to the old olive tree which stood in the middle of the village. Red Ralph was there with Long John, Dick Long Sword and Peter the Priest. They had some bread and Long John was portioning it. They were all shield brothers. Red Ralph was their sergeant. They had taken me under their wing. I put Badger where he was shaded. It meant I was in the sun but the horse was more important that I was.

I reached into my satchel and took out the ham and the cheese. "I found these. I thought the bone might make good soup." I handed them to Red Ralph. He was sergeant and he would distribute them.

He beamed, "It was a good day when Captain Tom took you into our company!" He nodded to Long John who cut a sixth piece of bread. Peter the Priest then divided the cheese into six and sliced the remaining ham from the bone. That too was into six portions. One was smaller than the others. That would be mine. I did not mind. He placed the portions on the bread and Red Ralph handed me mine. Treasure like this was too good to waste and we ate in silence. Even the crumbs were licked from our grubby, dust covered hands. The last piece of bread, cheese and ham was the largest and it was placed between two kettle helmets to keep the flies from it.

Red Ralph rubbed his bald pate, "Your father managed to find wine. How does he do that?"

I tapped my nose, "He divines it the way a horse divines water and his nose leads him there."

Peter the Priest laughed and said, "Aye it is red enough!"

Just then the Captain walked back from his conference with Sir Hugh and the Prince. Although he carried a wine skin he did not look happy. Red Ralph handed him the bread and Old Tom smiled, "Whence comes this bounty?"

The sergeant pointed at me, "Our newest member of the company is the most resourceful, Captain!"

"Thank you, Master Will. And Badger?"

I took out the remains of the barley from my satchel, "He has been watered and eaten barley, Captain. There was no grass for him to have."

He grinned, "Good lad. This will make up for the news I bear!" He bit into the bread, ham and cheese. We were all desperate to know what he had learned but we waited, patiently. When he had finished he took the stopper from the wine skin and drank deeply. He passed it to Peter the Priest and they all took a mouthful. When Red Ralph passed it to me I shook my head and handed it back. "Well lads, it seems that Peter the Cruel, now that we have won back his kingdom for him, baulks at paying the Prince the money he promised him. We have to march to Valladolid to try to get it from him there."

Peter the Priest said, "That is almost one hundred and forty miles from here. If every place has as little as this then we will starve to death."

Long John shook his head, "Or worse. Some of the lads have the bloody shits. That is all we need, no food, no horses and disease."

The Captain was an old wise warrior. "It is but sixty miles to Burgos and that is a big town. We may find more there."

"That is still sixty miles, Captain." Dick Long Sword was the youngest of the shield brothers and his boots had thin soles. Until he acquired a horse he would have to walk.

He shrugged, "Prince Edward has rarely let us down. We will have to trust to him." A horn sounded. "Time for us to march. Will, fetch Badger."

Although we had rested during the hottest part of the day the road still burned through the thin soles of my shoes. I had made them myself. I had found some thin leather and I fashioned them from it. The sandals I had worn before had offered no protection from the stones. Even so, the thin leather had not worn well. I had grown somewhat. My feet had burst the toes and the soles were as thin as the parchment the priests used. I longed for boots such as the others wore. I had not yet fought and I knew that when we fought there was a better chance of getting boots from one of the dead. This chevauchée into Spain and Portugal had already yielded good boots and fine blades for some. That was one way my father got the money to spend on wine. He always killed more men than anyone else and took more booty from the dead.

I walked next to Badger and the Captain. Ahead rode Sir Hugh and before them Prince Edward in his black mail surrounded by his household knights. We all followed the Black Prince because he was always successful. This campaign had been one filled with victories yet we had not received one piece of gold. The men were becoming restless. If they were not paid soon then they would seek coin themselves. They might raid towns and churches. My father fitted in well with these hard men. Most would fight for up to ten years and then retire back to England having made enough coin to be comfortable. There were many easier jobs in England. They could join the garrison of some rich lord and become old fat warriors recounting stories of their youth. Now, however, this was a good time to be out of England. They had the plague or black death as it was being called. It was called that because of the colour of the infection. Whole villages and towns had been wiped out. King Edward, Prince Edward's father, could do little about the disease and people fled in huge numbers. It was said, by men who joined us from England, that there was great discontent in the land. It explained why our numbers were always swollen by new recruits fresh from England. There was hope in war.

Red Ralph walked next to me. He saw me wince as I walked over a stone, "Fear not, Will, there will be more battles. This road is not yet finished. Burgos has many opportunities for us. Either Peter the Cruel will pay us or his town will suffer." He pointed to Sir Hugh. "Sir Hugh fights for one thing and one thing only, gold."

"Is that all there is, Red Ralph? Fighting for gold?"

"The alternative is to fight for land. It may come to that. There is, at the moment, peace between France and England but that will not last. The Welsh will creep from their mountains and we will have to fight them. The Scots still smart over the capture of King David at Neville's Cross and they will chance their blades. For the present, this is where the coin is to be found."

"I have never been to England. My mother had me after the Battle of Mauron."

He smiled, "She was a bonnie lassie. She still is."

"Did she not care for me? Is that why she left us all those years ago?"

His voice became sad and wistful, "She was young. She was little older when she had you than you are now. Besides the choice was Sir Alan Buxhill or your father." He shook his head, "I know who I would have chosen."

"Did he marry her?"

Red Ralph laughed, "Knights do not marry camp followers! She is there to warm his bed and to give him comfort. He has a hawk faced harridan for a wife. I heard she brought him land. It is the way of the world, Will, and the sooner you realise that you take your chances when they come, the better. Your mother chose life for had she stayed with your father she would have found death." He looked at me, "As would you had we not taken you under our wing."

We walked in silence while I took this in. I had heard a rumour that Red Ralph had been a knight once. I did not know if it was true but he knew much about the ways of lords. In the Blue Company you did not pry. If a man confided in his shield brothers then so be it. Otherwise, a man was taken for what he did for the company. His words reassured me. I felt better. I liked my mother. She was pretty, as far as I could remember, and she had been kind. She had oft times put herself between me and my father's hands. It was more than six years since she had left and her face was now a foggy memory. I remembered her songs and I had taken comfort in them when my father had beaten me. I had closed my eyes and heard the melodies.

"Red Ralph, can I ask you something?"

"Having given us the best meal in many a day I would say aye, ask away. I can only say nay."

"Why do they call you Red Ralph?"

"Because of my hair."

"But you have none!"

He laughed, "When I was young I had a full head of bright red hair. The Good Lord took my hair but left me my name."

"You beard is not red, it is brown."

He stroked it and said, "Aye, that has me confused too!"

"Will you go home when you have enough coin?"

"I will go to England, aye, but not to my home. The Black Death struck my home. My mother and father, brothers and sisters, all perished. They burned the buildings to stop the pestilence spreading. Barely ten of us escaped. I will not go back there. When I return to England I will find somewhere far from the Black Death. These shield brothers are my family now. When you get a shield then you will become family too." He ruffled my hair. "That will be some time off. There is still growing in you. I fancy you will be the tallest man in the company when you finally stop growing."

When we stopped for the night camp it was in another little village. The Prince and his knights paid for their food and wine. It meant there was none left for us. I thought it a mistake on the Prince's part but what did I know? I was the lowliest member of the company.

After I had seen to Badger Old Tom waved me over. "Will, the ham bone and the barley flour are a start. What else can you get for us?"

"Have you anything to trade, Lord?"

"The village is no good, Will. The Prince has paid for everything they had."

I smiled. I had learned much since my mother had left. I had learned that people often kept a little something back, "Let me try, eh lord?"

He nodded and handed me a rosary. He had taken it from a dead Castilian. "Here it is little enough but the people hereabouts appear to be more religious than most. It must be the proximity of Santiago di Compostela." The pilgrimage site with the statue of the saint drew people from all over Europe.

I took it and slipped it into my satchel. I had learned enough words to be able to barter. If I could then I would take. If I had to I would use barter. As I passed the other camp fires I heard my father's voice. It was raised. He had not been able to get wine and that made him belligerent. I was glad that Captain Tom was now my benefactor. I headed out of the village. I had spied a couple of lonely houses further away. Perhaps the Prince's men had not been there. My father's temper and heavy hand had taught me how to move silently. Despite my size, I could be stealthy.

I approached the first hut and I could not hear any noise. These simple huts had two doors. I went to the one which did not face the road. It was ajar. I drew my knife. As soon as I opened the door I could smell death. I clutched at my wooden cross and eased the door open. The interior was in darkness but, as I opened the door I saw the old man on the chair. He was dead. There was no sign of violence. I made the sign of the cross and said, "May you sleep in heaven and not worry about a young boy who seeks food. It can do you no good, my friend, and it may help us to survive."

I found some old onions and garlic. I put them in my satchel. The bread was mouldy. There appeared to be little else and then I sensed a movement above my head. I looked up and saw a rat gnawing at the leg of ham which hung there. I have quick reactions and a good eye. My hand flicked out and I pinned the rat to the roof beam with the blade of my knife. I put the ham in the satchel. This one had more meat upon it. I had to break it in the middle to make it fit in my bag. Then I took the rat. A man had to be desperate to eat a rat but there might be men hungry enough to give me a coin or two for it.

I left and headed towards the other hut. I was not making a noise and so they must have been watching the road for a man stepped out with a short sword. Before he could speak I held up my hands to show him my palms and I said, "Peace. Friend!"

His sword lowered a little.

I took out the rosary. We had enough food for a stew but the men would like wine. I proffered the rosary with my left hand, "This for wine? A skin?" I was not sure I had used the right word for skin but the man seemed to understand. He took hold of the rosary but I did not let go. I kept my right hand on the hilt of my short sword.

There was enough light for him to see its quality. He shouted, "Isabella! Wine skin!"

I realised I had used the wrong word but he had understood my meaning. A young girl, about my age, came out with the wine skin. I let go of the rosary and she handed it to me. Her eyes danced with mischief and she giggled when my hand touched hers. Her father shouted, "Inside!" and he stepped back and slammed the door in my face.

That was the first time I knew that girls and later women would find me attractive. I had never seen my face and so I did not know. The reflections in the pools we passed were all that I had seen. I had no idea of the quality of the wine but wine was wine and was better than the water we might find.

I made my way back to the camp. As I passed other fires I heard the belligerent voices of hungry men. I avoided them. When I reached our camp, I saw my father and he was arguing with Old Tom, "We have not been paid by the Prince and now we have no food. This is not right Captain!"

Old Tom was always reasonable. That was why he had been elected captain by the men. He could be trusted. "Look Harry, the Prince has yet to be paid. Peter the Cruel has not kept his word. We have thirty miles tomorrow and then we will be at Burgos. There will be food there."

My father suddenly saw me. His eyes narrowed, "Have you some food, you scraggy little shit?"

I braced myself for a beating but Red Ralph stood between us, "Will is now our camp brother and he forages for us now. Had you beaten him less then who knows you might eat tonight."

I saw my father's fists bunch. Ralph was also handy. If it came to blows I would not know who would emerge triumphant. Old Tom said, "What have you there, Will?"

I took out the ham, onions and garlic. "I found these." I slipped the wine skin from my shoulder. "I bartered for this." I took out the rat. It was a big one, "And this I killed!"

Peter the Priest clapped me on the shoulder, "By God but you are the best of thieves!" He took the rat and dropped it at my father's feet. "If you are hungry then eat this!"

In answer, he was backhanded so hard that he knocked me to the ground as my father struck him. Red Ralph reacted the quickest. He punched my father hard in the ribs with his left hand and then even harder with his right. I heard something break.

Before my father could draw a weapon, Captain Tom shouted, "Enough! You know the rules of camp. Will is now part of our camp. For what you did to Peter I could have you dismissed from the company. Take the rat and leave. Thank your son that you are not sent from the company."

He snatched up the rat and pushed by Red Ralph, "I have no son! The bitch who bore him gave herself to any. I am well rid of her!"

He stormed off. I felt so angry that I thought to race after him and finish what Ralph had started. Captain Tom restrained me and said, "They are empty words, Will. Your mother was innocent until she met your father. She left him because he was a bastard. Come, you have done well and our company eats well this night!"

Peter the Priest sat next to me as I ate, "When I was training to be a priest I learned to be patient and to tolerate weaknesses in others but your father tests even my patience. I know not why he is the way he is.

He had a beautiful wife and a fine son yet he drove one away and had the other stayed with him then I fear it would not have ended well."

I nodded, "He seems angry when he has no wine and to be possessed when he takes a drink."

"Some men are like that." He patted my hand. Peter the Priest was an enigma. He had studied as a priest and then just left the church. We never discerned the reason. He was the wisest man in our company and the most trustworthy. "I believe that each man chooses his own destiny. No matter where he begins we can all end up in a different station. I chose mine and I am happy with this band of brothers. "We will watch out for you. It is not as though you have lost a father, rather, you have gained four!"

Chapter 2

Burgos was a disappointment. The gates of the city were barred to us and we had to seek shelter at the monastery at Las Helgas, a mile out of the city. We had to camp, without tents. We had to make do with hovels. and there was precious little food. The mood of all of the companies, not just ours, began to turn ugly. We had fought for Peter the Cruel to help him regain his throne not because we wanted to but because we had been promised pay. We were not Spaniards. When neither pay nor money was forthcoming men grew restless. The men were also bored. The monastery where we were camped had little to offer us. There were neither whores nor wine.

I was not bored. I took the opportunity to make a scabbard for my sword. There was wood around and I did not mind crafting it to the shape and size of my sword. I enjoyed the work even though it took many days. There were some pine trees nearby and Peter the Priest showed me how to make glue from the resin. The monks had sheep and I found enough wool to line the inside of the scabbard to protect my blade. I really needed leather for the covering but I had none and so I used some old cloth I had found. Men had begun to die from what Long John had called, '*the bloody shits*'. It was an apt description for that is how they died. When they emptied their bowels, blood came too. None of our company had suffered for Captain Tom made sure that the water we drank was clean and we dug a cess pit well away from where we slept. Some of the other companies were not as scrupulous. That was where I found my cloth. One of the Red Company died and the warrior's torn and tattered cloak was discarded by his shield brothers when they divided his goods between them. It had been a red cloak but now had faded to a muddy brown. I found enough material to cover the scabbard. It would suffice until I could get leather.

I kept the sword sharp. I was desperate to use it to practise but Red Ralph would not allow me to. Instead, he had me spar with him using a branch from an olive tree. When I complained that it was heavier than my sword and did not swing as true he had smiled, "Then think how easy it will be when you do use your sword!" My father, had I said the same to him, would have fetched me a clout about the ear for my trouble. Ralph was right, the olive branch built up my muscles and made me think about how I would swing it.

"Don't use the point, Will! Use the edge and swing with your weight behind it. If your enemy has mail it is unlikely that your tip will pierce the rings but with your strength, a blow to the mail might weaken them and your opponent. When we fight the winner may not be the best warrior, it might well be the one who can keep going longer."

"How does my father keep winning?"

Ralph smiled, "He is as mad as a fish! He gets the blood lust in his eyes and he fights as though he doesn't care if he lives or dies. I have fought next to him. Often his opponent is so scared that he either runs or makes a fatal mistake." He lowered his branch. "That is enough for now. I am tired even if you are not."

I dropped the branch and felt the muscles of my shoulder burning. It was not the sun it was the exertion. "Fatal mistake?"

He took a swig from the water skin. We had boiled the water to make certain it was clean. He handed it to me. It was warm but I drank anyway.

"Aye, you have no shield yet but I have seen men fight well with their swords and then lower their shields." He took his sword out of its scabbard and demonstrated. "A wide sweep above the shield can either break a bone or cut the mail. Unless you are good then you cannot fight well without a shield. We would have shown you how to make one but the wood around here is poor. Oak is best, English oak or, at a push willow. It might be that we have to take one for you from one of our foes."

"I thought we had won the war!"

"We have but now we need to secure our pay and that might involve a few deaths. This Peter the Cruel thinks he has won but he does not know Prince Edward. By hook or by crook we shall have what is due us."

Three days later and we still had not had our money. Worse, Peter the Cruel had met with Prince Edward and told him that he could have his money but it would be at Valladolid. When we were told some of the men erupted. It was like a volcano. The Red Company had suffered the most deaths from disease and they were the unhappiest. They left the monastery and headed for the town of Burgos. Prince Edward and his knights were already packing up to head to Valladolid and Sir Hugh Calverley rode up to Old Tom, "Captain, we cannot have our men run riot. We have to pass through this town on our way home. Take your company and bring them back here."

"There may be blood spilled, my lord."

"Keep it to a minimum. If they do not return then they will get no pay at all."

"Yes lord." He turned to us. "Get the rest of the company together. We have a few heads to rattle. I won't need Badger today, Will. You can stay here."

"Captain, I am of this company, I would serve with my brothers."

The Captain looked at Ralph who nodded, "The lad is ready and it might do him some good. Practice is one thing but facing a man who is trying to hurt you is something else."

I was glad I had made my scabbard but I still had no helmet and no shield. Peter the Priest said, "Stay by me Will and watch my back!" The others all had helmets of different types and leather armour with mail or plates. I had nothing like that yet.

We were the largest company who served under Sir Hugh. He rode with us but I noticed that he stayed towards the rear. He had not earned the grey hairs by being reckless. The men we sought, the Red Company, would be in drink. Such men often lost all sense. The rest of our company all wore their helmets and carried shields. There was little to be gained in this action. There would be neither pay nor loot, only blood and enmity. We would get the job done and then head to Valladolid.

Captain Tom led us and as we were his closest comrades we marched behind him. Red Ralph, Long Tom, Dick Long Sword and Peter the Priest walked behind him. I was between Stephen of Gwent and Roger the Bastard. Neither were tall men and I was above both of them. Roger the Bastard, his father had been a lord who took Roger's mother, grinned, "Your head without a helmet will make a pretty target! We should be safe eh Stephen?"

He laughed, "Aye, at the very least your hair will get a trim!" The banter was good. It told me they accepted me.

We heard the fighting before we reached the town. They had a town watch and they had obviously taken exception to the rampaging men of the Red Company. "Right lads, pick up the pace."

Old Tom began to run. It was not a hard run but it would get us to the walls of Burgos quicker. There were two dead sentries at the gates and one of the men of the Red Company. He had been gutted.

"Peter, Will, see to this one."

We dropped out of line and the rest of the Blue Company ran into the town. The warrior was an older man. There were flecks of grey in his beard. From the smell which emanated from his breeks he had the bloody shits too. He smiled, weakly when he saw Peter, "You are too late to save my life, Peter the Priest, but you could save my soul. Hear my confession and then give me the warrior's death. I thought the shits would get me but that Spanish bastard has ended my life."

"I am no priest."

"But you were once and I need to have shrift."

"It is not right that the boy hears this."

He saw me for the first time, "I am Harold of Stamford. I know you, Will son of Harry. Your mother was a good woman. I have little left to give save this helmet and my shield. My shield brothers will have my sword, boots, dagger and coin. Take them, boy, and may they serve you better than they served me."

"Thank you, Harold, I will pray for you!" I took the helmet and shield. Peter gestured for me to stand off. I walked away and examined my new gifts. The helmet was battered and had no arming cap. It was a simple round one. There was no nasal but it would protect my ears and the back of my head. It would do. The leather on the shield was torn but they were mine. I turned and saw Peter the Priest laying down the dead Harold. He wiped his dagger on the dead man's breeks. I slung the shield over my back and hung the helmet over it. It still had the mark of the Red Company. I wanted to upset neither the dead man's friends or the Blue Company.

"Come, let us see what the damage is. That man had a wife and child in England. Why in God's name was he here?"

When we reached the town square it was all over. Four of the Red Company lay dead. I later learned that they had been drunk. They had faced my father and his cronies who were not in the mood for prisoners and I saw them rifling the dead men's belongings. We did not need that. There would be bad blood. I saw others who were nursing wounds. We arrived as Sir Hugh bellowed out his ultimatum. "You will now march to Valladolid as members of the Free Companies. You will obey orders. Do that and your sins here will be forgiven. If not, the Prince has ordered that you lose your right hands in punishment. What say you?"

The new leader of the Red Company, for the previous one had died, Captain John said, "What about our pay, Sir Hugh?"

"You will have it at Valladolid when the Prince receives his. You have my word that you will be paid. If not then I will lead you to take it from the Spaniards!"

That met with their approval and we marched back out of the town. The Red Company marched first with us behind them. The townsfolk glowered and glared at us all. To them we were all predators. We wasted no time at our camp. I saddled Badger and we headed south. As me marched Red Ralph saw my helmet and shield. He frowned. "Thieving Will?"

Peter the Priest shook his head, "He was given them. I heard the dying man's confession. All was done well."

"Even so some of his comrades may not think so. Put the shield in the wagon with our war gear. When we stop we will make it blue. Put the helmet there too!" He grinned, "It will make a good pot for cooking if nothing else."

"Leave the lad alone, Ralph. I had to wait years for my first helmet." Although younger than the others, Dick Long Sword had a fine kettle helmet. In this clime it kept a warrior shaded. I could see why they wore them in Outremer.

It was a cooler day for travelling and I was in good spirits. I looked more like one of the company now. I had a sword, helmet and shield. Boots and cloak would come next and then a leather jerkin. Only Captain Tom wore mail and that was a short hauberk. Sir Hugh had mail, mail chausses as well as circular plates on his elbows and shoulders. It was the way most knights went to war. While on the road we discovered that Peter the Cruel had gone to Seville to get his money. That did not bode well.

When we reached the town of Valladolid there was, at least, food waiting for us. Prince Edward must have realised the dangers in allowing his men to become discontent. We were only one third of his army but, the knights apart, we were the best. The food and the wine helped to make our new camp acceptable. I busied myself repairing my shield and helmet. I would have to wait until we had coin to make an arming cap. A helmet alone would protect from an arrow but an arming cap would mean I could endure blows to my helmet from a sword. I had seen men who did not wear an arming cap. Often, they died without a wound. My father had told me it was because the blow to the helmet had damaged the skull.

We camped and we waited, as did the Prince, for our money. The weather became hotter. It was now high summer and there seemed to be no air. The condition of the water deteriorated. Gradually we received less food and men began to die. The money was still not forthcoming and worse still was the news that Prince Edward was ill. Some said he had been poisoned. Rumours were rife. Once again, our small band seemed immune. The Red Company lost more than half of its number. The ones who survived just deserted. One night they were there and when we woke they were gone. We heard they became bandits and raided their way north.

Sir Hugh came to our camp one night. I was at the fire with the others. I was polishing my helmet. He spoke with Captain Tom. He looked at me with a frown. He saw my sword and the newly painted shield. "The lad is all right, my lord, he is not like his father."

"You keep your mouth shut about what you hear eh?" I nodded. I knew my future depended upon his good graces. The knight addressed us, "I do not think we will get our money any time soon. Prince Edward has the bloody shits too. He is lucky; he has healers and he is indoors. He is sending most of his knights home to Bordeaux. Horses were dying. You are lucky Tom that yours is so well cared for."

"That is all down to Will."

"Aye well the Prince has given us permission to take our pay from the locals. Leave the churches alone. The last thing we need is to upset the Pope. Anything else is fair game. Just leave the women alone and the churches alone. The rest of these people can pay for their King's lack of honour."

"Then you had better have a word with Will's father. You know what he is like."

The knight sighed, "Aye. It is a pity he is the best man in a fight that we have in the company. I will speak with him."

"When do we return to Aquitaine, my lord?"

"As soon as the Prince can ride!"

The rest of the company were summoned. My father could barely bring himself to look at me. "Blue Company, there is no pay forthcoming!" Men began to grumble and Long John banged his shield to get silence. "Sir Hugh has said that we can take it from the locals." He glared at my father who was rubbing his hands. "We are Englishmen. We do not kill or hurt women or children; understood Harry of Lymm?" My father nodded. "There is little point in shitting in our own nest. There are villages outside of Valladolid. We take those. They are close enough to us to walk. We have too few horses to risk losing them. We all go afoot!" I saw nods. "No churches!" The disappointment on the men's faces was palpable.

Before we left the men all prepared for battle in their own way. They all had their own rituals before they fought. Old Tom was our captain and had fought in the Crusades. He was a gentleman and had a mail hauberk. It had seen better days. His sallet helmet was well made and he had a coif about his neck. He had graves on his legs and the best sword in the company. Not as long as Dick's the others told me how well balanced it was. It had been a gift from Prince Edward. His ritual was to pray and then to kiss his sword.

Peter the Priest was the one who seemed to fuss over me like a mother hen but he was a good warrior. His kettle helmet and the long scar down his face, a memento from a Seljuk Turk were from that time.

Unlike many of the other captains, he did not wear mail. He had a leather jerkin with metal plates sewn on. He once told me that he could repair armour himself but a mail hauberk needed a smith. His ritual was to kneel and kiss the hilt of his sword. He always faced east when he did that. He had been the only survivor from his company and he honoured them before each battle. He had a mace at his side. He said it was the weapon for a priest. There were times when it was more useful than a sword and mail was no defence against its bone breaking head. Before he went to fight he chanted. It was in Latin and I did not know what he sang. It seemed to comfort him and he smiled each time he opened his eyes and donned his helmet.

Red Ralph was almost as old as Old Tom. He had no hair on his head and his once brown beard was now sprinkled with silver and gold. He had not been a crusader and he wore a conical helmet which had an aventail protecting his neck. His leather armour had mail across the shoulders. Often, he would take the broken mail he found after a battle and use that to replace his own when it was damaged. His belt was a wide one made of ox hide. His ritual was more practical. He had two swords: a longer sword in his belt and a shorter one in a scabbard over his back. He would take out a whetstone and sharpen all of his weapons. He sang as he did so.

Long John had a conical helmet with a nasal. Although slightly old fashioned he wore it over an arming cap and a coif with a ventail. He kept his hair cropped and he had no moustache, just a neatly trimmed beard. His armour was similar to Peter the Priest's save that he wore round disks. He had the simplest of rituals. He would not put his coif and helmet on until he was mounted. Of all of us he resented walking. He complained and moaned. I think it was because he could not complete his ritual.

Finally, there was Dick Long Sword. His sword was what they called a hand and a half sword. Close to the hilt there was no edge to it and he could use the weapon in a variety of ways. Because he often used two hands with the sword his shield was more like a large buckler. Despite his vulnerability he had yet to be wounded by either bolt or arrow. He was the youngest of the four and he was clean-shaven but he liked his hair long and it hung down below his conical helmet. His long sword hung across his back and he kept a short sword for those times when it was close combat. He liked to talk to his horse before a battle. As he had none at the moment he would come to talk to Badger while I held him for Captain Tom.

And me? I had no ritual yet. I was barely a warrior. In the many months since I had left my father I had not had to fight. We had lost men in the march south and so Captain Tom needed me to be ready to fight. Perhaps my ritual was that I was so terrified of dying that I had to make water. I did that and, as we marched, I prayed to God to save me for I had neither mail nor helmet. I had my new shield and pot helmet which I had to carry for it would get too hot on my head in the Spanish sun. I would go to war with an old short sword, a knife and the hope that an enemy would choose to fight a better warrior. I did not think that would happen. I had watched enough battles to know that men were more than happy to fight someone they thought they could beat. I wondered how many heartbeats I would last. All that I had going for me was my speed and quick wits. Dodging my father's fists would be good preparation for avoiding a sword or a spear.

Peter the Priest still looked like a priest even though it was ten years since he had left the monastery where he had been a novice. He shaved his face and wore his head tonsured. Unlike the other men he did not bother himself with women. I could never discover why he had left the monastery. Like Old Tom he had been on crusade and he wore a kettle helmet. The brim shaded his face.

I went with Captain Tom even though we did not take Badger. The horse was too valuable to be risked taking from the Spaniards. There were twenty of us. I stayed close to Red Ralph and Peter the Priest. It was not simply for protection it was because I wanted to do everything well. I slung my shield over my back as they did and my helmet from my sword. Those who had kettle helmets wore them. Those of the company who had the pot helmet pulled their hoods up for shade. I had no cloak and I still had no arming cap. I walked bare headed for the helmet would have boiled my brains to mush!

Doors were barred to us as we left Valladolid. The town guard fingered their weapons as we passed through the town gates. They knew what we could do. Word had reached Valladolid from Burgos. The Red Company had stained us all. It was why Sir Hugh had suggested we raid outside the town.

As we marched Red Ralph said, "I prefer campaigning further north. There we ride. Here there is precious little grazing and water for our animals. It is why Prince Edward sent his knights home. So, until we get more horses, we walk and soon you will be barefoot, eh Will?"

He was right. I could feel every grain of sand and soil beneath my feet. My toes, peeping through the end were permanently black. The nails were ragged and cracked where I had stubbed them. I bathed them whenever we passed flowing water but that was seldom in this hot country.

We had marched just over a mile to the north when we spied, in the distance, the walled house. A walled house meant a lord and that meant food and coin. It also meant guards. We stopped in the shade of some trees which had been planted for that purpose.

Captain Tom halted the men and waved at Peter the Priest, "Peter bring Will." I hurried forward with Peter. "I will lead half of the men north. The rest will hide in this stand of trees. You two take that gully yonder. Scout out the walls. Send Will back here with your news eh Peter."

Peter nodded, "You will lead your half of the men to approach from the other side?"

"Aye. They will have men watching. They saw us entering these trees and they will be watching for us to leave. Dick Long Sword can command the ones I leave here."

Peter said, "Leave your helmet and shield here, Will. You can pick them up when you return."

I hated leaving my treasures behind but I heeded his command and then followed him down the gully. It must have been a river once. Perhaps it still was but not in this furnace of a summer. The sun burned the top of my head. We were hidden from view. It meant we could not see the walls. I wondered how Peter would know when to change direction and get close to the hidden walls. I could not ask him. I knew enough about scouting to know that you did not talk. He moved lightly choosing large stones upon which to step. He had told me, one night by the fire, that a good scout left no tracks and learned to look for the tracks of others.

The voices from above us told me when we were near to the walls. They were Spanish and I recognised some of the words. 'English, bandits and lord' were three of them. Peter held up his hand and then began to creep up the side of the gully. I copied him. He used solid rocks and sturdy shrubs to pull himself up. He made certain that his footing was sound before he moved off. We peered over the top. The walls were less than forty paces from us. I saw four guards at the gate house. There was a small tower closer to us. It was empty. Peter would take in all that he saw before he sent me back and I did the same. In Aquitaine there might have been a ditch around the walls. Here there was too much rock but the gates looked sturdy enough. The walls were made of stone but they were only as high as Long John with someone seated on his shoulders. I did not see a keep within the walls. I saw a building which rose above the walls and there were two men on the top. It looked to have a fighting platform running around it.

We were close enough now for their words to be clearer. I did not understand them all but, from their gesticulations and the words I could make out I gathered that they had seen Captain Tom and our men marching north. The lord was Charles of somewhere, I could not make out the name of the place. We had not passed it. Perhaps it was the name of the place we were at. I heard rider and Valladolid. We waited until the four men dispersed. One came towards the tower closer to us and one went to the other tower. The other two remained over the gate.

Peter tapped me on the shoulder and we slithered down to the bottom of the gully. He put his head close to me and asked, "What did you learn from their words?" I gave him a surprised look. "You have a gift with words. I know that you heard some of what they said."

"I did not understand it all."

"It matters not. Tell me what you did hear?"

"There is a Lord Charles but he is not there. They think that our men are bandits and are raiding further north. They will send a rider to Valladolid."

He grinned, "Then you have learned more than me. Hurry back. Have Dick Long Sword ambush the rider. We gain a horse at the very least. Then bring the men back here."

I nodded. I knew it would take time to saddle a horse and for a rider to leave the hall. I skipped from stone to stone. I was out of breath when I reached Dick. As I recovered my helmet and shield I told him what I had learned.

"Good lad. Right boys, hide in the woods and the ditches. Long John you and I will take the rider. Will be ready to get the horse!"

"Aye, Dick."

I hid myself behind a tree and waited. It seemed an age before I heard the sound of hooves coming from the hall. The rider would be looking north and not south. He might fear some of the 'English bandits' might be returning south. I saw him as he emerged from the track which led to the estate. He was riding a small horse. He was a small man. I readied myself. Long John and Dick Long Sword rose like wraiths from the side of the road. I jumped to my feet too. It was me whom the Spaniard saw. He tried to rein in. Dick Long Sword swept his two-handed weapon at the man. His sword almost cut the rider in two. As his body fell from the saddle the frightened horse ran at me. I waved my hands and then spoke every Spanish word I could think of. I managed to grab the reins and swing the horse around. I stroked its mane and calmed it down.

By the time I had done that the body had been stripped of all that was valuable and thrown into the ditch which ran along the road. "Tie the horse to a tree. We will pick it up later." Dick Long Sword threw a pair of boots at me. They were rider's boots. "Here, for your troubles!"

I grabbed them and then led the horse into the shade of the trees. There was a little greenery for it to graze and I tied the beast to a tree. I saw that it was a mare. While Dick led the men down the gully I put my old shoes in my satchel and pulled on the boots. They were a tight fit for the rider was a very small man but I could stretch them. I hung my satchel from the saddle I donned my helmet and followed the company down the gully.

When I reached Peter and the others they had made a decision. "Will, you and Peter will be lifted up the wall. You will take the guard at this corner and then secure the gates. I will follow."

"Am I ready?"

Dick Long Sword nodded, "It is one man and Peter will be with you. You are light enough to lift." I nodded. He peered over the top. "We will wait until he walks to the gate." It seemed an age before Dick said, "Now!"

We clambered out of the gully. Forty paces did not seem a great distance but the ground was uneven. Had I been wearing my old shoes the stones would have made it harder. I reached the wall and Long John put his back against it. I heard footsteps on the fighting platform above me. The sentry had returned. I waited until they passed me and then I stepped away from the wall. I turned and, running towards Long John, put my right foot into his cupped hands. I saw Michael doing the same for Peter. I was boosted a moment before he was. I grabbed the top of the wall and pulled myself over. My new boots were almost my undoing. The heel caught on the wall and I landed on all fours. The sentry was just two paces away from me and he turned. Behind him, I saw Peter pulling himself up. The sentry drew his sword. He was opening his mouth to shout. I could not draw my sword in time and so I did the only thing I could. I used myself as a weapon. I lowered my head and sprang at him. My helmet hit him under the chin. My ears rang and I saw stars. I scrambled to my feet in time to see Peter's sword emerge from the sentry's chest.

He nodded and pointed to the gate. He passed me as I straightened my helmet, drew my sword and grabbed my shield. Our footsteps on the fighting platform alerted the two sentries there. Behind me, I head Dick Long Sword shout to the others, "We are discovered, get to the gate! We will let you in!"

I heard the shouts of alarm from the gate, we had been seen. Now that it came to it I was uncertain if I could sink my sword into a man's flesh. Red Ralph had warned me that it would be hard. I saw Peter hold his shield before him. I did the same and I watched Peter hold his sword behind him. I emulated him but I could not see why. Behind me, I could hear Dick Long Sword racing down the fighting platform to reach us.

The other two Spanish sentries stood together with their shields held before them. I had been too slow and now Peter would have to face them alone. Then I saw him lower his head, raise his shield and barge through them both. One reeled before him while the other was knocked to the side. As Peter swung his sword to strike at the dazed Spaniard I saw the other raise his sword to sweep into Peter's back. I had no time to think and I brought my sword up and into the side of the sentry. Even as I did it I could hear Red Ralph berating me for using the tip. I was lucky. The man had neither mail nor leather. My sword scraped off his ribs and then sank into something soft. The Spaniard's sword dropped to the ground and he began to die.

Dick Long Sword had left the fighting platform and leapt down to the ground. He was racing to the gate. Another two sentries were running towards him. Just then the sentry on the north wall shouted and pointed. It had to be Captain Tom that he had seen. Peter shouted, "Down the ladder, help Dick!"

I scrambled down the ladder. Dick was swashing his long sword before him and keeping the two men at bay. My sudden appearance made one turn. He swung his sword and hit my shield. I reeled backwards and was lucky to keep my feet. As Dick's sword smashed into the other sentry's shield, breaking his arm, Peter appeared and shouted to the other, "Yield or die!" He said it in English but the three of us made our meaning clear. He dropped his sword. Dick turned, lifted the bar and opened the gate. The rest of our men entered.

Long John said, "Captain Tom is here."

We formed a semi-circle of swords. Five guards appeared before us. They thought better of tackling the ten of us and ran back to the hall. Peter turned and said, "Thank you, Will. I owe you a life and now you are blooded."

I looked at the blood on my sword. He was right. I had killed a man. It had happened so quickly that I had not had time to think of it.

Captain Tom appeared, "Well done, lads. I am sorry it took us so long. Right, let us get to the hall. Red Ralph go with Will and find the stables. There may be horses there."

As we hurried towards the pungent-smelling stable Ralph said, "We found three men working in the fields. They made the mistake of fighting us. Did you have trouble?"

"I killed a man." He nodded understandingly. "And I have boots and a horse!"

"You have a horse?"

"Well, I tied it to a tree."

"Let us see what else we can find."

As we went we heard the sound of axes on wood. The stable was unguarded and there were five horses. Four were palfreys and one was a sumpter. The one I had captured was a rouncy. I pointed, "There are four saddles!"

"Good then at least five of us get to ride home. You saddle them and then join me at the hall."

After I had saddled them, I went to the hall. The door lay splintered and shattered. Silent Michael stood on guard. He grinned at me. "You have much luck, Will son of Harry. I will fight close to you. A man cannot have to much luck when he goes to war!"

I stepped inside the hall. It was dark and it was cool. I heard screams, squeals and shouts. By the time I reached the main chamber, I saw that our company had captured the household.

A dark-haired Spanish lady stood with her arms folded across her body. She was jabbering away in Spanish. Captain Tom looked exasperated, "Will. Talk to her!"

I tried my Spanish, "We do not speak Spanish good."

She changed to French, "You barbarians will pay for this. My husband is with King Peter. You will all lose your hands for this!"

Captain Tom nodded. He could speak French, "If your King had paid Prince Edward then we would not need to do this. We take from you because your King has no honour and did not pay his debts! If you do not try to stop us then you will come to no harm. I promise you that."

"You are not a man! You are an English bastard!"

He laughed, "Then you know my father! Will watch them. The rest of you, you know what to do!"

The woman and her ladies slumped into the chairs around the table. Their hatred and disdain for these English bandits was clear. They began to talk. I had an idea what they were saying for they pointed at me and then to the other rooms. I began to make sense of what they were saying. Some of the words I did not understand; I guessed they were curses but, as I waited for the others to return I picked up more Spanish. I learned that her husband was a cousin of the King but the two of them were many hundreds of miles away. I saw now why they had resigned themselves to the ransacking of their home. I did not feel so bad about the robbery for it was the King's fault. He had only regained his throne because we had won it for him. Had we still fought for his brother then Peter the Cruel would have had nothing.

The hall filled with goods they had taken from the other rooms. Men were sent to load the sumpter and two of the palfreys. Finally, Captain Tom came into the room and nodded to me, "Off you go Will. I will speak with the lady."

When I reached the outside Peter and Red Ralph were waiting for me. They had a cloak, an arming cap, a sword and a bag. Peter spoke, "The cloak, arming cap and the sword came from the man you killed. We found these clothes in the hall. They look to be your size. Welcome to the Blue Company!"

They clapped me on the back. "Put these on the horse you left on the road. If you get to it first the Captain may let you keep it."

I almost ran down the track to the road. The horse was still there and the flies were buzzing noisily around the corpse. I untied her reins and led her to the road. I made my bags secure and hung my shield and helmet from the saddle. I examined the saddlebags and discovered ten silver coins. I put them in my purse. Until then it was an empty purse! Then I mounted her. She was a little on the small side but she would do. Riding was better than walking.

When the others arrived Captain Tom and Dick Long Sword were riding. Captain Tom grinned when he saw me on the horse, "You learn quickly, Will, son of Harry, but they tell me you have earned it. You may ride the horse for it is too small for the rest of the Company. Are you happy with your share?"

I almost felt guilty about the coins but I said, "Aye Captain, there will be more chance for us to take coins I think!" I knew that any food or drink would be shared out. If the lady was related to the King then she would have had jewels.

As we walked Dick Long Sword said, loudly, "We shall have to watch this young warrior, Will. He uses his head when he is fighting but I have never seen a man use it as a weapon!"

They all laughed and I was content. As soon as you were mocked it meant you were accepted. I had joined a band of brothers. I had a family once more.

Chapter 3

We were the most successful of the companies. The men who had gone with my father had found food, wine and a little money. We had taken a chance with a walled hall and we had reaped the reward. We did not need to scavenge again. Dick Long Sword even found me some thin leather with which to cover my shield. I would be a proper warrior. I had even killed a man. I had not had time to think about it else I am not sure that I could have done it but I could not undo the act. The horse I named Spaniard for that was what she was. She was hardy and able to endure the climate better than Badger. Dick, John, Peter and Red Ralph were given the other horses. My new brothers in arms did not mind my horse but I could see the covetous glances from my father and his associates. I would not say friends for my father was a solitary man and had no friends. As he had disowned me as a son and his wife had left him there was little I would have from his life.

The Prince recovered a little but the deaths amongst the company continued. We had marched into Spain with twelve thousand men in the Free Companies. Just over five thousand remained and after a month of enduring the heat, the order was given to head for home. Home was Aquitaine and Bordeaux. Home was four hundred miles away and safety, the pass of Roncesvalles, was still a two-hundred-mile march. It would have been shorter heading further west but there we had enemies. We would be retracing our steps through Burgos and Pamplona. We had not made any friends in either place.

The Prince stayed with us until Pamplona. I did not know the man as well then as I came to know him. I wondered if he felt guilt about not paying us. He rode with our company. Although we had lost men we had lost the fewest of any company and with our seven horses, we would be able to augment the household knights who accompanied the Prince. On the second day out of Valladolid he seemed to notice me for the first time.

"Sir Hugh, who is this young warrior? He seems a little young to have a horse and to be a member of the Blue Company." The Prince paid Sir Hugh but he was not our lord, at least not then.

Sir Hugh looked at me and smiled, "Will, son of Harry is young, my lord but he is something of a lucky charm. You remember his mother, Mary, Geoffrey's daughter, Sir Alan Buxhill took her to his bed." The Prince nodded. "He has a horse for he has some skill with one and he has shown that he can use a sword. On his first combat, he killed a man and saved the life of a brother."

Captain Tom laughed, "Aye Prince, his helmet is a terrible fierce weapon!" The rest of the company joined in the laughter and the Prince smiled. He was a warrior and knew the value of such banter.

"Tell me more." Peter the Priest took up the tale and told the Prince of all that I had done. The Black Prince turned to me, "I shall keep my eye on you, Will, son of Harry. A prince or even a king needs all the luck he can get. You know I have two sons now?"

"Aye, Prince Edward."

"Edward and Richard. When they are old enough I may have you be their servant and bodyguard. We will see how you do on this journey home."

Sir Hugh asked, "You think we may have to fight, my lord?"

"If we do not then I have underestimated the two brothers. Peter the Cruel would rather we were dead than pay the debt he owes and you and your men betrayed his brother. It will be an interesting journey."

Sir John Chandos, who rode at his side said, "My lord you are in no condition to fight a battle or even a skirmish. You should not even be riding."

"If I am in a carriage then it will be an even slower journey. If we can reach Pamplona safely then we have a chance to escape without further losses."

I dropped back for this was not my business and I rode behind Captain Tom, next to Red Ralph. So it was that I heard the next conversation even though Sir Hugh spoke quietly, "My lord, I know not about the other captains but my men are still unhappy about the lack of pay which was promised them."

"I know and I will pay them. They need to be patient."

"They have shown patience, my lord and many of their friends have died."

"As have mine."

Captain Tom realised we had heard that which we should not and we dropped back a little further. Red Ralph said, "Your star is on the rise Will. A lord like the prince could see you a gentleman."

I laughed, "I think not, Red Ralph. He was just being polite. I think he said it to make us fight for him. He will need us before we reach Bordeaux."

Old Tom laughed, "You are suddenly wise, Will, what makes you think so?"

I gestured a thumb behind me. "The way that our company marches. It shows they have pride and spirit. The rest are strung out in a ragged line."

Peter the Priest said, "I agree with Will. It explains why we follow the household knights."

We had little trouble until we reached the bridge over the Arakil Ibaia just west of Pamplona. We had not been welcomed in any of the towns and villages through which we had passed. That was because many of our men took what they wanted. The further north we went the less there was to take for word spread and people went into the hills when we came through their towns and villages. The water from their troughs was all that we found. We also lost men on the journey. It was not to war, it was to disease and sickness. Another two hundred died in the six days before we reached the bridge.

The bridge was contested by a large force of French and Spaniards. They were led by Arnoul d'Audrehem. Prince Edward and he did not get on. The Prince had said that the French Marshal had broken his word by fighting against the Prince. Captain Tom saw this as revenge for the accusation. There was a barricade across the bridge backed by Spanish crossbows. The mounted French waited beyond the river.

Sir Hugh was called to a council of war. We had our own views. That is to say that the others had their views and I listened.

"We cannot ford the river."

"Aye, we should head west where it is shallower."

"You are wrong. We head to Pamplona. That is friendly territory."

"It was friendly. Do you think they want us in their town? If the French stop us it saves them having to put up the prince and feed his army."

Captain Tom silenced them all, "It is simple enough. The Prince will use his archers and then he will send in men at arms to clear the bridge."

My father had been listening nearby, "And yet we get no pay? Let the knights force the bridge." There were murmured comments which seemed to agree with him.

Captain Tom said, "Any man who does not wish to follow Sir Hugh then leave now! When we are paid it will be more coin for us."

My father and his new cronies had failed to think their argument through. We were stranded far from safety. We had to stay together and fight, not for money but for survival. We were waiting just two hundred paces from the bridge. We stood by our horses and watched the enemy prepare for an attack. Their crossbows rested upon the barricade they had built. They would be accurate. They suffered from the same defect they always had; they could not use them to send their bolts indirectly at us. The archers could.

In the end, Captain Tom was proved right. We still had four hundred archers. They hated the men who used crossbows and they had a greater range. Captain Jack led them to within range of the crossbows. The White Company was sent with them to hold their pavise behind which they could take shelter. As the pavise were set up and moved closer there was the crack of bolts into the wood. It sounded like hailstones. Two of the White Company were hit.

Long John rubbed his hands together, "Now we shall see the Spaniards squeal. A wager anyone? The crossbowmen die within eight flights."

Red Ralph laughed, "No bet! I have seen our archers. They are deadly."

Captain Jack shouted, "Nock!" We watched the archers each put an arrow to their string. "Draw!" You could hear the creak of the bows as they did so. They drew them all the way back. I had seen them before. Captain Jack could not wait too long for the next command, "Release!"

The arrows soared high in the air. When they reached the top of the arc they would plunge to earth. A barrier before you was no protection to plunging arrows. Accuracy was not as good but as the archers sent five flights in the air before a man could count his fingers and toes it mattered little. Two thousand arrows scythed into the crossbows. The men of the White Company who were the closest to the crossbowmen all cheered and shouted.

Sir John Chandos himself led the knights and the White Company to attack the wooden barrier across the bridge. The archers continued to rain death on the defenders. As the men of the White Company pulled at the tree trunks across the bridge they were attacked from the sides by men armed with crossbowmen in boats. The archers switched targets but as the crossbows were less than forty paces from the casualties were high. The White Company managed to tear down four tree trunks and hurl them into the river. It cost them dearly. Their captain, Richard of Nottingham, ordered them back.

Sir Hugh shouted, "Captain Tom, take the Blue Company and support Sir John!"

We tied our horses to the nearest trees. I was trying to control the fear I felt rising within me. The White Company were all veterans. How could I do what they had failed to do?

Peter the Priest said, quietly, "Just do what you have practised with us. Keep your shield high and your sword behind you. Do not try to hack at mail. Every man has some flesh that you can find. Use your height. You may be young but you have grown tall in the last weeks."

I nodded, "I will try not to let you down."

He laughed, "You cannot."

"Forward the men of the Blue Company."

I was not at the fore nor even the fourth rank. I was at the rear with the old men and other young warriors. I was the youngest. There were men behind me. They were the ones who were afraid. For many, this would be their last battle. When they had their money, they would find something safer. Others were there who were still recovering from the bloody shits. I was in the middle and I took comfort in that. I did not know the two old men next to me. I had seen them in the camp. They both had grey hair and scars.

One turned to me, "Just keep in step, young 'un. You'll do alright. It is in your blood. Your father is a ferocious man in a fight. Just don't be as reckless as he is."

We began to march. The archers broke ranks to allow us through and then resumed their archery.

The other old man said. "Just watch your feet. There are bodies here."

Even as he said it I looked down and saw one of the White Company with a bolt in the middle of his forehead. It was either a very lucky or a skilful hit. It had struck him above his nose and between his eyes. Only a full-face helmet could have saved him. Ahead of me I heard the first clash of metal on metal. I was not with Peter, Ralph and the others. I felt guilty. My fear left me and I hefted the shield tighter to me. We made another eight steps and then we stopped. We could not push any further forward. Then the wounded began to pass back between us and we took a step forward. I was closer to the action. I saw my father. He was to my right and two rows ahead of me. He was shouting and waving his sword recklessly. It was almost as though he didn't care if they hit him. He seemed impervious to blows. The man next to him suddenly reeled around. I saw a bloody tear across his chest and he screamed as he plummeted over the parapet and into the river. And then I took another step forward.

I saw, below me, Long John and Peter the Priest pulling at a tree. Peter saw me, "Slip your shield on to your back and give us a hand. We are going to give these Frenchmen a surprise."

I sheathed my sword and slung my shield. I knelt down. I could see that they had worked one of the logs so that they could pull at its widest end, towards the bole. It was bizarre for above us men were fighting and dying. I heard my father. He had stepped on to the top and was defying the enemy to get at him. We pulled together. Nothing happened. We pulled again and nothing happened. The third time I felt a movement. The fourth saw us pull half the length of the tree from the barricade. The last pull made it pop out and it left a hole. Long John was too big to fit but Peter and I could.

I copied Peter as he took off his shield and placed it on the ground. He used it like a sledge in the snow and pulled himself through the gap. On the other side, the French were too busy fending off our men who were standing on the top. Peter waited until I had crawled through before pulling out his dagger. I copied him. Suddenly he grabbed a leg and ripped the blade across the back of the Frenchman spearman's knee. As the blood spurted and the Frenchman screamed in pain he stood up and rammed his dagger into the throat of the man next to him.

I slashed with my knife and tore through the tendons of another Frenchman. I lifted my shield from beneath me and rammed it upwards into the jaw of a second. We had now disabled four men and we had a foothold.

Above us, I heard Red Ralph shout, "Now we have them!" He leapt down into the gap Peter and I had created.

The French reacted quickly and I barely had time to bring up my shield. I still only had my dagger. The mace smashed into the shield. It forced me to my knees and my arm became numb. As he pulled back his arm to finish me off I rammed my dagger upwards. I struck his groin. He squealed like a pig being butchered. His mace fell from his hand. I pulled back my right arm and, standing, stabbed him in the neck.

Dick Long Sword had joined Red Ralph and the two of them swung their swords to enlarge our enclave. It bought me the time to take out my sword. I was just in time to block the blow from above me. My sword and the Frenchman's clashed. My left arm was useless. Behind me, more men had joined us and pushed. My sword arm became jammed against the Frenchman. I found myself face to face with him. He stank. I saw him open his mouth to bite off my nose. I brought my knee up so hard between his legs that I jarred it. He doubled up and I sawed across his neck with my sword as his head was lowered.

The two old men who had been with me at the start of the battle were now behind me, "Keep going young 'un we will watch your back."

Their presence gave me confidence. I just left my shield hand at my side knowing that there was another warrior who could lift his shield to help me. I was aided by the fact that the three Frenchmen before me were all shorter than I was. I swept my sword in an arc. The newly acquired Spanish blade taken from the hall outside of Valladolid was well made. Two reeled backwards while the third was too slow. He had a pot helmet like me and my sword opened his cheek and his nose. I must have struck something vital for he fell. The old man to my right suddenly swung his war hammer and the beak smashed through the helmet and skull of the second Frenchman. The battle had grown smaller. I was not aware of my father, Red Ralph or anyone. I just stabbed, slashed and hacked at any who stood before me.

I heard a horn and a voice shouted, "Make way! Sir John and his knights!"

The sound of thundering hooves made us back towards the parapet. I realised that we were almost across the bridge. I saw the knights charge and disperse the last of the men on foot. Captain Jack led the archers to follow them along with the last men of the Green Company.

Captain Tom shouted, "Clear the bridge!"

We were not fighting knights. We were fighting French mercenaries. There would be no quarter. As I was following our men there was little for me to do save to watch their backs and feel the blood return to my left arm. In a short time, all were dead. I joined the two old men in searching the bodies of those we had slain. We took their arms, helmets, coins, jewels, crosses, in fact, anything of value. Then we tossed their bodies over the side of the bridge into the river. I heard a cheer and looking across the river saw that Sir John had driven the French from the other side of the bridge. They were fleeing west. We had won.

"Will! Come get your horse!"

I nodded and turned to the two old men, "Thank you. Without you I would have perished. I owe you."

One of them put his arm around my shoulder, "No Will son of Harry, we owe you. This will be our last fight." The other held up a purse. "We have enough here to go back to England. We will open a tavern. We will call it the Blue Company. You killed most of these men and the coins should be yours."

I shook my head. "I am just beginning. Take it for you have earned it." They nodded their gratitude.

I made my way back across the bridge. Near to the place where the barricades had stood I saw the body of Michael the Silent. There were other shield brothers dead too. We had paid a price! I put the two swords and the helmet I had taken into the company wagon. The sumpter we had taken meant that we did not need to use men alone to pull it.

Red Ralph said, "If you make two more scabbards then you could keep your swords on your horse."

"Thank you. The helmet I took is a better one too. It has a nasal and strengtheners on the crown."

"They are a little old fashioned and do not give as much protection to the neck; still it is your choice."

As I mounted I saw that my father was crossing the bridge to the northern side. He was wounded but he was smiling. He had a wine skin. One day his luck would run out.

The battle yielded many horses. They were not war horses; they were palfreys, sumpters and rouncys but, as we had done the hardest fighting, our company claimed them. Captain Tom offered me a better horse than Spaniard but for the time she would do me and I declined his offer.

We spent the next six days in Pamplona. Prince Edward had a relapse. He was too unwell to travel. I sold the sword given to me by the soldier from the Red Company and one of the ones I had taken from the battlefield. They both fetched a better price than I had expected. I was able to buy a winter blanket and a cloak. When I had lived with my father I had often shivered in the Aquitaine winters. Red Ralph told me that the English ones were much worse,

We were in the town square enjoying some decent wine, bread and cheese. We were there with Peter the Priest. I did not understand why they spoke of England. I had never been there. "But we fight in Aquitaine and Gascony, not England."

Peter shook his head, "King Edward is old. Already he has ruled for longer than most kings. If Prince Edward returns to England he will have need of men he can rely upon. In England we can be more certain of our pay. As the King of Castile has shown us some of these foreigners are not to be trusted." I was learning about politics. The men who were now my shield brothers were thinkers.

It was my shield brothers who had advised me what to spend my money on and I did as they advised. I quite enjoyed Pamplona. The last few months had seen me grow. Soon I would need new boots. Ralph put it down to the fact that I was eating more regularly. When I had lived with my father I had scavenged more than he had provided. If he had spare coin it went on wine and not on food. Only Long John was taller than I was. I had yet to broaden out but the short leather jerkin I had first worn was now too tight. I had to leave it unfastened. As such it was of little value. We did not think we would need to fight again for a while but it was a worry. I spent wisely.

Long John asked around the camp and discovered that there was a leather maker who might be able to furnish me with a leather jerkin. He proved more than helpful. My Spanish had improved on the journey north. Captain Tom used me to negotiate with the locals. We haggled a price. I had Long John with me and that helped. I was able to afford metal disks which were sewn on to the leather. There were not too many to make it too heavy but enough to protect the leather.

I paid him half and he said, "Young Master, you might consider, before I make it, a padded gambeson to be worn underneath." He shrugged, "My armour can save you from cuts but blows can still break limbs. My brother, two doors away, has a wife who makes them." He saw my hesitation. "Go and get a price and then return. It does not bother me but I will need to adjust for the size if you have a gambeson too."

"There will be no extra charge?"

He smiled, "You haggle well, sir. There will be no extra charge."

The gambeson was not as expensive as I had expected and she had one in my size. If I grew then I could use it unfastened. The leather armour would have thongs to tighten or loosen. I returned to the armour maker and he promised it to me in three days. Two days later Prince Edward left. Sir John had decided it was not safe to stay longer. That left the Free Companies with the task of getting home without the protection of the heir to the English throne. I wondered if I would have time to have my armour finished. Luckily Sir Hugh set about buying provisions. He had been assured, Captain Tom told us, that Prince Edward would pay us the money he owed once we reached Aquitaine. I was not convinced but it allowed me to collect my armour. I wondered if I would need it before we reached Bordeaux.

Chapter 4

The last miles to the pass of Roncesvalles were uneasy ones. We were fewer in number. We had lost men at the bridge as had the other companies. More men died of sickness. The only horsemen now were Sir Hugh, his squire, the standard bearer and us. Our men had managed to capture some horses after the battle. We rode at the fore. If men thought it strange that a youth who had seen barely fifteen summers should be riding with the lord they said nothing. Word of my courage, or as some would say foolishness, at the bridge had raised my standing amongst these swords for hire. Part of me hoped that my father might make peace with me but it seemed to make him angrier. We heard that he half beat a man to death in a drunken rage before he was pulled from him. Had he not shown so much bravery at the bridge then I think Sir Hugh would have cut him loose.

Once we reached Gascony there was relief and yet the journey was far from over. We had the mountains to negotiate and we were running short of food. The good news was that the weather turned cooler once we crossed the Pyrenees.

The Gironde river was a welcome sight. We saw, to the north west of us, the city of Bordeaux. Sir Hugh would not risk a camp close to the city for he still feared that some of the men might try to take their money directly from the Prince. We made a camp far enough away so that men would not be tempted to bother Prince Edward. As it was close to the river men could bathe and we could water our horses. As I had a horse I was one of the men who accompanied Sir Hugh to Bordeaux. At that time, it was the Prince's home. He ruled Aquitaine from that mighty stronghold. Passing through our camp I saw the hatred and resentment from my father. He pointedly spat as we passed.

Peter the Priest saw the gesture and shook his head, "Your father is a troubled man."

Red Ralph did not share the same attitude of Christian forgiveness as the former priest, "I would end his troubles with a knife in the guts. He is a force of nature in battle but he does nothing for the spirit of the men around him. He is the bad apple. Sorry Will, he is your father but…"

"Perhaps it is the fault of me or my mother. He seemed to think his troubles began when I was born and made worse when my mother left."

Captain Tom must have been listening and I saw him shake his head. "Your father is still a relatively young man. I remember when he first joined the company. I was not a captain then. He was wild even as a young warrior. Captain John of Blackheath who led us then hoped that he could mould him into someone who could lead the company. He failed and the wine won."

I reflected the rest of the way to Bordeaux. Had I such a flaw in me? When I had crawled beneath the barricade and fought with Peter I had been as reckless as my father. Would I succumb to the power of wine? Would I become the warrior whom others shunned? Wiser men than I said that the body was controlled by humours. We all had the same humours but some were stronger than others. Peter the Priest appeared to have more humility and forgiveness in him than most men. My father had more anger. Which did I possess? The thoughts troubled me for some time.

Sir Hugh's standing was such that we were admitted to the castle immediately we arrived. Captain Tom went with Sir Hugh and his squire. We went to the guard room. Red Ralph had recognised the sergeant of the guard. They had both served in the London Company.

"Red Ralph, you are still alive. Where has your mop gone?" he patted Ralph's bald pate. "Come out of the sun. We have fine wine here!"

Ralph nodded and spread his arms, "This is Walther of Southwark. He looks civilised now but when he was a young warrior he was as wild as they come!"

The sergeant shook his head and laughed, "Do not disillusion my young guards." He pointed to the door, "It is time to relieve those on the walls. Leave real warriors the table."

As the chamber emptied we sat. I was the new warrior and the young warrior. I remained silent and I listened.

Walther of Southwark raised his goblet, "Here is to Prince Edward and death to the French!" We all toasted. The wine was good but I did not drink as deeply as the rest. I was still thinking of my father and the humours which lay in my body. "I hear that the companies suffered badly. We counted ten thousand of you leaving to head south. We hear that most lie dead in Spain."

Red Ralph nodded, "Aye, had it been in battle that would have been one thing but it was disease and hunger that did for us." He lowered his voice, "The Prince was not paid and he did not pay us. That is not right."

Walther of Southwark leaned forward, "He has asked his parliament for a fouage, or hearth-tax, of ten sous for five years. If it is passed then there will be your money." He leaned back. "I am not sure that all of the lords of Aquitaine will agree. There are many in Poitou who have French sympathies."

"Perhaps a few raids on their lands might encourage them to pay." Long John believed strongly in the right of Kings and Princes to rule as they saw fit.

Walther shook his head, "Let sleeping dogs lie. The last thing we need is a revolt in the north. We need peace."

Dick Long Sword laughed, "Which is contrary to our line of work, Walther of Southwark. We earn our livelihood by war!"

He laughed, "Aye you are right. I have missed those days. Do you remember Ralph when we left England all those years ago? We were little older than the youth who sits silently at the end of the table."

"I remember and do not disparage Will. He has climbed a wall to help us to enter a stronghold and with Peter the Priest was instrumental in forcing the bridge at Arakil Ibaia. He was rewarded with a horse."

The sergeant looked impressed, "Yet he is barely old enough to shave. Still, he looks big enough. If he has the skills he may become a captain."

Peter the Priest said, "Perhaps but not all men choose that road. Perhaps he would become a gentleman."

Walther shook his head, "That is a dream we all share yet it is just that, a dream." He winked at Ralph, "Like being paid regularly!"

The relieved guards appeared in the door. Ralph rose, "Let the working men sit. We are at our leisure. It was good to see you, Walther."

"And you. I nearly forgot. I have a woman now and four children!"

Ralph clapped him on the back, "I see why you stay here then! I have yet to be tied but I am pleased for you."

We stepped outside the guard room and waited in the outer ward for Sir Hugh and Captain Tom to return. Red Ralph was in reflective mood. He turned to me, "Perhaps I should take a wife too eh?"

I listened much and I took in what men said. I was unique among my shield brothers I had been a child in this land and this was one area where I was the expert. I shook my head, "If you are in the Company then I would advise you not to." I gestured with my thumb towards the distant camp, "How many of the women who followed their men survived the march to Valladolid and back? How many children were buried? I was lucky. I know that. Go back to England find a lord with a castle."

Dick Long Sword said, "Wise words from one so young but of all of us you know best the perils of following swords for hire."

Red Ralph rubbed his beard, "I might return to England one day, Will, but that will depend upon the Prince and his promise to pay."

Our lord and captain were within for a long time. When they came out they both looked glum. They were with the Prince and his two sons. The two princes were young. Edward was just five and Richard, three. Their father held their hands. When they reached us he bent down, "These, my sons are the back bone of England. With doughty men like these behind you then the world can be yours." He stood and looked at me, "Will son of Harry, Sir John Chandos said good things about you. When you fought at the bridge of Arakil Ibaia it was you and Peter the Priest who won the day." He took out two gold coins and gave one to me and one to Peter. "Take this as a reward. I have told Sir Hugh that you need to wait but a little time to be paid." I could almost feel the disappointment amongst those around me. I felt guilty about having received the gold piece. "How old are you, Will son of Harry?"

"I am not certain, my lord."

Red Ralph said, "He has seen almost fifteen summers, lord."

"When you have seen two more I would have you as a bodyguard for my sons. What say you?"

There are times when you know not what you ought to say. This was one such time. I was not sure I would wish to be a bodyguard. I enjoyed the friendship of my company and I had much to learn. On the other hand, if I turned down the future King of England then my future would be bleak.

"I would be honoured, Prince Edward although I have much to learn."

"And Captain Tom is just the man to make you into a gentleman."

He turned and returned indoors. We mounted our horses and left the castle. Sir Hugh said, "I have some business at the river. I would ask that you do not tell the Free Companies what transpired. I will gather the captains and tell them myself."

Captain Tom nodded and said, "We will visit the town too, my lord."

We found an inn with a stable and sat ourselves around the table. It was quiet. There were no other men at arms in the town and the Gascon was keen for our custom. He took our order and I said, "Would you change this coin for me? A gold piece is too great a sum to carry."

I watched him weighing up his choices. A gold piece was harder to use. On the other hand, if he did change it for me then a young man like me might well spend it all on ale and wine. Greed won, "Of course, young master."

Long John said, "It will not sit well with the men to wait for pay."

Old Tom leaned forward, "And we will not have to wait. The Prince suggested that we might have a chevauchée. He wishes us to take our pay from the French. We can head north, across the Loire and raid Maine."

"Then we will not receive our pay from him."

The wine and ale arrived. Tom leaned back and said, "Put simply no. We must accept that and make the best of it. There is little alternative. We are Englishmen all and we would not fight our future King, would we?"

The tavern keeper handed me the ten silver coins. When he had gone I gave two coins to each of them. I did not give any to Peter. He had had the same bounty.

Dick Long Sword said, "Why do you do this, Will? You earned it and we did not."

"You did for you took me in and you were kind to me. I have learned much from you. Regard this as payment for my apprenticeship."

They smiled and Peter the Priest said, raising his beaker, "Will son of Harry, you are already on the way to becoming a gentleman. Here's to Will."

"Will!"

"And as an act of friendship I will pay for this round of drinks."

Red Ralph laughed, "Who needs a wife with friends like these!"

We enjoyed two drinks and then headed back to the camp. I did not need to make any more purchases in Bordeaux. The two coins I had gained would go in my purse with the others I was squirrelling away. If the day ever came when I was a gentleman then I would need coin. I would need clothes and a horse which was better than Spaniard. I had grown since I had first acquired her and my feet were closer to the ground. Soon she would be too small for me.

When we reached the camp Sir Hugh had yet to arrive and we were assailed by questions. Captain Tom fended them off by telling them of the offer Prince Edward had made to me. He successfully diverted the attention on to me. I had to endure a hailstorm of questions before Sir Hugh rode up. He gathered the captains in his tent.

I saw to the horses and headed down to the river to fetch more water for them. As I turned to return to the camp my father sidled up. He was drunk. I laid down the bucket.

He snarled at me, "So the son of a whore is to become a gentleman! Your mother thought she was too good for me and so do you."

"Do not speak ill of my mother."

I saw him bunch his fists. I had had many beatings and I recognised the signs. "You little shit! I am your father!"

"I thought you disowned me!"

All the time I was speaking I was watching for the look in his eyes which would tell me he was about to attack me. When I had been younger that had been my signal to run. I was no longer a boy. I was a man and I had faced enemies in battle and slain them. He might still give me a beating but I would not accept it without a fight. I recognised the signs and I was ready. As he launched himself at me I avoided his swinging right hand by ducking and hit him hard in the ribs with my left. He was passed and even as he winced in pain I punched even harder in the same side with my right. I heard something crack. I had broken ribs. He was a street fighter and, as he swung around he suddenly head butted me. I saw stars but I managed to retain my balance. He swung his foot at my groin. I moved backwards, cupped my hands and, catching his boot, threw him backwards. Even as he tried to rise I picked up the bucket of water and swung it at his head. There was a crack and he fell at my feet.

Dick Long Sword and Red Ralph appeared. They saw my father and grinned. Red Ralph said, "With any luck you have killed the bastard!"

Dick knelt next to him and put his ear to his mouth. Shaking his head, he rose, "No, the devil looks after his own! That is the first time in a long time I have seen him bested."

I shook my head, "He was drunk!"

"And that is when he is at his most dangerous. Until we head north, Will, we will watch your back. Your father is a vindictive and sly man."

Red Ralph said, "We could always slit his throat and slip him into the river."

Dick rubbed his chin and then said, "We had better not. Sir Hugh values him as a fighter. Come, Will, we need to tend your eye." The butting head had caught me above the right eye and already it was closing.

By the time we reached our tent, the meeting had finished and few noticed my swelling eye. Peter the Priest frowned until Ralph said, "Fear not! It was his father did this and when you see him you will know who the victor was."

As Peter tended to the wound with vinegar and then witch hazel Captain Tom gathered the rest of the company around him. There were fewer than five hundred of us now. We had begun with more than a thousand. Desertions, disease and death had claimed the rest. He had just finished speaking with them when my father staggered up from the river. His head was bleeding and he limped. He glared as he passed and pointed a finger at me and drew it across his throat.

Red Ralph shouted, "Will has our protection, Harry of Lymm, if you come near him again you will find more than a fist!"

Captain Tom frowned until Ralph explained what had happened. "Ah, perhaps it was for the best." He sat on one of the logs we used for seats, "And now we had better plan where we head for our chevauchée."

Dick said, "The Loire?"

"It is too far and there are targets closer to home. The land around Bergerac is rich. The town itself has a wall and a castle but it is not far for us to travel and the benefits are obvious."

Red Ralph shrugged, "So long as we get coin then I am happy!"

The Captain had maps and we sat and planned what we would do and where we would go. We had horses and could travel further than some of the other companies.

We left for the chevauchée two days later. Most of the company now had a horse of some description but they were not the best and our speed was still that of a walking man. We needed more horses. As we rode I asked Peter the Priest about Sir John Chandos. He seemed, to me at least, to know what he was doing. "Why is he not here now? Surely the Prince needs him."

"The Prince needs coin and until parliament agrees to his request he cannot pay anyone. Who would Sir John lead? He has no men to command and he is back in Normandy on his estates. When the Prince gets the coin he will return."

"Is it his family's land?"

Peter was patient. "No Will. He does not come from noble stock. He was a gentleman who earned great honour at the Battle of Sluys. He was made a knight banneret."

"Then someone who is not of noble blood can become a knight?"

He gave me a curious look, "I suppose so but it is rare. Men such as us can hope to become a Captain. That gives both prestige and honour. Do you wish to become a knight?"

"I will settle for gentleman."

He shook his head, "I fear Prince Edward has put strange ideas in your head. Set yourself lower targets and you will not be disappointed."

I liked Peter the Priest but I would strive to reach the highest rank I could. I had begun life at the bottom. Each step I climbed was an achievement. God smiled on those who tried and I was a trier.

As we were riding in a land we did not know well Captain Tom sent Peter and myself to ride a mile or so ahead of the company. That suited me. I felt more like a warrior now that I was armed like Peter. While we had been camped at Bordeaux I had made myself a scabbard for my saddle sword. When time allowed I would make a second. I also had a knife in the top of my boot. I had seen others use the strategy. I was still unhappy about my shield. The dead man from the Red Company had not looked after it well. Nor had he made it well. Each time we passed a stand of trees I looked wistfully at them. I did not need much wood and a newly hewn oak would be perfect.

The river determined our route. There was a bridge at Bergerac. Too deep for men on foot to ford we had to find somewhere to raid which was north and west of Bergerac. Captain Tom had told us to find rich houses rather than walled cities and towns. At the end of the first day we had found nothing worthwhile. We had discovered a farmhouse. The farmer and his family had fled and we used it for our first camp.

Peter made a suggestion to Captain Tom, "Captain, why don't you get what you can from the farms around here. Will and I will ride all day and see what is further afield. If we travel at the speed of men on foot we will get nowhere." He was right. The farmer had fled on the only horses on the farm. We would have plenty of food and, as the farm also made wine, there would be wine too. The handful of coins was less than the Prince had paid to Peter and me.

"Very well. Find us a good target!"

We left before dawn. Peter had a nose for these things and we headed north across fields. There were trees for cover and it allowed us to ride further without discovery. We found one small target within eight miles of our camp. It was a small settlement. I might have passed it by but Peter noticed a track leading from the handful of houses. We skirted the village and headed through the woods. There was plenty of game. We startled a small herd of deer. Peter reined in and smiled, "Where there is a wood with plenty of deer then there is a lord who likes to hunt."

"Does that not mean a castle?"

"It used to but who knows? Let us approach cautiously. Be ready to flee if we are discovered."

I followed Peter's lead. I think that all the years of meditation and silent reflection had given him patience. He never seemed to hurry. I smelled the wood smoke and knew that there was a dwelling nearby. As the trees thinned we stopped and, tying our horses to a tree, we advanced carefully and cautiously towards the edge. There was a house. It was one hundred paces from us. There looked to be a ditch around it for I saw a bridge. It was a grand house with a wall protecting it. There were fish ponds and it had a tower. Even I knew they added up to a noble. Peter pointed and I saw the two men on top of the tower. The tower would be sanctuary in case of a raid. It also had the advantage that any sentry who watched from its top would be able to see an enemy approach.

Peter signalled for me to back off. As we remounted and rode back to the village he said, "There is one target. The men in the tower are there to watch the road which leads to the village. If Captain Tom approaches through the woods we can be upon them before they have time to take refuge in the tower."

We continued down the road and headed east, away from the village. Peter thought that we might have been seen. He wanted the villagers to think we had headed east. Once we had travelled for a couple of miles we turned north and headed up a small stream and shrubs. Peter was just trying to hide from prying eyes. He seemed confident that we could find another place to raid we just had to be patient. As we climbed through the trees which gave us welcome shade he said, "The purpose of this chevauchée is also to draw out the French. If we can mask our numbers and make some knights and men at arms try to oust us then we can gain more treasure."

"How so?"

He used his fingers as he listed each reason, "Armour, horses, ransom. If we can capture a couple of knights then we will be rich men!"

We reached the head of the stream and there was an open area. We dismounted to let the horses drink. Peter spied a large tree. "Shin up there and see how high you can get."

He seemed to have more confidence in my ability to climb than I did but I complied. I took off my cloak, belt and sword. The hardest part was getting up the lower part of the tree but Peter helped me by letting me stand on his shoulders. I pulled myself up through the tree. There was full foliage and I could not see much. I kept climbing. Amazingly I reached the top. The branches there were thinner and while holding on to the thickest branch I tore away the thinner ones. In this way, I cleared a space and I was rewarded. I spied smoke and the roofs of houses. There was a town. It looked to be no more than three miles to the north east of us. I gingerly turned around but could see little else. Getting down was harder than getting up.

"Well?"

"Three miles north east is a town."

"Then let us investigate eh? If we can take back two targets we will have done well. Was there a wall?"

I buckled my belt and fastened my cloak, "I could not tell."

We picked our way down the slope. We soon found a hunter's trail and we followed it. The trail joined a track which had the marks of wheels upon it. Although the road led east and not north Peter was confident that it would lead us to the town for it descended. We stopped when we heard the noise of people. The noise came from below us. The voices were heading south. We slipped from our horses and crawled through the trees. There below us was a cobbled road. Men, women and horses moved along it. There were one or two heading north but most were heading south. As we lay there, hidden by the undergrowth we listened to the conversations. It soon became obvious that the small town had a market. The name sounded like Saint Meard. When the road became empty Peter slipped down to the road and said, "Keep watch!"

He disappeared, leaving me alone. It seemed an age until he returned. I pulled him up and he nodded, "Come, I have seen enough. The town has a wooden wall and a gate. It is nothing. There is no town watch. We have our two targets."

It was almost dark when we reached the farm. Captain Tom was worried, "We thought you had been captured?"

Peter laughed easily, "The lad is a natural. We have two targets. One is a town and the other a small hall and village."

"Could we take them both on the same day?"

"I don't see why not. Will, you could find the hall again couldn't you."

"Aye."

"Then he can lead you to them. We will need to leave before dawn for the men to reach the town but it will be worth it. They held a market today. That means there will be coin aplenty in the town. It has a small wooden wall and gate but nothing to worry us. The hall has a tower."

Captain Tom gathered his leaders around him and explained his plan while we ate. Red Ralph came over, "We are leaving four men to watch this farm." He grinned at me, "One is your father. He has still to recover!"

I did not feel as happy about it as Ralph. I had hurt my father. Was that a sin?

Chapter 5

Captain Tom and Dick Long Sword went with Peter and the smaller part of the company. Red Ralph led the rest of the men with us. There were only a hundred of us. More than half were archers. The majority of our men were with the captain and the larger target that was the town. I knew that we had the shorter journey but much was expected of me. As we rode at the head of the marching men Ralph asked me more questions about the places we had discovered. They were astute questions and would determine our plan of attack.

"Long John you take twenty men and cut off the village. If we secure that then no matter what happens at the hall we will have something for our pains. We will use speed to take the hall and tower."

We split up close to the village and I led, walking Spaniard. We stopped well shy of the edge of the wood and I tied my horse to a tree and put my cloak over the saddle. I would need my helmet and my shield. Red Ralph could see the hall and he waved our men forward. We had fifty archers with us. When we reached the edge of the trees, he pointed at the two men at the top of the tower. "I will take the rest of the men and run to the gate. You have to stop those two from raising the alarm."

Edgar, who led the archers, nodded, "They are dead men already!"

We moved to the treeline and watched the two men. They walked the walls and eventually would turn away from us. When we could no longer see their faces, he waved his sword and we ran. We covered half the distance before the two guards turned and saw us. Six of the arrows found a mark and the men died. Unfortunately, one died noisily. He plunged over the side of the tower and screamed. There was a thud as he hit the ground. We were just forty paces from the gates and I felt sure that they would be closed but, amazingly, they were not. The reason became obvious as a rider galloped out of them. He was going for help. The cleverness of Ralph's plan became apparent. The rider would be stopped by Long John's men at the village. More importantly, the defenders were struggling to close the gate.

"Run Will! Stop them!"

I was young and I was fast. I hurled myself at the gates as they came together. With my shield before me, I crashed into them. My weight meant that they could not close them and when Red Ralph threw his weight behind me they burst open! The force of our charge knocked the three men to the ground. I drew my sword and turned to face the one to my left. He had no shield. He picked up his pole axe and swung it at me. I dropped my head below the swashing blow. My battle was with him. I flung up my left hand and my shield hit the shaft of the pole axe, knocking it upwards. I stepped forward and swung my sword. At the same time, he attempted to bring the pole axe head down on my head, but I was inside him and just the haft hit my helmet. My sword hacked into his leather armour and it stopped the blade from penetrating but I had hurt him I could see. I brought up the edge of my shield under his chin and his head jerked back. Hooking my right leg behind his left I punched him in the face with the hilt of my sword and he fell over.

I had my sword at his throat, "Yield or die!" I think he was surprised to be given the choice. That made him think he could still win. His eyes flicked to his left where his pole axe lay. I pushed harder with my sword and blood trickled down his neck. "I will not ask again!"

His eyes closed in resignation. "I yield."

I looked around and saw that the others had managed to overcome the remaining men at the gate. The archers had made up for the noisy despatch of the sentry and they had stopped anyone taking shelter in the tower. I gestured with my sword for the man I had captured to stand. I saw that he had a mail hood, a good baldric, scabbard and sword. I sheathed my sword and began to take them from him. He stiffened. I shook my head, "Do not try anything. You surrendered and the other men have lost. Accept it." His shoulders slumped. He had seen my youth and regretted his decision to yield but the sight of my comrades appearing in large numbers deterred any further resistance. I took his purse. He had twelve silver coins. His hand went to his neck. He had a cross. I smiled, "Your cross is safe! Now move to the others." I watched him walk over to the rest of the captives and I returned to Spaniard. I hung my treasures from the saddle. Now I could have a second scabbard on the saddle. As I led my horse to the hall I realised that Spaniard's days as a riding horse were numbered. She was simply not big enough.

When I reached the hall, I regretted going back to my own horse. We had captured more than twenty horses. Had I been with them then, as I had captured a man, I might have been able to claim one. I smiled to myself and gave myself a mental telling off. I had done well enough and I would find a good horse. I just had to be patient.

There were two plough horses and we used those to pull a wagon with all of our booty. We headed back to the farm. We reached it first. We had plenty of food and wine as well as the treasure of the house. The ladies had had rings and jewels. There had been a chest of coins buried beneath the floor of the tower. All was well!

Captain Tom and the others returned just before sunset. Although they too had found horses, weapons, food and wine, they had also found more opposition. Whilst we had lost none he had lost thirty of his men. The good news was that we now had almost enough horses for all of us. Only my father and those who had guarded the camp were without horses.

Captain Tom was dismissive of his complaints that he had no horse, "When we travel back to Bordeaux in the morning you can ride in the cart."

None of my band of brothers had been hurt. I knew that I was lucky to have such friends. Peter the Priest, however, was a little worried about the ramifications of the raid. "The French will not sit idly by while we raid their land. The sooner we are in Bordeaux the better it will be."

Long John said, "We have not had all the money promised to us. At a shilling a day we still have far to go before we are fully reimbursed."

I fingered, guiltily, the coins I had taken from the Frenchman. I had counted them on the way back. I had six week's wages already. When I added in the money I had already taken I was not owed anything by the Prince. I kept quiet.

Red Ralph shook his head, "We will get our pay. I have known men wait a year or more for pay." He pointed at my father who had found a wine skin. "What would we do with the coin? Most men would waste it on wine and doxies! When I am paid off it is back to England for me."

Dick Long Sword looked at his friend in surprise, "I thought you would end your days as a captain, Red Ralph."

"I tire of this life, I want a bed at night and sheets which are changed at least once a month. I want regular food and an outhouse in which to take a shit!"

Long John laughed, "If an outhouse is all it takes we will build you one!"

They bantered into the night. Like all swords for hire they had dreams. Red Ralph had been doing this the longest. I was young but I knew enough to realise that all of them would reach that viewpoint eventually. The two white beards with whom I had fought at the bridge had shown me that. Would I be left alone when they departed for England?

It took time to break camp. We stripped everything of value from the farm. All of the chickens and fowl had been eaten already but we had two pigs who shared the wagon with my father and the wounded. Laden with booty, we moved slowly. Captain Tom was no fool and he had scouts with the van and at the rear. It was the ones at the van who discovered trouble. Robert the Breton galloped back. "Captain Tom there are French horsemen ahead and they would dispute the road."

"How many?"

"We spied five banners and there are over three hundred horses."

Five banners meant at least fiver bannerets and they might have up to five or six bachelor knights with them. Had there just been men at arms we could have swept them away.

Captain Tom turned to Captain Jack. "We will form a battle line. Ride behind us and then place yourselves on the flanks when we meet them. Let us see if we can make them charge."

Captain Jack was a confident man, "Aye Tom, we will do that. You have no lances." It was a statement of fact.

"I know. We can do little about it now. We are in God's hands." He turned in the saddle, "Harry of Lymm, you and the men guard the wagon!"

"I can fight!"

"We all know that but you have no horse and you have wounds." He smiled at me. I had inflicted the wounds. "Blue Company. We ride!"

When we reached the Frenchmen, I could see that they had chosen the place for the battle well. They had, to their right, the river. That flank was secure. On their left flank was a small knoll. There were fifty crossbows there, hidden behind pavise and shields. Their leader, he had a rampant blue gryphon on a red field on his shield, was using the knights as a battering ram. There were thirty of them with squires and men at arms behind. The knoll and the river constricted the field. They waited. They could afford to. Peter had said to me, as we approached, "There will be more men coming behind us. The ones ahead are to stop and hold us. This is an ambush. They mean to have us all slaughtered. We are swords for hire and not worth ransom. All that we are worth is our horses, weapons and the coins in our purses."

Captain Tom said to me, "Your horse is too small to be in the front rank. Ride behind me." He smiled, "You can be my squire for the day eh?"

I nodded and walked Spaniard behind Badger. I did not like it but it made perfect sense. This was a day for men who knew what they were doing and not a boy who had barely begun to shave. One in two of the men in our front rank had spears. The lances of the French knights would hit them first. The knights had slightly longer shields and would be able to protect their legs. They also wore helmets with visors. A blow to the head was normally fatal but not when the enemy wore a visored helmet. The odds were in the Frenchmen's favour. What we had going for us was the ability to fight. As my father had shown when he had fought me by the river the Blue Company did not follow any rules when they fought.

I was pleased that Captain Tom was flanked by my four shield brothers. I was also honoured that he had asked for me to ride behind him. The rest of the front rank were also our most experienced men. We had a slightly wider frontage than the French but we were shallower. I saw the archers dismount. The ones by the river had nowhere to flee if things went awry. The ones on our right would have to eliminate the crossbows first.

Peter the Priest said, "Captain, if they are waiting then they have men coming from behind. The longer we wait the less chance we have of success."

"Aye, you are right." He stood in his saddle and raised his sword, "Captain Jack! Now if you please!"

"Aye! May God be with you!" I saw men making the sign of the cross.

Captain Tom shouted, "For the Blue Company! Prince Edward and England!" He spurred Badger. Badger was a war horse. I knew not how Captain Tom had come by him but he showed his breeding by opening a lead. Captain Tom pulled back on the reins, "Not so fast my black beauty."

Ahead a horn sounded. We had forced the French knight's hand. He could not take a charge at the stand. They had to be moving. Suddenly I heard the whoosh of arrows as Captain Jack's men sent their first missiles into the air. There were shouts and screams as they fell first amongst the crossbows and then in the serried ranks of men at arms on the French right. They had poorer protection. Our archers were our greatest advantage. They might not win this skirmish for us but they could give Captain Tom the chance to do so.

Our horses now had their legs open and were galloping. Poor Spaniard was doing her best to keep up but she was struggling. I was lucky in that the ones behind me had the poorest of horses and they were falling back too. The only advantage I could see was that we would not be hard on the heels of those before us. We would have time to react. I was able to observe Captain Tom. He had lowered himself in his saddle to make himself as small a target as he could. He had his sword resting across his saddle. He could not out reach a spear. His shield covered his body and half of his face. I realised that those of our men who wore the kettle helmets which had been so useful in Spain would now be at a disadvantage. The pot helmet I wore and which had been scorned by my friends would be less likely to be knocked from my head.

We were closing rapidly now as the French horses built up their speed. With the crossbows eliminated the archers were now thinning out the ranks of men and horses. As the French knights came in range I saw them taking hits. Some had leather armour and caparisons on their horses. Even so, some were struck. I saw a man at arms pitched from his horse. He caused the two horses behind to baulk. One of the knights was struck in the neck by an arrow. It was almost comical the way his shoulder slowly lowered and then the weight of his helmet and mail dragged his body from the horse. He was still alive and his left foot was in the stirrup. His weight dragged the horse to the ground and the fall knocked two other knights to the side. I saw that it was where Captain Tom and my four friends would hit. There was a hole. As they reached the fallen horse, which was trying to rise, Captain Tom and Red Ralph made their horses leap over the horse and rider.

I had time to move Spaniard to the right and avoid the dying knight and flailing hooves of his horse. As luck would have it one of the knights who had been knocked to the side was struggling to control his horse. His lance was waving uselessly up and down. I had my sword across my saddle and, as I passed the knight I swung my sword backhanded. I hit behind his upper arm where there was no metal plate. The edge of my Spanish sword hacked through to the bone. The lance fell. I passed the horse with my bloody blade. A lance came towards me. A knight had seen what I had done to his fellow and he sought vengeance. My shield was on my left and I just had a sword for protection. It would not be enough. It was the size of Spaniard which saved me. That and the metal disks on my armour. I was lower than the knight expected and he aimed at my head. I lowered my head as the lance came towards me. My helmet would give me some protection. The wooden lance hit my helmet hard but I managed to move my head to the left and the lance head slid off and hit my right shoulder. It felt as though I had been hit by a hammer but the metal disks held and the lance head broke. I felt dizzy but I was alive. I lifted my head and saw that Captain Tom, Red Ralph and the others had now stopped. They were fighting the squires.

Arrows still flew over our heads. I saw a squire swing his sword towards Peter the Priest's unguarded back. An arrow suddenly struck his shoulder and drove deep into his body. If a knight fought he would not kill a squire. We had no such compunction and I saw boys, a little younger than I, trying to fight greybeards like Captain Tom. Their lances and spears were useless because we were too close to one another and my friends' swords found gaps in mail.

I dug my heels in Spaniard's side and headed to a man at arms who was trying to get at Dick Long Sword. He was already fighting two others and his back was unprotected. I managed to force Spaniard between the Frenchman and Dick. I took his blow on my shield and used my knees to wheel the agile Spaniard around. I brought my sword across the Frenchman at arms' chest. His left hand had the reins too and he struggled to bring up his shield. My sword hit his chest hard. He reeled. He was above me and I stood in the stirrups. As he struggled for breath I brought down my sword from on high. My height helped me. Even though his sword came up it was a weak block. The edge drove deep into his shoulder. Dick Long Sword had seen off his two opponents and his Long Sword lunged to drive into the body of the Frenchman and come out of his back. He slid from the saddle.

Dick Long Sword shouted, "This is no place for you. I thank you for your help. Take the horse back to our wagon! You have acquitted yourself well."

I was about to refuse and then I realised that if I stayed I might put others in jeopardy. I had been lucky and a warrior had only so much luck. I think Dick saved my life that day. I sheathed my sword and grabbed the reins in my right hand. I saw that the men who had been behind me were either dead or had advanced to fight on. As I rode towards the wagon I saw that my father had disobeyed his orders. He was running through the battlefield with a sword and a dagger. As I passed him I saw him drag a man at arms from his saddle and hack him to death. He did not see me for the blood was in his head. He would not stop now until there were no men left to kill.

I reined in at the wagon. John of Talacre was there. Three dead Frenchmen lay around the wagon. I knew not where their horses were. He grinned, "You did well young Will. It is good that you are here for your father has abandoned us." He pointed, A handful of men at arms had managed to break through and were heading for us. I wondered where the archers had gone and then I saw them in the midst of the battle doing as my father did. They were dragging men from horses and using their short swords and daggers to good effect.

Spaniard was spent and so I dismounted and climbed on the horse I had captured. It was a bigger horse. Spaniard wandered off. She would not go far. John Talacre and the others were using the wagon as a fighting platform. They had pole axes and war hammers. My task would be to keep the French horses at bay if I could. I know not where I had found the ability to ride. Since I had been four years' old I had found it easier to ride than most men. I grabbed the reins and, drawing my sword, rode at the horseman who was closest to the wagon. We approached each other shield to shield. As his companions rode around me I jerked my new horse's reins to the left as I punched with my shield. He reeled and that allowed me to swing my sword. I hit his back but I did not manage to cut through his leather armour. The blow was hard and I saw him grunt in pain. I continued my turn and I was almost behind him. As he tried to turn to face me I swung my sword. The blow was weaker for I was tiring. I caught his hand with my sword. He had leather gauntlets but I drew blood. I would not be able to keep this up for long. I had to end it. I stood in the stirrups and swung my sword across the Frenchman's chest. His arms went in the air and his back arced as he fell from the saddle. There was an ugly sound as his neck hit the ground. I knew that he was dead. Two of the men at arms had also been slain by John and the others. The rest had fled. As I grabbed the reins of the dead man's horse I saw that the battle was over. We had prevailed. Losses looked to be about even on both sides but the knights had realised that they could not win and they retreated. We would get no ransoms!

I sheathed my sword and took off my helmet. John Talacre said, "That was well done, Will. The horse is yours. We shall have the others."

I shook my head. "I have Spaniard and this one. They will suffice. But, with your permission, I shall search the dead man!"

"Go ahead. We have enough from those that we slew. Your father shall have no share. He abandoned us. A man does not do that." He shook his head, "He has bad blood within him. You must have yours from your mother."

The dead man at arms had a sword and scabbard which I could probably sell. His dagger was a long narrow one and I did not have one of those. It would be useful. His leather armour was no longer any use but he had shoes which looked like they might fit me. His purse had silver in it. I took his helmet as it was conical with a peak and flared back. It was designed to make a sword strike slide down it. I took off my pot one. The blow from the spear had dented it. I smiled. It might end up as a cooking pot after all. I tied my new horse to the wagon and fetched Spaniard. The new saddle was better than my old one. I would use Spaniard as a sumpter. I transferred my scabbards to my new horse. I stroked her mane. I had ascertained that it was a mare. She had a lovely golden colour and her mane was almost blond. "I shall call you Sunrise."

Captain Tom and the rest of those who had fought, and survived, came back from the battlefield. I saw that my four shield brothers lived. All four of them led a horse each. On their saddles hung the armour, helmets and weapons they had taken. John Talacre spoke with Captain Tom and I saw him pointing at me. The other four dismounted and began to examine the horses they had captured. I was honour bound to ask the question of Dick Long Sword, "You killed the warrior who rode this horse. Do you want her?"

He cocked his head to one side, "You defeated him. All that I did was to clear the saddle for you. Besides I have a war horse I captured from a knight."

Just then my father wandered back. He was besmirched and bespattered with blood. He had found, on the battle field, a skin of wine. Captain Tom dismounted and stood with his hands on his hips, "It seems, Harry of Lymm, that you are incapable of following any orders. It is fortunate that your son does. Had he not returned then the men left to guard the wagon might be dead and we would have lost all that we collected on this raid."

My father laughed, "At least the river rat is good for something." He gave a mock bow, "Thank you, your lordship."

Red Ralph was going to go over to him and strike him but Peter the Priest restrained him. "He is troubled and does not have long for this world, I fear."

Ralph said, "Do you tell fortunes now?"

He shook his head, "It does not take a seer to know that drinking so much wine and eating so little food can do you little good. He will not see England again."

I had not thought of that. He was still my father. John Tallboy had said that he had bad blood. Perhaps it was not that. There were daemons, men said, and they grew inside a man and took him over. My father was fighting a battle with something inside him.

Chapter 6

The other companies had had varying degrees of success. Sir Hugh was happy for, when we returned to our camp at Bordeaux then there was peace. Men had coin, food and wine. As our company was now fully mounted, once more, then we could move faster if we needed to. A month after our return our leader visited us again. He and the captains were in conference for half a day. Captain Tom gathered our company around him. "Prince Edward asked for a hearth tax, fouage, on the estates of his richest lords. He did it to pay us!" There was a cheer. "However, they have refused to pay and are in revolt against their lawful prince."

There was an uproar. I heard men saying that we could take their estates and get the money for ourselves. Others made dire threats against every lord. It did not take much to turn men into a mob. The mood was ugly.

Captain Tom raised his arms for silence. "Worse, the King of France, Charles has sided with the rebels and demanded that Prince Edward should come to Paris and receive his judgement, as his liege lord."

There was a stunned silence.

Captain Tom smiled, "Sir Hugh was there and heard his answer. *'We will willingly attend at Paris on the day appointed since the king of France sends for us, but it shall be with our helmet on our head and sixty thousand men in our company!'"*

Once again there was a cheer for this was our kind of language. We hated the French and as we had defeated their King and his armies at every turn we were more than willing to go to war. Men shouted that we would march on Paris ourselves. I was able to watch and take all of this in. I was almost detached. Sir Hugh and the Prince had been very clever. The men would fight for no pay. Captain Tom had not promised money. We would fight for our Prince.

"Sir John Chandos is bringing troops from the north. King Edward has sent the Earls of Cambridge and Pembroke, and Sir Robert Knolles to assist his son. Sir Hugh will lead the six thousand men of the Free Companies with Prince Edward and we will attack from the south! We go to war! Prepare yourselves."

Now that we were going to war we had to prepare quickly. I managed to sell my spare equipment. Men in other companies were willing to pay. As it was winter I used some of my money to buy warmer blankets and cloaks for the journey. I had learned much since I had joined the Blue Company. I also bought two spears. I had never used one but I knew that they would be useful. When time allowed I would have Red Ralph teach me how to use one.

My father had no horse. He was one of the few who did not. Our battle with the French had resulted in losses amongst our men but that was more than compensated for by the large number of horses we had taken. My father, and the other men without horses, were given the company wagon. With the exception of my father, most were weak warriors and that was why they had not gained a horse. They feared him and the four men became his followers. It seemed to improve his humour. He did not care that they were poor men at arms whom no one else would countenance as shield brothers. He moulded them into his own. As I had Spaniard to carry my war gear I did not need to use the wagon.

We headed north towards the Loire. With two armies heading from Brittany and Calais we hoped to catch the rebels between us and destroy them completely. Prince Edward was not a well man. He had not recovered fully from the illness or the poisoning from the Spanish campaign. He would not, however, ride in a wagon. He rode his horse. Each company took it in turns to be his escort. He had always done this. It was why we fought for him even when he did not pay us. He was a warrior and we loved him.

He liked our company best of all. Captain Tom had been with him at Poitiers and the two chatted easily as old friends. That was despite the difference in their births. As usual, I was riding behind Red Ralph. Prince Edward suddenly turned and waved me forward, "Ride next to me, Will son of Harry."

As I rode forward Peter the Priest said, "Give me Spaniard." I handed him my horse's reins.

"Captain Tom has told me that you are one of the best warriors he has. That is high praise indeed."

"I am lucky, my lord, to serve with such good teachers and in such a fine company."

The Prince nodded, "Modest too. You have grown apace and I hear that you have killed almost ten men."

"I have not been keeping count, my lord."

"You should for they were enemies all! I asked you once if you would serve as my sons' bodyguard. I did not give you the chance to say nay. You may answer freely now. Would you be as someone who can teach my boys how to become men? There will be others to teach them to read, to write, to dance, to speak languages, to eat correctly," he used a hand to dismiss those as irrelevancies, "a warrior does not need such things. He needs to be able to stand his ground with men about him who are of a similar humour. What say you?"

I had a choice and I guessed, or hoped, at least, that he meant what he said. Since he had first spoken to me I had enjoyed the advice of my four shield brothers. Red Ralph and Peter the Priest were both of the same opinion. If I wished to be a gentleman then this would be my best chance. I would learn all those things that the Prince said were irrelevant. For me to become a gentleman they were vital.

"I can put my hand on my heart, lord, I would be honoured to protect your sons and to pass on the little I have learned."

The relief on his face touched me, "You will not regret it. When my son, Edward, becomes King and is fully grown you may do as Sir John Chandos does for me. You may lead his men to war."

That night, as we camped, there was a discussion amongst my friends about my decision. Peter and Ralph were pleased but Long John just shook his head, "I do not envy you, Will. Courtiers are treacherous bastards. They would knife each other in the back and smile when they were doing it. You will need eyes in the back of your head. Prince Edward's younger brother, John of Gaunt, has made no secret of the fact that he would be king one day. He has a son too, Henry. Mark my words there will be blood on the crown and you had better be careful that you are not spattered with it!"

As events turned out his words were prophetic but, as we headed north my life seemed to be taking an entirely new direction. I had seen the worst of life and now the best beckoned.

Once we reached the Loire we had reached the extent of friendly land. There had been a time when the mighty fortresses of the northern bank, Chinon, Tours, and Saumur had been part of Henry the Second's Empire. Now they were French. The bridges would be held. We needed a crossing and so we headed east to find somewhere we could ford. We had enough horses to ford the river and then force one of the bridges across the mighty Loire. Despite our equine gains we still had some men who marched on foot and guarded the baggage.

We headed east and passed Tours yet still found nothing. Then one of the scouts returned with the news that he had found an island in the middle of the river. It meant a ford and then a swim. Prince Edward came to us. "Those without mail can cross here. The scouts say there is a small town with a bridge two miles upstream. We will head there and you can take the bridge from the north. They will not expect it."

Sir Hugh nodded, "I will take the Blue Company."

The men who would be crossing the river prepared. We hung and secured our helmets and shields from our saddles. We checked the girths and reins. We spoke to our horses.

Despite his seniority and his wealth Captain Tom still wore a leather jerkin studded with metal disks. He led us. We headed down to the water. As we entered the shallow southern arm I saw movement in the trees downstream. We were being watched. Riding at the head of the column I was close enough to see that Captain Tom did not appear worried. He rode with Sir Hugh.

Peter leaned over as we clambered up onto the sandy spit of an island in the middle of the river. We had managed to get into the water easily for it was not a steep bank. On the north bank it looked a little steeper. "It does not matter if they see us coming. Once we reach the other bank we can gallop. We will out run any watchers. Now hang on to your saddle when we enter the water. Swim upstream. You have a strong horse. I fear Spaniard would have struggled here."

We had more than forty paces to swim and the current was strong. I took my lead from Red Ralph ahead of me. As we stepped down into the river he kicked his feet free from his stirrups and lying along his horse's back, turned the animal's head to face upstream. I did the same. As Sunrise stepped into the water I felt the force of the river. I held on to the saddle as well as the reins and I shouted encouragement to my horse. She was powerful and she kicked. The water was cold, almost icy. My breeches became soaked and I saw why Prince Edward had sent the riders without mail. Thomas the Welshman fell from his horse. He managed to cling on to the reins and he bobbed to the surface. Long John moved his horse closer to the struggling man at arms and Thomas scrambled back to the saddle. Had he had mail he would have been dragged beneath the waters of the Loire.

When Sunrise's hooves found solid ground I was relieved. Once on the other shore I put my feet in the stirrups. I felt the water sloshing around in my boots. I would be uncomfortable until I could find the time to empty them.

Captain Tom wasted no time in heading down the road which ran along the northern bank of the Loire. We galloped hard for when we reached the town we would be leaving our horses to fight on foot. Ralph said, as we galloped down the road, that he hoped we would catch them with their gate open. That would make our life easier. A year or two earlier and I might have been worried about attacking a walled town. However, since then I had scaled a wall and gained entry. There was no unknown to frighten me. I was close enough to Captain Tom to see the empty road ahead of us. It did not remain empty for long as we caught up with those fleeing from the sound of our hooves. There was little to be gained from drawing our swords and striking down at the people who dived into the undergrowth at our approach. Our blades were for warriors.

The fleeing populace helped us for the town watch kept the gates open as long as possible. In the event it was too long. Badger's long legs took Captain Tom through them with the rest of us close on his heels. Sir Hugh was next to him. He too had a good war horse. Old Tom's sword swept down to hack into the arm of the Frenchman who tried to bar his progress. There was a garrison. Many were on the walls while others were guarding the bridge. Captain Tom shouted, "Red Ralph, take some men and secure the bridge. The rest of you dismount and secure the gate."

Sir Hugh returned to the outside of the gate to encourage those of our men who were tardy.

"Will, Dick, John, Peter, Harold, Robert; with me. Peter, take the tower!"

I dug my heels and Sunrise leapt after Red Ralph. There were two small towers at the town end of the bridge. I could see the standards and banners of Prince Edward and the rest as they snaked their way along the southern side of the river. The French had a gate between the two towers. I looked up and saw a crossbow. It was aimed at me. I heard the crack and I lowered my head. My new helmet saved me. The angle and its shape deflected the bolt. I heard it hit my saddle. I was just grateful that it had not been Sunrise. I kept my head down as we galloped towards the gate. It took time to load a crossbow and they are inaccurate against moving targets.

Red Ralph reined in and shouted, "Dismount! Get the gates. The Prince awaits us!"

Normally we would have tied our horses but they had nowhere to go. I slipped from my saddle and pulled up my shield. I was just in time for a bolt slammed into it. The tip protruded through. It made me angry. I would have to repair the shield. I ran towards the right-hand tower. There was a door at the bottom. One of those who had been watching us turned to run in. I was young and I was fast. I reached it before Peter the Priest who was behind me. The Frenchman tried to close the door. I had grown in the last two years. I had eaten better. I was big and I was strong. Making certain that the crossbow bolt was not near my arm I hurled my shield, with the weight of my body behind it, at the door. The Frenchman had managed to close it but not yet bar it. I heard him cry as the wooden door smashed into him. He crashed into the wall. It was dark and stygian inside. I just lunged at the form which lay close to my left leg. I must have struck flesh as there was resistance and then my blade slid along bone. There was a scream.

Peter stood behind me, "Well done! Watch my back!" Holding his shield above his head he began to clamber up the steps which led to the fighting platform.

We were lucky. Those on the walls were too concerned with trying to stop the rest of our men who were galloping up to the gate. Peter burst through the trapdoor and I heard the clash of steel. He moved to the left and it allowed me to clamber through. A spear came from my right. It was aimed at Peter's unprotected back. The top of my shield, more by accident than intent, deflected it in the air. I instinctively stabbed with my sword. The interior of the wooden tower was dark and an accurate strike was impossible. I sliced through his breeks and blood flowed from his thigh. The man's momentum carried him forward and, as I stepped through the trapdoor, my helmet rammed under his chin and he fell inside, unconscious.

The door to the fighting platform was enticingly open and I stepped over the Frenchman and into the light. After the dark of the tower it was almost blinding. There were men further down the fighting platform. I saw the man who had hit my shield with the crossbow. He was loading the weapon. I ran at him. A crossbow is heavy and hard to lift. He was still raising it when I hit him with my shield and he and his machine of the devil fell from the wooden walkway to crash on to the cobbles below.

The blood cleared from my head and I remembered that I was supposed to be watching Peter's back. I turned and ran back. The tower remained empty. When I reached the other side, I saw Peter making the sign of the cross over the Frenchman he had just slain. I glanced to the bridge and saw that the Prince and the rest of the men were advancing across it. A quick glance told me that Peter the Priest had used his mace to cave in the side of the French defender's head. Below my feet I heard the heavy gates as they creaked open. Peter was searching the body of the man he had killed. I said, "I am sorry I did not stay behind you. The blood was in my head!"

He nodded, "You did as I asked. That spear would have ended my life. Go check his purse and the other I slew!"

I sheathed my sword and slid my shield around my back. The tip of the bolt scraped across my leather. I would have to remove it when I could. I searched the man who was unconscious first. His purse contained a few silver coins. He wore good boots but his feet were too small. He had no sword but he had a long, pointed dagger. The Lombards called them a stiletto. I put it in my boot and then dropped the Frenchman through the trapdoor. The one Peter had killed had a sword, a helmet and a full purse. I took them and went back to Peter. I handed them to him.

He nodded and said, "I will split his purse with you later." I was not expecting that. I smiled. "You earned it. You have another to search!"

I headed back down the ladder. The man I had struck with my sword had bled to death. He lay in a pool of sticky blood. He had a sword and I took it. His purse was heavier than the other two. I took that also. He had boots but, again, they were too small. The Frenchmen were like midgets. Long Tom called them monkeys. I had never seen a monkey but heard of them. There was little else of value and so I stepped outside. I was just in time to see Prince Edward ride through the gates. Even with his visor down he could not be mistaken. He was the only knight with black mail. Red Ralph thought it a foolish indulgence for it drew enemies to him.

Raising his visor, the Prince said, "Well done, Red Ralph! Once again I am indebted to the Blue Company!"

He and the knights who followed him rode to the centre of the town. Red Ralph took off his helmet and turned to me. "Young Will, you have more courage than sense. Next time wait for another to join you. You could have been killed!"

Peter the Priest was walking behind me, "He was right to do so Ralph. Had the Frenchman barred the door then we would have had the devil's own job to break it down. It was my fault for being too slow!" He handed me a gold louis and five silver pieces. "Here, Will, you are becoming a rich man!"

Long Tom and William the Welshman came out of one of the houses. They had a ham, two loaves, a wine skin and a cheese. They raised them and Long Tom said, "To the victor!"

The town was now filling up and I saw my father. Hatred and envy oozed from every pore of his body. He was a lonely figure now. He was shunned by almost all. The one man who could bear him had died of the bloody shits as we had crossed the Pyrenees. No one wanted a violent and unpredictable drunk as a shield brother. The four men on the wagon were not friends, they were terrified of him. I knew that the only reason Captain Tom allowed him to stay with the company was because of me. He had burned all of his other bridges and was now a lonely and desperate figure.

As we had been the first ones in the town we naturally claimed the best accommodation. Our men had suffered wounds in the attack and the Prince did not object when we took over a merchant's hall. He and his knights naturally chose the lord of the manor's hall. I believe we had the better of it for it was the home of a rich merchant. We searched it when we entered and even my father followed the rules and rituals of the company. All that we had taken from the dead was placed in the centre of the table and Captain Tom divided it equitably. He was our leader and all trusted both his judgement and his fairness. My purse was growing heavier day by day. If and when the Prince paid us I would be rich. Red Ralph now had enough for his inn in England.

Once we had claimed our sleeping spaces we saw to our horses. The merchant had stables. Our mounts were crowded but they had grain, water and shelter. I found a hammer at the blacksmith's forge and I hammered the bolt out of my shield. The shield was not ruined but it was weakened. I would need to replace the leather. As we were moving the next day that would have to wait. While I was at the forge I sharpened my weapons. I now had two good swords in my saddle scabbards as well as the one hanging from my new baldric. I was no longer the ragged boy who had been barefoot and with torn clothes. I now looked like one of the Blue Company.

The five who shared our cooking pot all acted as my guardians. I drank ale and wine with the rest of them but if I looked to have too much then one of them, normally Peter or Ralph would take the beaker from me. It was as though I had lost one father and found four substitutes and a grandfather. Captain Tom was summoned to a meeting with the Prince and so we all shared in the cooking duties. There was a kitchen in the hall but we used the fire in the centre of the hall to cook that which we had found. Peter the Priest had found some flour and, with a pot of ale we had found, he kneaded dough for bread. There was a bread oven in the town and when the dough was ready we would cook it there. Fresh, hot bread was a luxury. We used the ham bone, some sausage and a scrawny chicken to form the basis for a stew. I searched the town and discovered a garden. I picked greens and herbs to augment it. When Long John found some dried beans, the stew was complete. It would bubble and simmer away all day. We had the ham we had taken from the bone, the cheese and day-old bread. Along with the wine skin that would tide us over until the stew and the bread were ready.

We took off our leather armour and hung our weapons. They were close to hand but the Prince had set the Yellow Company to watch. They had had the easiest of marches. It was almost civilised to sit on chairs, watch a fire, drink ale and wine and just talk. I knew nothing. I was a boy and so I would listen to these wise warriors who had being fighting longer than I had been alive.

"It is fortunate for us that these French were piss poor warriors. They did not put up much of a fight."

Peter shook his head, "This is not the hard part of the chevauchée yet, Long John. This border belonged to the Prince's grandfather until relatively recently. The French have barely claimed it back. Wait until we reach Maine and Normandy. There they will fight to hold on to what they have taken. The King of France is an ambitious man! King John lost much of his father's Empire. The French wish to keep it that way." He turned to me. "And this one needs better armour."

Ralph said, "I have some mail I took from a knight when we were in Spain. You could do as I do and put it across your shoulders. You really need a coif or aventail. The protector for your head will not stop a sword across your neck."

"Thank you, Ralph."

"You will need a stitching awl. I think Captain Tom has one. Ask him when he returns. I think one of the dead Frenchmen was wearing a thin leather vest." He laughed, "My sword went through easily enough. There may be enough for you to make the thongs to attach it."

"Where was the body?"

It will be with the others. The Prince had them piled by the north gate. He intends to burn them tomorrow!"

I hurried out. Already men were drinking. Those who ran inns and taverns had just hidden when we had ridden in. They were practical people. They would sell their wine and services to our men. As I passed one such inn I heard the moans from the upper room as one of our men satisfied his carnal cravings. Heading across the town square I saw a disconsolate Harry of Lymm, my father, drinking alone. His back was against the water trough.

I thought him asleep but he was not. I was ten paces from him when he shouted, "Whorseson! You think you are so clever. You steal my friends as that noble stole your mother. I shall have my revenge. You just watch!"

There was a time when I would have run away but I had killed men and I knew my own worth. I turned and faced him, "Do not insult my mother or you and I will exchange blows and, as you discovered the last time, I am not so easy to beat these days. If you talk to me then use my name, Will son of Harry. It is not a name I am proud of but until I am given one by my shield brothers than I will have to live with it."

I saw his fists bunch. He placed them on the ground as though he was going to push himself up. I took a step towards him and he looked up at me. He decided it was not worth the effort of rising and he slumped back against the trough and waved a dismissive hand at me. "You will come to naught! You will end your life in a ditch with your throat cut as your grandfather did."

"That may be your fate but it is not mine. I shall end my days as a gentleman or better."

He laughed and then began to convulse. He brought up a little of the bread he must have eaten earlier. It spilled down his chest and he coughed to clear it. I had seen him do this often. He shook his head. "And I will dance on the River Styx when Hell freezes over!"

I turned and left him. I determined that I would not end my life as he had. He was waiting to die. I now understood why he was so ferocious in battle. He was seeking death. Red Ralph was right. I had been reckless.

There were guards on the gates. They recognised me and waved me through. One said, "You are not thinking of running are you Will?"

I shook my head and laughed, "We are promised pay! I will wait until then before I run!"

They both laughed, "I can see that you have learned sense since you join the Blues but I fear coin will be a long time coming."

I pointed to the pile of bodies. Others were sifting through them. Some men liked to collect teeth. When they reached London, they would be able to sell them to those who made teeth to lords and ladies whose own teeth had rotted. They were light to carry and worth gold rather than silver. "I just wish some leather to make thongs to attach mail to my jerkin."

One pointed to a body by itself. "That one is a Gascon. They use thongs as laces for their boots. It will save you cutting them."

I found the body and took off the boots. The Gascon was an old warrior and had fallen upon hard times. The boots were well made but the soles had worn through. The thongs, however, were in good condition. I took the boots from his stiffening malodorous body, "I am sorry old man. I mean no disrespect but you shall not need them and I can use them." I would not have said such words to any other body but I had not killed this man. He might have even fought for us. Gascons fought on both sides of this war. I turned and headed back to the hall.

My father had gone from the water trough. I was wise enough to keep to the main part of the town. If he had had enough drink then he might decide to hurt me by attacking from behind. There would have been a time when he would have faced me but our last encounter had warned him that I was now a man and not a boy. Each day I grew stronger and I had seen that he was getting weaker.

By the time I reached the hall Old Tom had returned. I put the boots with my war gear. I saw the two long strips of mail already there. Red Ralph did not speak but nodded. Old Tom said, "I have just told the others that we leave tomorrow. Each company has been allocated an area to raid. We have half a moon and then we head north west to Poitiers. We are meeting at the manor of La Roche-sur-Yon." I saw that the others were already looking at me and now Old Tom gave me a sad smile, "It is the manor of Sir Alan Buxhill. Your mother will be there."

I did not know what to say. Would I recognise her? Would I be able to even see her? She was the kept woman of a noble and I was a mercenary, a sword for hire. Peter the Priest said, quietly, "We are your shield brothers now, Will. All will be well."

I knew that they were waiting for me to say something. "It is my father I worry about. If he knows we are going to where she lives then there might be trouble."

Captain Tom said, "There will be no trouble. He is a lonely man without friends. We will watch him and if he looks like causing trouble then we will dismiss him."

There would have been a time when I would not have dreamed of speaking up to Captain Tom but I had changed. Killing a man does that to you. "I fear that would do no good. In fact, it might put my mother in danger. He told me he will have vengeance. If he has nothing to lose then he might choose to take my mother with him."

"Or you Will."

I nodded, "I have thought of that Peter but I am tougher now than I was. It is my mother I worry about."

"Then we will all be on our guard." Old Tom laughed but it was a sad laugh, "If your father could get the hate from his eyes and the wine from his veins he might see what a fine son he has produced. You are a man I would be proud to have as my son."

Red Ralph laughed, "More like grandson, Old Tom!"

It was said with humour and Tom took it as such, "You could well be right!"

I took the stitching awl and, as they talked of the days when they would retire I sewed the two mail strips over the shoulders of my leather. It was harder than I had thought but I was pleased with the result. Each day I was better prepared for war. One day I might reach an age when I would think of retirement but that would be many years hence and I had much to learn.

Chapter 7

We headed north and west towards the castle of La Flèche. It was a strong castle and we did not relish the thought of taking it but Prince Edward wanted us, as the strongest company, to draw other forces towards us. It would mean that the other companies would have an easier task. We did not have to take La Flèche, we just had to make the French think we intended to. Now that we were all mounted, we moved much more quickly. We left guards at Cour sur Loire as well as our baggage. We would be striking swiftly. We had eighty miles to go and Captain Tom intended raiding all the way to La Flèche.

He sought out the five of us before dawn. "I want you four as scouts. With the boy here, you have someone with good ears and eyes. He is the best forager we have ever had and he is quick thinking too. Find the French and stop them finding us. We need somewhere to stay. A village or small town will do. I know the Prince has asked us to draw the French to us but I didn't earn these grey hairs by being stupid. We will let them think we intend to attack La Flèche but I want to avoid castles."

Red Ralph said, "A couple of archers would help us out."

Captain Tom shook his head, "Let them think we don't have any archers. When we unleash them, it will come as a real shock. Besides they won't help you if you are ambushed and you, Red Ralph, are too canny to get caught."

"Don't try to butter me up. We get first choice of house and no guard duty?"

"Aye all right. Now go. We will be an hour behind you."

This was the first time I had scouted. The short trek up the gulley with Peter did not count. As we saddled our horses Red Ralph said, "Keep your head bare. Have your shield slung over your left leg and the saddle."

"What about a sword? Should I carry it?"

Peter the Priest shook his head, "You have three of them. If you can't get one out before a Frenchman then you should be just guarding horses. You will be fine. You and I will be the arrow head of this patrol.

I am relying on your eyes and ears. Any sound which is not made by us then let me know."

I pulled myself up into the saddle. I hung my helmet from the sword in my saddle scabbard and my shield over the saddle and my other sword. I kicked Sunrise in the flanks and Peter and I led the others through the gates. Long John rode at the rear. As soon as we were out of the gates we were in French territory. They would know we had taken their town. How would they react? We were the only company which left early. We were bait. It was a compliment but one I wished we had not been paid.

As we trotted into the dark, for the sun would rise behind us, I realised that we were in open country. There would be woods but this was rich farmland. The fields were largely treeless and five horsemen would soon be spotted. I felt the responsibility on my shoulders. I had foraged and knew how to hide close to an enemy but here I had four others with me and I was on a horse. I forced myself to relax and calm down. I sniffed the air. I listened for noises and my head swivelled to take in as much as I could.

My nose found the French. We were five miles from Cour sur Loire. The smell was a mixture of wood smoke, animal dung and horses. The wind was bringing the smell to us and I knew it was not our horses. My ears detected, to the north, the sound of someone shouting. I could not make out the words but I did not need to. The smells and the sounds were enough. I just pointed north. Peter pulled his horse around. He had seen a hole in the hedge and he slipped his horse through. I followed him and we rode in single file. Red Ralph made a signal. They would wait on the road. There was a hill before us. It was terraced with grape vines. They gave us enough cover so that we could zig zag our way up through them. The noises grew. It was either a village or a large farm.

Peter was older than I was and his senses were not as acute but he had common sense and when he slipped from his saddle I did the same as did the others. As he landed on the ground he drew his sword. Now the vines, which were old and twisted up on supports, truly hid us. We walked through a couple and then Peter took Sunrise's reins and gestured for me to crawl. I had to sheathe my sword. I squirrelled my way through the vines. The ground was becoming flatter. I reached the top and saw, below me, a large farm. They had a wall and a gate. There were horses. They also had a hall and the door was half way up the wall. It was a place that could be defended. I knew that Red Ralph would want as much information as I could give to him. I counted thirty-two men. They were not all engaged in the same task but I saw that they had weapons close to hand. I heard the neigh of horses and saw that two of them were being exercised. This was a manor. Where was the lord? Then I saw him. He was the one giving the orders and his breeches were well made. He was stripped to the waist and helping his men. They were castrating young bulls. That was why they had so many men. Four were holding each one to stop them moving. There were also women. They were bringing food and drink to the men. I heard the ring of hammer on metal. They had a forge and a blacksmith. I could not see those but they would be men and they might increase the numbers who might defend the place by four or five. I had seen enough and I slithered back down the slope to the horses. We walked back down the terrace to the road and I did not speak until we joined the others.

I told them what I had seen. Red Ralph nodded, "A goodly target. Long John ride back to the column and tell Captain Tom. We will ride along the road. There must be a track or road to the farm from the north. We have not seen one here. We will stop any escaping."

Long John rode back and we donned helmets and urged our horses on. We rode quickly and galloped along the road. We found the entrance to the manor. It was almost a mile from where we had scaled the terraces. I could see why they had chosen the site. The wine terraces faced south and would have the maximum sun. The other fields were filled with cattle, pigs and sheep. This was a rich farm.

Across from the entrance was a stand of trees. It was not a wood. There were no more than a dozen trees. I guessed they had been left there to give some shade. We dismounted and tied our horses to the trees. They were not completely hidden but it would have to do. Drawing our swords and taking our shields we headed to the entrance. There had once been two large oaks. They had been cut down leaving a pair of trunks as high as a man. The bark had been stripped and a bull's head carved into each of the trunks. A small wooden fence marked the boundary. It was not an obstacle. We split into two pairs and stood next to the trees. We had little to do but wait.

I was with Peter. He drew his sword. He would have room to swing and would not need his mace. I took my Spanish blade. I held it in two hands. Fighting alongside these veterans had taught me to think even before I fought. If we were needed then it would be because men were fleeing and they would be mounted. The only way to stop a mounted man was to strike at his horse. That required a sword held in two hands. With our backs against the two tree trunks and our faded cloaks we were almost invisible. We were patient and we rested there. I caught an occasional glimpse of one of the horses as they grazed behind the stand of trees but they looked natural.

The noise of battle, when it came, seemed unnaturally loud. There was a clash of steel and screams. There were shouts. I heard the shouts of anger as men fought and the screams of terror as women and children fled. Peter said quietly, "Be ready. If we are needed we will have little warning."

I nodded and adjusted the two-handed grip on my sword. The fingers of my left hand wrapped over those of my right. I had made a new grip with cord covered by thin leather. It would not slip. I moved my feet so that I had a wider stance. I would be swinging from left to right. It was not a natural movement for me yet. I had not fought long enough with a sword. I was becoming more skilled. All of my shield brothers had said so. I was not as good as they were but I was still young and had time.

The sound of galloping hooves told us that someone was coming. None of the others risked peering around the side of the tree and so I restrained myself. I concentrated on listening to the horses. There was more than one. As they drew closer I detected the sound of three horses. I could not look around but I could see Red Ralph's face as he readied his sword. The hooves grew closer. When would we strike? Red Ralph held up three fingers, then two and then one. Peter stepped out swinging his sword. I moved towards the wood to avoid his swinging sword.

The three Frenchmen came down the trail at a gallop. Dick Long Sword swung his sword first and it hacked into the chest of the first rider. The second, in an instant I saw that he was a lord, veered towards Peter and me. I pulled my arm back as Peter hacked his sword into the side of the lord's horse. It stopped, reared and threw the rider to the ground. It galloped off away from us knocking Red Ralph to the ground. The third rider was a good horseman. I saw him urge on his horse and the beast rose to clear the prone Frenchman and Red Ralph. Horse and rider landed just two paces from me. As the horse veered to the right to avoid me I swung my sword. I was aiming at the horse but its movement took it away from me. My blade was sharp and I was strong. The upward swing tore through the Frenchman's leg from the knee all the way to the thigh. Bright blood arced like a fountain. The tip of my sword rasped off bone and the rider began to tumble from the saddle. He was a big man and he clung to his reins. The horse could not remain upright and the two crashed to the ground.

"Will, grab the horse!"

I jammed my sword into the soil and ran after the horse which had risen and shaken itself free from the mortally wounded Frenchman. It began to move away from the smell of blood and the cries of its dying master. I managed to grab the reins but it still pulled and I was forced to run next to it. I began to talk in French, "Steady, my sweet." I clicked my tongue. "Slowly, slowly." It began to slow. As it did I risked leaving go with my left hand to pat its flanks. I began to sing, in English, a song my mother had sung to me, "Baby, baby, rest your head. Baby, baby, time for bed." I kept singing until it stopped. We were close to the stand of trees and I led the horse, I could now see that it was a mare, towards them. The horse would be reassured by the smell of other horses rather than that of blood. After tying her to a tree, next to Sunrise, I returned to the others.

I picked up and sheathed my sword. Red Ralph was being tended by Peter the Priest. Dick Long Sword was searching the French for they were all three dead. The lord had landed badly. The one who I had struck lay in an almost black pool of blood. The injured horse and the other one were walking down the road away from us. Red Ralph looked up. "You had better get after those horses. They are valuable."

"Aye. Are you badly hurt?"

He laughed, "I suffered more in Poitiers when the whore there shoved me from her bed! You did well. Now get the horses."

I ran back to Sunrise and mounted. The two French horses had stopped half a mile down the road and were eating the cow parsley which grew at the side of the road. I did not gallop, that would merely alarm them, I walked my horse. When I reached them, I saw that one was bleeding from the side. Peter the Priest's sword had hurt the beast. I tied Sunrise to a tree and also the one which had no wound. I took the reins of the other and led it to the shade of the tree and tied it off. There was a water skin on its saddle. I took off my helmet and poured some water into it. The wounded horse lapped it up. The blood was not pouring from the wound but it was bleeding. I went to Sunrise and took out the vinegar skin and the small pot of honey. The French horse ate some of the leaves from the tree. I took the blue cloth from around my neck and poured some vinegar on it. I sang as I wiped the wound. The horse whinnied but did not rear. The cloth came away bloody and dirty. I put my fingers in the pot of honey and smeared some along the wound. I waited until I was sure that the bleeding had stopped and then led the horse back to the others.

Dick Long Sword was smiling, "You are worth your weight in gold, Will. You have a way with horses."

"I know not whence that came."

Red Ralph had been bandaged and he nodded, "We are glad that you have the skill. We have your share and that of Long John. This French lord had a full purse." He handed me the sword and scabbard of the Frenchman I had slain. "This is yours by right. You do not need it and, if I were you I would sell it. Wait until we reach La Roche-sur-Yon."

We recovered our horses and the three captured ones. Captain Tom led the men from the farm. There was a wagon filled with supplies and wounded men. He nodded to Red Ralph, "You have done well but you are wounded."

"It is nothing. I have broken my coxcomb is all."

"Nonetheless I have others wounded and I need a man to command. Take the wagon, the captives and the captured horses back to Cour. We will push on. Long John can rejoin his shield brothers."

Red Ralph did not want to leave us but he would not refuse Tom. "Aye, Captain." I handed him the halter which held the three captured horses and he waved at the wagon driver to follow him.

Captain Tom said, "Peter, take your men and scout out the road. We need a bed for the night and it should be closer to la Flèche."

"Aye Captain."

Our horses had had a rest and we rode quickly down the road. It was mid afternoon and I doubted that we would make more than ten miles. I wondered if we should have stayed at the farm. I said nothing for the others had more experience than I did. What did I know? I was still young and inexperienced. We passed a farm which was also on a track which led from the road. Peter decided not to take it for it was narrow and there were no wheel ruts. It was too small to be of concern to us. The road we were on began to descend. It twisted and turned making it hard to see ahead. Trees and bushes along the side also obstructed our view. Peter rode slower and slower. It was fortunate that we did. We turned a corner and saw some houses. They were not the danger. Ahead was a bridge over a narrow river and a castle. There was a stone gate and the tower within was made of stone. It made little difference that it was not a large castle, nor that the wall was not high. We could go no further without the rest of the company for the end of the bridge was less than fifty paces from the gate. We would be seen and crossbow bolts could be deadly at that range.

Peter turned, "Back to the farm we found. That looks like a good place to stay. Will, ride back to the captain and bring the company there. We will secure the farmhouse."

"Aye Peter." Turning Sunrise, I galloped back along the road. I rode faster for I knew there was no danger between the column and me. I passed the track which led to the farm and three miles further on I saw Captain Tom.

He reined in, "Well?"

"There is a castle ahead, Captain. It is stone and guards a bridge over the river. We did not risk searching for a ford. We have found a farm for the night."

He rubbed his beard, "That will have to do." He waved the men forward and I fell in beside him. "Are you sure it was not La Flèche?"

I shook my head, "From what you said, Captain, La Flèche has a broad river and is a mighty castle. This is a narrow river, a small bridge and a single tower. There are but one or two houses south of the river and you said there was a bastion."

He smiled, "You are a clever one. I was not certain you were listening the other night. If you can curb your reckless nature then you will go far."

When we reached the farm, I saw that it was a modest dwelling. There was a farm and a large barn. The ground floor was for their animals and the upper floor was accessed by a ladder and a door half way up. Peter and the others must have surprised the occupants. Long John was guarding the farmer and his family. The farmer was nursing a bloody nose and glaring at Long John. The farmer's wife and four children were seated on a log. It faced west and I guessed that it was a favourite spot to watch the sunset. The children ranged from a boy of ten summers down to a toddler.

Peter was eating some bread, "There is little here, Captain. The farmer has a few vines, a milk cow and the rest is made up of land he farms for crops."

Captain Tom nodded, "We have enough from the manor. Tell them they can sleep in their house we will use their barn but if they attempt to leave they will be killed." There was iron in his voice.

Peter spoke to the farmer. He nodded and looked relieved. They went to the ladder and ascended. Peter pulled it away, "That will ensure they obey your orders Captain."

We lit a fire outside the farm but on the side away from the castle. As it was dark any sentries would not see the smoke and the wind was from the south west. Captain Tom interrogated us about the bridge. "Is it guarded at both ends?"

"The castle guards the north end but there is no gate at the bridge." The Captain nodded. Peter continued, "The river looks narrow. We might be able to ford it upstream."

"I like not being trapped at a narrow bridge. La Flèche should be less than thirty miles away. As soon as we are seen they will send a rider and we could be surrounded by the end of the day."

This was where we missed Red Ralph. He had a cunning mind and came up with innovative ways to beat our foes. I said nothing for I was inexperienced. They danced around the problem and then Peter said, "We could cross the river with a few archers and men at arms. If you brought up the company to the south side of the bridge then those who crossed the river could stop any from escaping."

Captain Tom nodded gloomily. "We will still lose men and we have perilously few now."

Long John said, "Then the alternative is to go back but that will not endear us to the prince. He wants us as bait."

A depressing silence fell upon us. It seemed that no matter what we did we would suffer. I saw a solution but I was loath to speak it. There must have been something about my manner which gave my thoughts away for Peter said, "Will, if you have a suggestion then make it. Better a foolish one which we can reject than silence. Whatever you say we will not think less of you."

I nodded, "It seems to me that we can do as the Prince says and yet not risk men's lives." I could see I had their attention. "If men cross the river and show themselves then the French will send for help." Captain Tom nodded. "We let them. Make them think that we are going to attack but all we need to do is hold the southern end of the bridge. If they attack we fire it."

Silence fell again but this time it was a reflective one. They were thinking through the problem. Peter, eventually, smiled, "There are houses to the south of the river. We capture them and take what they have. The ones who cross the river can easily get back. I like it, captain. When we have drawn the French, we withdraw to the manor. We could defend there."

Captain Tom gave his assent, "It is a better plan than I could conceive. We will do it but I need you, Peter and the best men that Captain John has to cross the river. You need to have enough men to make them send a rider."

"Do we attack?"

"There will be houses outside the walls. Take what they have and only withdraw if reinforcements arrive."

And so it was decided. Captain John chose ten archers and Captain Tom gave us another ten men at arms. My father was not amongst them. The sergeant who commanded the archers was Oswald of Oswestry; a dour man, he knew his business. He was happy to follow Peter the Priest. The ex-crusader was known to be a good leader.

Once again, we left before dawn and headed up stream. None of us wore mail and so the fording of the river would not be a problem. The archers carried their bows and strings in leather sheaths. They all had a full quiver of arrows. Despite the fact that the plan was mine I was not confident. We rode two miles before we found a suitable place to cross. The banks were shallow and there was a sand spit in the centre of the narrow river. The water came up to my thighs but no higher and Sunrise was able to walk across.

Once we reached dry land we all tightened girths and made certain that our weapons were dry. Peter and Dick led. This time they did not need my sharp ears and eyes. The aim was to surprise them and make them panic. Dawn broke behind us and we headed down the road which flanked the river. We ignored the houses. If time allowed we would raid them but the priority was to get to the castle. As luck would have it we discovered that it was a market day and we began to find farmers heading to market. As soon as they saw us they fled. They were on foot and they took to the ditches and hedges. We ignored them.

When the sun broke we were less than half a mile from the castle and the sun glinted from the spears of the two men on watch at the gates. I heard Oswald of Oswestry shout, "String your bows!" They could dismount, nock an arrow and send it towards an enemy before a man could count his toes!

Peter drew his sword and urged his horse forward. The people before us ran directly for the gates. It was a race they could never win. One farmer, slower than the others slipped and fell beneath Dick's horse's hooves. Dick could not avoid him. I heard a sickening crunch as the man's skull was shattered. We were a hundred paces from both the bridge and the castle when they tried to close the gates. Oswald and his men dismounted. The two sentries on the fighting platform fell. Two riders who had obviously been sent for help barged through the gates, knocking a couple to the ground. It worked against the defenders for they lay between the gates and as much as the French tried to close them they could not for others clambered over the bodies to gain entry. Captain Tom led the rest of the company across the bridge.

Peter, Dick and myself, hit the gate at the same time. I saw a hand on a door and I hacked down. I sliced through three fingers. Dick Long Sword drove his blade into the neck of a second and Peter the Priest placed his horse between the gates. They were not closing. Oswald and his archers kept the gatehouse and fighting platform clear and we rode into the town. The castle was on a mound and there was another wall around it. We had done more than we had expected. We had taken the gates.

"Dismount and protect the archers!"

Until Captain Tom and his men arrived we would have to hold off any attack from the tower. I slid from Sunrise and hefted my shield around. The rest of our men spread out on both sides of the three of us. I heard the creak of the bow behind me as an archer drew back on the mighty weapon. As his arrow flew over my head I braced myself for the defenders had seen how few we were and were now rushing towards us. Clearing the gate meant that Captain Tom and the rest of the company had not been seen.

A French man at arms ran straight at me. He had a pole axe which he raised as he ran. The archers were clearing the gate to the tower and the tower walls. I would have to endure the attack. I had long arms and a long sword but a pole axe could strike me with impunity. I held my shield before me and angled it. I was taller than the Frenchman. It was, as far as I could see, the only advantage. I held my sword behind me. Once he was committed to the blow then I could strike. I saw that he intended to bring it down from on high. A sideways blow was more dangerous but he was running with others and could not risk sawing sideways without hitting his comrades. On such tiny details are battles won and lost. As the pole axe came down I did two things. I shifted my weight to my right leg as I stepped forward. I lunged with my sword. My move almost negated the effect of the axe for it was not the end which struck my shield but the bottom part of the blade. Even so it was a mighty blow and had I not had my shield angled then I might have had my arm broken. The axe head slid harmlessly down the leather of the shield. The man wore a mail covered padded jacket but I was strong and the tip caught in the mail and then ripped along the links. It must have been old mail for they gave way and I ripped through his padded jacket. As he tried to raise his pole axe again quickly, not an easy thing to do, I punched at him with my shield. The edge of his axe must have damaged my shield or perhaps it was the bolt hole, whatever reason the shield split and splintered in his face. One splinter drove up into his eye and he screamed. I grabbed hold of his ventail with my left hand and, as I hooked my left leg behind him pushed him over. He fell to the ground and I took my sword in both hands and brought it down hard. I split his body in twain. The men next to him recoiled and that allowed Peter and Dick to kill them.

The three men in the centre were like the keystone in a bridge. Their line was broken asunder and it coincided with the arrival of Captain Tom. He shouted, "Break ranks and let us through!" Peter and I turned away from each other and stepped backwards as the rest of our company galloped after the men we had broken. As I had no shield I drew my second short sword from behind me. It was a precaution only for the French were fleeing to the castle. The men who had fled did not make the castle. It would be without the twenty men who had sallied forth. I suspected it would not have a large garrison.

Leaving Captain Jack and his archers to thin the ranks of those in the castle Captain Tom rode back to us, "Well done, now search the houses.

Will and Dick, see if you can find a wagon and horses. I would be away from here sooner rather than later. The castle and gate are too strong to take and we would gain little. Peter, we will leave after dark. Have the rest of your men lay faggots under the bridge and we will burn it before we leave."

I used my nose to find the wagon and the horses. There was a stable. The sign above the gate suggested it was a carter who lived there but I could not read the French words. I could speak French but not read it. There was no one in the yard and I wondered at that. Dick must have thought it strange also for he said, "Perhaps they fled inside the castle. The man who lives here has money." He pointed to the door which was finely carved and made of oak. It was open and not barred. Had it been barred we would have found it very difficult to break it down. "You are the horseman. Get a wagon and hitch the horses. I will find our pay."

There were four horses in the stable but one of them was lame. We would have to use one of our horses to help pull the wagon. Long John had the biggest horse. It took me some time to prepare and hitch the three horses. I led them out. Dick was piling rich furnishings and treasure in the yard.

"I need Long John's horse."

"Go and I will load."

I saw Long John's horse. Long John was emptying a house opposite. "I need your horse for the wagon." He frowned, "It is to pull the wagon with the treasure."

"Then I will drive!"

"As you wish." I led Blackberry, Long John's mount. She was a very docile yet powerful horse. She had the sweetest nature of any horse I had ever tended. Long John wished for a more aggressive horse. God had made her gentle for a purpose. She allowed me to hitch her to the wagon. I had found a bag of apples in the stable and I gave each of the four horses one. I wanted no disputes between them. Then I helped Dick to load the wagon. Men began to bring us items they had looted from the buildings. There was mail, helmets and weapons as well as food, pots and trinket boxes. Some carried purses. We would share all when we reached safety.

Long John came into the yard. He was carrying a chest over his shoulder. "Best hurry lads, the Captain is going to fire the town to cover our escape. He fears the French from La Flèche!"

Dick shouted, "Then help us load. We are almost done here!"

It did not take the three of us long and as Dick and John loaded the last few items I went to recover our horses. Peter the Priest was waiting at the horses. "Hurry! The Captain has men watching the road. There are knights coming from La Flèche!" He pointed to the buildings close to the castle. Smoke was billowing from the roof of one of them. He has fired the town. As soon as you move then the rest will mount and follow us."

Dick and I mounted quickly and then slapped the rumps of the horses pulling the wagon to make them move. The wagon was laden. We would not move quickly. As we left the stable I saw that Captain Tom had men with brands entering the houses and setting them alight. The archers of Captain Jack prevented a sortie from the castle. Once we had passed through the gates then it was easier for the ground led down to the river and the wagon was quicker. Peter dismounted as we reached the bridge, "Move! I will fire the bridge."

The wagon rumbled on to the wood of the bridge. Peter's act was not reckless. It would take time for the flames to take hold. The rest of the men could, if they had to, ford the river but it would be better if we could cross together. Long John had the mastery of the wagon and he headed down the road to Cour. We would have to reach it. The small farmhouse was indefensible., The manor was not. Dick and I waited for Peter. The former priest and the last men at arms galloped across. Captain Jack had his men send another flight of arrows over the wall and then they galloped. They had to ride through smoke. Captain Tom and Peter were the last across and I could see the flames licking at the wooden parapet. I doubted that the bridge could be saved.

As we followed Peter and Captain Tom, Dick said, "Now all we have to do is fight knights and a French garrison! Whatever we have taken we will have earned."

Chapter 8

It was a hard ride back. The manor was empty. The lord's wife and his family were at Cour sur Loire. They could be ransomed. Captain Tom made sure that we were defensible. Sentries were mounted at the gate and men watched the road. Peter came to me, as I checked our horses, "We have the first watch at the road." He smiled, "The Captain trusts your young eyes and ears." I must have looked unhappy, although I had not intended to do so for he added, "He is doing us a favour. The first and the last watches are the easiest. Your father has the middle watch. He always hated that but the Captain is punishing him."

As we had ridden back I discovered that my father, once we had broken in, had found some wine and become drunk. He had been found by Harold of Stamford about to ravish a young girl. He would stand the middle watch and he would not receive a share of the booty from the town. He would have to make do with that which we had taken from the manor. He would not be happy. I thought back to Peter the Priest's words. He was indeed a troubled soul. Being on guard first meant that we would have to have food kept for us. That was where our comrades came into their own. Dick and John would make certain that we had more than they did. They had been given the last watch of the night.

Our watch was at the gate. Others watched in different places. We would not need our shields but we would need our cloaks. We walked down the track to the entrance. Even in the half dark of twilight we could still see the spattered blood on the trunks of the two dead trees. As we had walked down Peter had told me how we would watch. "We hide behind the tree trunks. Even the French will have the sense to send good scouts to follow us. It is dark but if they are good enough they will smell the piss of men who could not wait to get to the manor and they will see the piles of horse dung. We wait and we listen."

It seemed good advice to me and I squatted next to the tree trunk and the wooden wall. I was used to watching in the dark. I had waited often enough for my father to return, usually drunk, and with fists ready to pound into me. He would usually be seeking vengeance for having lost money at dice and I would have to bear the brunt of his anger. When my mother had lived with us she had often placed her body between us. That was how I remembered her, tears pouring from her cheeks and her frail back being struck by my father. I was too young and too small to do anything. I did not blame her for leaving. I was just amazed that she had stayed as long as she had.

I knew to keep still and to look for movement rather than a person. I saw a fox, its eyes looking somehow red appear from the woods. It sniffed and, I daresay, detected us and moved back into the woods. Bats and moths fluttered around us. They were a distraction but I ignored them. It was peaceful. I did not expect danger. The bridge had been on fire and the knights and men from La Flèche would have had to stop to douse the flames but I would do my duty. I had heard stories of sentries who had slept and whole companies had died. A couple of hours watching would not hurt me.

When the noise came I doubted myself. I was imagining things. I forced myself to look again where I thought I had seen a movement. I was right. I saw a shadow move. It was not on the road but was moving down through the woods. There were no friends north of us. It was an enemy. I could not speak for that would alert the French. I could not draw my sword, it would make too much noise. I slid my right hand behind my back and pulled my dagger and, with my left hand, pulled the stiletto from my boot. If Peter had not seen the two shadows which crept towards us then I would have to deal with them. I could not let down my comrades. I wondered how I would take them. I was seated. Then it came to me. I was invisible. So long as I did not move then I could not be seen. They would, perhaps, investigate the track. Then I thought again. They were on foot. They knew where we were and the French had sent out scouts to find us. They would come up the trail. I did not have much of a beard but I was dirty and I hoped that my face would remain hidden. There was no moon yet and all was dark but I could see their shadows as they moved closer.

I then began to worry if I would be able to stand quickly enough. I dismissed the thought. They were scouts. There would be no one nearby. I just had to kill and kill quickly. Killing with a knife would be harder than with a sword. You were closer. The blade would not rip as deep and yet your hand would touch flesh. The two shadows stopped and I heard a murmur. I prayed that Peter would hear it too. Then I would not be alone. The murmuring stopped and the two shadows detached themselves from the trees and headed across the road. They held swords before them. Did that give me an advantage or not? I was panicking myself. I would not let down the company. I might die but I would take one with me and Peter would avenge me.

It became obvious that they had not seen us for they looked not at the tree trunks but at the track. I had a dilemma. When did I strike? It was decided for me. As the man on the right approached, he glanced down. He must have seen my foot. If he had used a dagger I would have been dead but he had a sword and, as he swung it I launched myself. I used my left hand as a spear and aimed at his crotch. I slashed at the back of his knee with the dagger in my right hand. His sword struck my back but the stiletto had driven up through his groin and into his bowels. Faeces, blood and entrails poured out and down my left arm. My dagger hacked through his hamstring but by then he was dead, twitching his life away in a pile of piss and shit. I jumped to my feet. The other lay dead. Peter put his finger to his lips and pointed for me to stay there. He disappeared. After what seemed like an age he returned with two horses.

"You did well, Will. I feared you might try to speak but you did not." He sniffed and smiled, "You smell like a cess pit but that will wash off. Help me put their bodies on the horses and I will take them to the Captain. You stay here. I think we have earned a shorter watch!"

When he left I felt so alone. I had been so close to the Frenchman that I had smelled his last meal. I knew that he had not bathed in a while and, when I had looked in his face, I had seen that he was little older than I. It was strange.

Two others returned and said, "You have done well Will son of Harry. Go back to camp. We will take an early watch."

The other sniffed, "But take a wash first!"

The manor had a well and I used six buckets of water to wash the blood and the excrement from me. It cleaned off easily from my mail but my shirt and tunic seemed to have absorbed both the blood and the mess into the fibres., There was still a smell. When I reached the fire around which my shield brothers slept I saw that they were waiting for me. Dick had a bowl of food for me and John a beaker of wine. Peter sniffed, "Better but you will need those clothes washing. When daylight comes we will see if there are any to fit you inside the hall."

I ate the food and nodded.

Dick said, "If there are scouts then the French will not be far away. It looks like we will fight again tomorrow."

Long John took out a whetstone and began to slide it along his sword. "We have had places which are harder to defend. These will be knights who come. They do not relish fighting hired swords. When they have bled enough for honour they will have to let us go."

Peter shook his head, "I am not so certain. This French King sees weakness. It has been almost fourteen years since they were trounced at Poitiers. Perhaps they think Prince Edward is weakening."

There was truth in Peter's words. We all knew that the illness which had beset him in Spain had hurt him. He was still a mighty warrior whom few would face in battle but who knew the effects of such a disease? I finished the food and the wine. I took off the soiled tunic and laid it next to my leather mail. My cloak had managed to avoid any mess and I wrapped myself in it. The others had been waiting for me and we all curled up around the fire. Dick and John would wake us when they went on watch. We would have dawn's early light to search for clean clothes.

It seemed just moments before Peter shook me awake. I rose and shivered. The air was cold. "Come we will go into the house. You can search for clothes and I will find food."

Pulling my cloak tighter around my shoulders I followed him. The sun was rising and we could see the sleeping forms on the floor. While Peter headed for the kitchens and larders I went to the stairs. Captain Tom had taken the lord's bedroom for his own and I was loath to disturb him but I saw a light from beneath the door and heard movement. I eased the door open and said, apologetically, "Captain, Peter the Priest thought there might be clothes within. My shirt and tunic are badly soiled."

I saw that Captain Tom had been at prayer. He was rising from his knees. He smiled. "There is a chest there, Will. You earned the right to take whatever is within. I have taken that which I need. We will need the chest to take the rest of the booty from that castle." He stood and buckled on his sword. "I will go and rouse the men. If the French allow we will head back to Cour and thence to La Roche-sur-Yon." He made the sign of the cross. "That is in God's hands." He left me alone in the chamber.

We had taken no prisoners and still did not know the name of the town we had burned. Knights and lords might know such things. It did not matter to us. Sir Hugh would probably tell Tom when we returned but all we knew was that we had done that which we had been asked and, thus far we lived. Time alone would tell if we were to reap the rewards of our endeavours.

The clothes in the chest were all well made but the lord of the manor had been bigger than I. It was not until I reached the bottom that I found a good shirt and a tunic which fitted. They were both finer than any clothes I had owned before. That was not a surprise as I had had cast offs for my whole life. These too were cast offs but they were a noble's cast off and of high quality. I was about to place the other clothes back in the chest when I spied a good pair of breeks. They fitted. Dressed more like a lordling than a hired sword I descended. The hall was awake. I carried my cloak and I had to endure the comments of the others as I walked back to the door. I was used to it now. It meant I was part of the company. When I was the beaten child of Harry of Lymm then they would have left me alone. They felt sorry for me. I had proved myself a warrior and now I was Will. I still needed a name but that would not be my choice. Some shield brother would name me and it would stick.

Peter had food going and he shouted, as I approached, "Fetch wood for the fire."

I busied myself finding the wood and then building the fire. We ate whatever we could and often had an eclectic stew which might have turned the stomach of someone who was fastidious. We ate what we could when we could. By the time John and Dick returned from their duty, the stew was ready and all were awake. Four archers rode out to scout the road which led back to the burned bridge. Captain Tom was cautious. He did not want us to be caught on the open road by knights and men at arms. The manor was defensible and we would only leave and head back to Cour when it was safe.

Once we had eaten I sharpened my swords and daggers. We saddled our horses for the archers had not returned. I began to believe that we might reach the safety of the Gascony when an archer galloped into the yard of the manor. "Captain Jack, a conroi of knights and men at arms approaches. They had ten banners!"

The two captains looked at each other. We all knew what that meant. There would be at least ten knights and that could mean as many as two hundred mailed men. These would not be so easy to defeat.

"Men at arms to the lower wall. Archers behind them." It was a simple enough plan. The manor had a low wall which ran around the perimeter. It was what they called in England dry stone in that it was not mortared but it would, with shields and spears behind it be a barrier. As it was on a slope the effect of the war horses would be negated. Our task would be to protect the archers. As I hurried with Peter and Dick, Captain Tom shouted, "Will, son of Harry, you have no shield. Today you carry the standard!" The Captain himself normally bore the faded blue standard. I suspected that he was protecting me. I obeyed. I went to the wagon where the standard was stored and took it out. By the time I reached Old Tom our company had deployed. We looked perilously few to endure an attack by knights and mailed men at arms. Tom looked across at me. I was slightly taller now than the old captain. I had grown or perhaps he was shrinking. "Do not fear, Will, there may be ransom from this. Just defend the standard. If it falls then we are lost."

With those chilling thoughts in my head I drew my freshly sharpened sword.

I heard horns in the distance. The French had found us. As they moved up from the road I saw the sun's rays shining on mail and helmets. These were the knights from La Flèche. The castle guarded the eastern approach to Angers and, as such, had a good garrison. These had not fought as we had and they were both better mounted and mailed. I looked down at the perilously thin lines preparing to receive them and knew that I would lose comrades. My elevated position behind them allowed me to see all of them. My father was on the right-hand side. I could hear him shouting insults and challenges to the French. That was his way. I saw Old Tom kiss his sword and knew that battle was imminent.

The road was just two hundred paces from the perimeter wall. Captain Jack would know the precise moment to unleash his arrow storm. They had not had to use many thus far and our archers always had spare quivers. Some of the men at arms had found spears but there was not a continuous line of them. The French had lances and spears. This would be a true test of the shields of our men and the strength of hearts behind them.

The French had no crossbows. That was understandable. They had ridden hard to catch us and crossbowmen marched on foot. They might well be on the road hurrying to catch the hated English but they would arrive too late to decide this battle. The vine terraces through which we had climbed did not suit the knights. Inexperienced as I was I deemed that they would have been better waiting for their crossbows but perhaps the lord we had slain and the ones in the unnamed castle were important men. These French knights sought revenge. The French showed some intelligence by dismounting their men at arms. Their knights and squires liked to charge into battle. A horn sounded and the ten knights and their squires charged through the vines to our wall.

Captain Jack waited until the French horses were less than fifty paces from our wall before he unleashed his arrows. They were able to loose their arrows between the men at arms. With a flat trajectory and at such close range the bodkin tipped arrows were knight killers. Our captain of archers ignored the men at arms and concentrated every bow on the horsemen. Inevitably some horses and men were struck by multiple arrows while others, miraculously escaped without a mark. Twelve horses and riders fell but the survivors reached our wall. As Captain Jack turned his archers on the men at arms our men began to die. The lances and spears jabbed down to find gaps between shield and mail. I saw that the veterans at the front chopped the lances and spears in half. They had done damage. Ten of our men had been struck. Once the spears had gone then the knights and squires drew their swords.

The arrows began to thin the men at arms but they were men like us. They marched with shields held above them. Some of them still died as archers used a flat trajectory to send the steel tipped missiles into chests and faces. I saw Dick Long Sword swash his sword towards a squire's horse's head. As the squire reared the horse, Long John lunged with his own sword and found the beast's chest. The horse fell backwards, crushing the young squire.

Just then three horsemen managed to jump the wall. One was surrounded and slain by the men at arms and archers who stood there but the two other horsemen survived and rode straight for us. I had no shield. Captain Tom stepped before me to give me some protection from his shield but I saw the squire on the horse lower his spear. He thought to have glory. I lowered the standard slightly. It had a rounded end but it was made of sturdy wood. It was not the best of weapons but it was a weapon. I stood stock still. I needed to make an easy target for the squire. I wanted him over confident. The knight who rode at Captain Tom rammed his lance at Tom's shield. Tom knew how to deal with it but, in turning the lance he exposed me. The squire saw his chance and he rammed his spear towards my chest. I did two things at the same time. I swashed my sword at his spear head while punching with the standard at his head. I was lucky that it was a rouncy he rode for it was small. The spear head moved harmlessly to the side and I saw the look of disappointment on the squire's face. It was replaced by shock as the head of the standard rammed into his jaw and knocked him from his saddle. He landed awkwardly and was dragged a few paces. His horse knocked me to the side and continued beyond me. I ran to the squire but his eyes were open and he was dead. The archers who had butchered the other rider cheered and the knight who was sparring with Captain Tom turned his horse and charged back towards his own men.

Captain Tom looked at the dead squire and said, "What a strong blow. You have a mighty left hand, Will Strongstaff." And with that one blow, I had my name. I ceased to be Will son of Harry. Just then I heard a roar from the right and looked to see my father stand on the wall and then leap into the middle of a mass of men at arms.

Beside me, I heard Old Tom mumble, "Reckless fool! He has the death wish!"

Reckless or not the sudden attack on the French left had an effect. He whirled with sword and shield. It seemed he bore a charmed life for while Frenchmen fell he remained untouched. They feared death whereas my father sought it. Encouraged by my father's success and anticipating treasure from dead Frenchmen the whole of our right flank left the wall and fell upon the men at arms.

Captain Jack turned his archers in the centre and the French right. When two arrows struck the leader and he turned to flee the battle was over. The other knights and squires turned and rode after their leader. The men at arms who were not engaged also managed to escape but the rest did not. Their mail worked against them for they could not run quickly encumbered by mail, shields, swords and helmets.

Captain Tom cupped his hands and shouted, "After them! Stop at the road!" He turned to me and took the standard, "Go help your shield brothers!" I needed no urging and drawing my sword and dagger I ran towards the wall. I saw the bodies of the men who had fallen to the spears. It was a sobering sight.

I had fresh, young legs and I soon caught the older men. This was not a tourney between knights this was a battle to the death. There were no rules. I saw a Frenchman fighting with Long John. Without breaking stride, I rammed my sword into his back. Long John nodded his thanks and then turned to follow Peter the Priest and Dick Long Sword. I found no more Frenchmen before we reached the gate.

I saw my father running down the road, chasing the horsemen. Peter shouted, "Harry of Lymm you are ordered to return. He ignored Peter's words and continued to run.

Long John said, "Let him go Peter. He wants to die."

Peter shook his head, "We were shield brothers and took an oath. We cannot leave him. We have to save him from himself. Come."

Sheathing our swords, we ran. The others slung their shields over their backs. I was fresher and I began to catch my father. The drink and poor diet were having an effect. I saw him catch up to a squire. He swung his sword at the horse's rear. The squire, angered no doubt, turned to face my father. It was a fatal error. Even as the squire's sword came down my father's, wielded two handed, bit into the squire's side. The squire's sword still came down and struck my father square on the helmet. He collapsed. Three French men at arms turned and thought to end my father's life but then saw the four of us and thought better of it. They fled down the road.

"Will, see to the horse. It can carry your father back."

The horse was sweating and its wide eyes told me of its panic. I stroked it and spoke to it. Holding the reins, I looked at the wound. It was clean and not deep. Already the blood was congealing. The horse had been lucky. I took the water skin from the saddle and poured some in my helmet. The horse drank it. I did not give it too much just enough to calm the beast. Peter and John lifted his body on to the horse's saddle while Dick stripped the squire. They were honourable men. My father would have all: the horse, sword, mail and purse. Once a shield brother always a shield brother.

Captain Tom wasted no time in leaving. We had been lucky but there would be others hurrying to follow us. My father, still slung on his horse was tied to the back of the wagon driven by Long John and we rode as fast as we could for Cour-sur-Loire. We reached it before dark and I saw that Red Ralph and the others who had been left there had made it defensible. Some of the other companies had returned. The Grey Company had not fared well. They had met a larger body of French and been bested. They had left half of their company to the east of the town. Worse they had lost their captain. We learned all this from Red Ralph as Captain Tom divided the booty. "I think many of them wish to join our company."

Peter said, "That will depend upon Captain Tom."

"Aye I know but I have been talking with some of them. I know the ones who would be an asset. The others can join the other companies." He pointed to the two wagons we had taken and the string of horses. "We have done well. I can understand why they wish to become part of the Blue Company." He looked at me, "And you have lost your shield I see."

Peter laughed, "Aye but he has a name, Will Strongstaff!"

He told him the story and when he had finished Red Ralph put his arm around my shoulders and said, "This calls for wine! Come I know an inn and the woman who runs it seems to like me! We will celebrate!"

Part Two- Harry of Lymm

Chapter 9

Prince Edward did not join us at Cour. He rode directly to la Roche-sur-Yon. He had been taken ill again. Sir Hugh took charge of the Free Companies and we marched due west to our new base. He told Captain Tom that the Prince was pleased with our efforts. We had done all that we had been ordered. For ourselves, we were happy for we were richer and our numbers made up by the best of the Grey Company. As their leader, Walther of Lincoln said, "One advantage of a grey cloak is that it can become any colour and I like blue!" They were sworn in and became part of our company. The ones who were not chosen were resentful for it was a slur on both their character and skills. The fact that none tried to do anything about it confirmed that Captain Tom and Red Ralph had made the right choices.

We had more than a hundred and fifty miles to march. We had managed to sell our captured horses to those in the other companies and we had no men on foot. My father never thanked us for saving his life and giving him the horse and loot from the squire. I might have resented that but Peter and the others just found it sad that he had fallen so far. As we rode Red Ralph said, "Do not be upset about your father. We are not. He is like Lucifer. His fall from grace has been spectacular. He always had a temper but he had a kind side too. The first months after he and your mother were wed he was as happy as any man. Even after you were born he was happy. I know not what changed him."

That answer did not satisfy me for I began to think that I was the cause of my father's change. He had been a good warrior until I had come along.

We rode in Gascony and kept south of the Loire. We should have been safe but our raid north might have inspired the French to seek revenge and so we camped each night by the castles which guarded the border. As we moved further west the land changed. It became flatter and even more fertile. This was the land King Charles wished to have for his own. This area produced great quantities of food and had a very agreeable climate. I could see why Prince Edward was happy to have this as his own domain. As we rode west I learned more of the Prince's younger brother, John of Gaunt. It seemed that he was unhappy for his brother to have Gascony and be heir to the crown. The English crown had ever been a source of conflict between brothers. I wondered if it would result in a bloody battle for the crown. King Edward had ruled a long time. Would the brothers fall out? John of Gaunt had great influence in England. There might have been a time when such matters did not concern me but Prince Edward had said, on more than one occasion, that when time allowed I would be the bodyguard of his two sons. That would place me in the centre of any dispute.

La Roche-sur-Yon was a prosperous little place. The people looked well fed and content. Sir Alan's castle was a sturdy one with a curtain wall, a keep and a strong gatehouse. As we saw it in the distance I grew more nervous. I was not even certain that I would be allowed to see my mother. Perhaps Sir Alan had discarded her already. What if she was not even in the castle? The point was a moot one for we were given a field to the west of La Roche as our camp.

We would be here for some time as the Prince was not a well man. He had returned to Bordeaux and we were given some of the pay we were owed. Sir Hugh was happy for us to be given the chance to regain some of our strength as we had spent almost three years campaigning. Our horses looked lean and weary. The grazing would help build them up again and we had been promised regular supplies of food. I could see why we had been sent there. We were close enough to the border to respond to an attack and yet close enough to Bordeaux for us to aid the Prince should someone try to attack him while he was weak. As the land around la Roche-sur-Yon was fertile and we had money there would be no disputes with the locals.

It took six days for us to make the camp to the satisfaction of Sir Hugh and the captains. When it was done we were given permission to go into the town. I asked for leave to walk to the castle. It was outside the town and Sir Alan, it seemed, valued his privacy. Captain Tom asked, "Do you mean well, Will Strongstaff?"

"I will not cause trouble if that is what you mean, Captain. If I see Sir Alan I will doff my cap and bow. I will speak politely. If I am not allowed to see my mother then so be it but I cannot come all this way and not try to get a glimpse of her."

The captain stared into my eyes as though trying to divine my thoughts. Eventually, he nodded, "You have shown yourself to be a man of his word. Just be careful. Do not let your father follow you. He will know, as well as any, that your mother lives close by."

"There is wine to be had in the town and the coin he received for the mail and the squire's weapons will be burning a hole in his purse. I mean well, Captain and I will not damage the reputation of the Blue Company."

I went back to the tent I shared with Red Ralph and the others. They had already left for town. They had money to spend but they intended to make purchases which would be of use to them rather than wine which, as Red Ralph said, most men just pissed away. I changed into my best clothes. They were the ones I had taken from the manor north of Cour. When I wore them, I felt like a gentleman. Peter the priest thought they must have belonged to the lord's son. He had died along with his father. I had taken a cap too and it was adorned with a feather I had found on the battlefield. I had scraped the upper part of my cheeks and used a sharpened dagger to trim my beard. I did not wish my mother to think I was a vagabond. With my sword in my scabbard and a dagger in a sheath I had taken from a dead squire, I felt I looked like a young gentleman. It was a part I was playing.

The rest of the men had hurried to the town and I had the road to myself. I passed farms with men tilling the ground and examining the fruit on their trees. They did not raise many animals here. Closer to the sea, where the salt marshes lay, they reared wonderfully tasting lamb and mutton. Our tent had decided to buy a lamb and enjoy a feast. Normally when we captured an animal we butchered and ate it so quickly that it was almost tasteless. We would cook this one well for we had time. We wanted to enjoy our food.

As I drew closer to the castle I became more nervous. What would my mother call herself? Would she still be Mary daughter of Geoffrey? He had been a member of the Blue Company but he had died long before I had been born. I know that he was held in high regard by the men who had served with him. Where would my mother live? I was unsure of how these arrangements were made. He had a wife. Would she suffer a concubine in her husband's bed? Peter the Priest surmised that she might well be in England. Many nobles' wives preferred that arrangement. I felt my steps slowing as I neared the gatehouse. I was afraid. There was no moat but a dry ditch. The low-lying land meant that in wet weather it would become a temporary moat. There were two men at arms sitting on the bridge over the ditch. They watched me approach. Had I been going to the town then I would have taken the main road. The only place I could be going was the castle.

They spoke to me in English. That was not a surprise for Sir Alan was an Anglo Norman. "Have you taken the wrong turn, friend?"

I shook my head, "I am here to speak with Mary, daughter of Geoffrey."

They looked at each other and the older one said, "Be off with you. Sir Alan could have you whipped for such impertinence."

I pulled myself to my full height. I was taller than the two of them and they were definitely garrison soldiers. The older one had heavy jowls and the red nose and cheeks of a drinker. The younger could barely contain his gut with his baldric. "Mary daughter of Geoffrey is my mother. It is not impertinence."

"I did not know she had a son, another one that is. She and Sir Alan have three children." He chewed his lip nervously.

The younger one said, "Surely it can do no harm and Sir Alan is not in the castle."

The sergeant at arms shook his head, "It is more than my job is worth. Keep him here and I will see his lordship's steward."

When he had gone the younger one said, "You are of the Free Companies?" I nodded. "A rich life is it?" He rubbed the sleeve of my tunic with his fingers. "I could not afford such a garment."

I knew that I needed a friend and this was as close as I was likely to get in the castle. I smiled, "It can be but if there are rich rewards then they are offset by risks. We lost more than six thousand men in Spain."

"Still to be as young as you are and have such fine clothes and a good blade; I imagine the older ones are almost lords."

I thought of the complaints about pay and I smiled, "The wiser ones save their coin and the foolish ones do not live long enough to enjoy it."

Just then the Sergeant at Arms returned with a greybeard. It had to be the steward. I saw him appraising me as he approached. "You do not appear like a ruffian or a brigand but, with his lordship away I am responsible for the castle and all those within. What mean you by this visit?"

I did not want to confide in them. It was private but I knew that if I wanted to speak with my mother then I would have to. "My mother left when was little more than a baby. I would have her know that I have turned out well."

The steward nodded, "That you have but we can tell her that."

"If it were your mother then you would wish to speak with her would you not?"

The steward made the sign of the cross, "My mother and the rest of my village in England are all dead. The plague." He studied me, "But you make a good point." He wagged a finger at me, "I will allow one visit. Do not return. This is your hello and your goodbye. I know that seems harsh but Sir Alan… well, let us just say that if he finds out about this I will incur his displeasure but Mistress Mary, your mother, is well thought of and I know that she would speak with you. Come."

I followed him through the gates. They had not a mark on them. The walls looked as though a mason had just finished carving them. This castle had never known a battle. It explained the condition of the guards. They were not warriors, they were overpaid servants who carried swords.

"What is your name?"

"Will Strongstaff."

"Your fellows gave you that name?"

"They did."

"How extraordinary."

We entered the keep and he took me not to the Great Hall but what looked like a chamberlain's room or guard room just off to the side. There was a rough table and two benches. He was keeping me hidden.

"Sit there and I will fetch her."

I took off my cap and smoothed the feather. I laid it on the table. My sword felt uncomfortable and so I took off my baldric and scabbard and laid them next to the hat. I was filling the time for I was nervous. I heard the sound of voices. They were children's voices. Then I heard my mother. I had not heard her speak for so long and yet I knew it was her tinkling tones I heard. "You go with Robert. I have to speak with a visitor. He will show you the stables."

The voices and footsteps faded and I wondered why my mother did not enter. Eventually, the door opened and she stood there. She was beautiful. Every four-year-old believes his mother is beautiful. I was now a man and I knew that she was beautiful. I stood. It was an automatic response for she was a lady with beautiful clothes and long, combed tresses hanging down her shoulders. She had a necklace with a single jewel and a ring on each of her hands. I took that in and then stared at her. I dropped to one knee, took her hand and kissed it. I could not speak. Had I done so I would have unmanned myself. I felt my eyes filling.

She lifted me up and I saw that she was weeping, "My sweetheart! How I have missed you!" She put her arms around me and hugged me. I did the same and we stood there in silence save for the sound of her tears as they dripped on my expensive tunic. She coughed and forced herself away. "We do not have long and there is so much I need to say to you. Sit." She held my hand in hers and looked at me. Perhaps it was my imagination but I think I saw pride in her eyes. She reached up and moved an unruly lock of hair from my forehead. "You have grown into a handsome man. You have the look of your grandfather."

That made me smile for men had said that I did not look like my father and now I had an explanation. "And you are still beautiful. Did I hear the Steward say you have three children?"

A frown briefly passed across her face. Then she smiled, "You have two brothers and a sister but you cannot tell them that. Sir Alan does not like that I had a child before he... well, you know."

I shook my head, "No mother I do not know. Did I drive you away? Was I the reason you left?"

Shock and dismay filled her face and she put her hands on the side of my face, "I left to save you! Had I remained then your father would have either beaten me to death or you and that would have been as good as me dying. I knew that if I left then the reason for his anger would go."

"No, mother, it did not go. I was beaten every day after you left. If not for Red Ralph and the others I would have died."

"Then I will add Red Ralph to my prayers for he was always a good man."

"What made my father change for he was not always thus."

"I am not certain of the exact cause but I think he wanted more for the two of us than he could give. Instead of doing something about it he just felt sorry for himself and fell into a pool of drink." She tapped her breast, "It was something in here. Perhaps bad blood, who knows?"

That was what Peter the Priest had said, "Then I have the bad blood in me too?" It was a genuine fear. Would I turn into the monster that was my father?

She smiled, "I do not believe that. You have too much of me and my mother and father. Besides, I believe we make our own fortune. I am, well not quite a lady, but I live better than my mother. I am called my lady and I have servants."

"But you are not married."

No, Will, I am not married. Does that make you ashamed?"

"Of course not, I was thinking of you. What happens when Sir Alan tires of you?"

"He may tire of me but not his children. His wife is in England. She is a cold barren woman who should have become a nun. Sir Alan told me that she did not enjoy coupling with him. You are right. One day he will take a younger woman but I will still be the mother of his children and I will be looked after. But what of you?"

"You mean will I end up as my father and be a man at arms waiting for death?"

She stroked my cheek again, "Such pessimism does not sit well with your face my son."

"And I hope for more. I will become a gentleman."

I told her what the Prince had promised and she reached up to hug me. "Then I can sleep easy at night. I have prayed for you each night. The Lord has answered my prayers."

"But he may change his mind. Still, I have coins now and I know how to use a sword. Even if he does not take me as guard for his sons then I will become a captain."

There was a knock on the door and a servant put her head through, "The Steward says it is time."

"Thank you, Maryanne, give me a moment." I stood and she hugged me and then drew my head down to kiss me on the cheeks. I have little to give you save this." She slid my dagger from its sheath and cut a lock of her golden hair. She kissed it. "I still have your first lock of hair. Know that before I sleep each night I pray to God to watch over you. I will do so until my time on this earth is over."

"And I pray for you."

"One more thing, think kindly of your father. He was not always such a tormented soul. If what you say about his drinking and reckless attacks then I fear he has not long on this earth."

"I have tried to build bridges…"

"But he burns them. I know." She straightened her back and brushed away the last of her tears. "And now I will be Sir Alan's concubine once more. You cannot write to me but I can ask others of the fortune of the Blue Company. How are you known?"

"Will Strongstaff."

"A fine name and, I daresay, honourably earned. Farewell my son. If I do not see you again then I will be waiting for you in heaven. I am so proud of you I fear I will gush once more."

The door opened and the Steward stood there with the three children. I strapped on my baldric and donned my hat. The two boys stood open mouthed. One said, "Are you one of the Prince's men?"

I smiled, "I am, I am Will Strongstaff of the Blue Company. Farewell lady and thank you for your kind words. Thank you, Steward, for your kindness." I strode from the room, the keep and the castle with a confident stride. Will son of Harry was dead but, in his place, walked a warrior with a future.

Chapter 10

We spent three months camped in that field and we recovered well. I tried to speak with my father many times but to no avail. Eventually, I gave up but my mother's words stayed with me. I would learn to be more tolerant of my father. I had not had his journey. Perhaps my own journey might change me. Who knew?

I found a man who worked in gold and silver in La Roche-sur-Yon and I gave him two gold pieces. I had taken them from the dead knight. One was payment and the other was to be fashioned into a locket for the lock of my mother's hair. When it was finished I hung it from my neck and never took it off. It gave me comfort in the hard days which were to come.

Our pleasant rest was interrupted in late autumn when the French invaded Aquitaine. The Prince was still ill, he had the dropsy, and so Sir John Chandos left his home to lead us. He set up his headquarters at Poitiers. We marched to join him. The rest had done us all good. The fine food we had eaten added to the training I had enjoyed with my shield brothers meant that I was bigger and stronger than I had been. Indeed, I was now one of the largest men at arms. I still lacked the skill of Peter and Red Ralph but I was catching them up. I had sold Sunrise and my Spanish horse in order to buy a palfrey. Goldcrest was a large horse but not yet a war horse. She could easily carry me and, if I had had it I would have been able to wear mail and plate. I had also bought two spears. I did not trust myself with a lance. The months in the camp had allowed me to make a new shield. I took advice from the others and was well pleased with my efforts. The bright colour I had stained it made it stand out and Long John feared it would draw enemies to me thinking that I was a novice. I did not mind. I had stood with others and fought for the standard. I would cope.

The rest had not done my father any good at all. Whereas we had trained and prepared for war he had spent all of his coin on wine and ale. It was sad to see. Ralph and Peter were particularly upset for they had joined the company at the same time as my father. They had been young warriors together and they spoke of a different Harry of Lymm to the one I knew.

Sir John Chandos was a popular leader. He led from the front and he was intelligent. Men liked leaders they could trust. We trusted him. We all wished the Prince to be with us but if he was ill then he was of little use to us. We would make do with Sir John. He commanded as many knights and their retinues as there were in the Free Companies. Accordingly, he just used Sir Hugh as a go between. Sir Hugh then briefed the captains and Tom told us.

"Well lads, we are heading east towards the Vienne river and Chauvigny. Sir John wants to threaten the road from Lyons to Orleans." That made sense to me. When we had been at La Roche-sur-Yon the others had explained the geography of France to me. I knew that the food from Lyon and the south continued to travel to the north until Christmas. By cutting off the supply Sir John hoped to weaken the French. "The Free Companies will be spread amongst the knights and their men. Sir John knows our value. We are attached to Sir John himself. We will not take wagons. As soon as we cross the Vienne then we forage for ourselves. Sir John intends to fight defensive battles where we can. That way we use our archers. Those of you with two horses can take them but there will be no wagons."

Stephen of Kent asked, "What do we do with the treasure that we take?"

"If you can carry it then all well and good but we will not be slowed down by wagons."

"And are we to be paid?"

"Yes, Owen the Welshman, Prince Edward has sent coin and it will be distributed tomorrow before we ride."

As we returned to our camp to prepare Ralph said, "You have to hand it to the Prince. He times things well. There will be no desertions and men will travel east in good spirits and with full purses. He and Sir John are doing all in their power to ensure victory."

The campaign began well. We left in the late morning and headed north and east. By ensuring that everyone was mounted we made good progress and reached the bridge at La Roche-Posay by dark. Sir John himself led our company and forty household knights to charge the bridge. The sun was setting behind us as we galloped towards the bridge. I was using a spear for the first time. The lack of a wagon meant I had only been able to bring one spear. Once it shattered then I would have to use my sword.

As I was tucked in behind Captain Tom, Sir Hugh and his squire as well as the household knights of Sir John, I could see little ahead of me.

I heard the clash of spears on shields and metal on metal as the knights hit the end of the bridge. There were screams and shouts but we kept moving albeit more slowly. The clatter of Goldcrest's hooves on the wooden bridge were interrupted as she stepped on the bodies of the men Sir John and his knights had slain. Surprise was complete and we managed to enter the town before they could close the gates. Sir John shouted, "Spread out! I want this town!" And we obeyed!

I rode with my four shield brothers down an empty street to our left. It was wide enough for three men only and I rode next to Dick Long Sword. I was desperate to use my spear. I had practised with it but the real test would come when I used it in action.

Men emerged from doorways but when they saw our mighty horses thundering down the narrow streets they ducked back inside. We were riding to reach the far gate. The more townsfolk we could capture the greater the reward. Red Ralph lunged with his spear as one soldier, braver than the rest tried to bar our progress. It was futile. It was the sort of act my father might try. He had the luck of the devil; the slain Frenchman did not. The French had had time to organize a defence at the town gate. They formed a shield wall. It was just one rank deep. To be effective they needed at least two and preferably three. As the street widened to the gate entrance Dick and I were able to close with Peter and Long John. We struck the shield wall like the tip of an arrow.

I punched with my spear as the Frenchmen who were at the left side of their line struck at me. Two spears against one should have meant that they won but I was above them and both flinched behind their shields. They did not have long spears and my head and face were safe. It allowed me to choose my target. The one at the extreme left of the French shield wall had his shield covering his left side. His right shoulder was enticingly defenceless. I plunged the ash shaft towards him. He wore no mail and the sharpened spear head tore through the leather as though it was not there and into his shoulder. He had made the mistake of using thin leather and it would cost him his life. I wore ox hide! His companion's spear hit my shield and the other slid across the back of my right hand. Blood flowed. As Goldcrest's chest struck the two men they fell. The falling Frenchman pulled his body clear of my spear.

Red Ralph shouted, "Will, secure the gate and stop them leaving!"

My charge and strike had taken me close to the gate and I urged Goldcrest on. I turned her so that her body filled the gate and my shield was facing any who would try to breach it. More townsfolk and men at arms ran towards the gate. I pulled back on my reins and stood in the stirrups. My horse reared. I thrust my spear towards the face of the man at arms whose sword flailed before him. I did not strike flesh but heard my spear head ring from his helmet. He reeled and the two with him stepped back to avoid the hooves of my horse. Peter and Dick galloped into the back of the three of them. Two fell and the third dropped his sword and fell to his knees crying, "I yield! I yield!"

Seeing the soldier surrender took the flight and the fight from the others and they all stopped. Peter said, "Dick, Will, close and bar the gate. We have the bolt hole!"

It was dark by the time we had secured the town. Our small band was left to guard the gate. Long John said, "I hope Captain Tom knows that we have done service here."

Red Ralph snorted, "Do you trust our Captain so little, John? We will get our share."

We had already taken the purses and weapons from the dead and the captives. It was not a fortune but it was enough. At least I thought so but John, Ralph and Peter were coming to the end of their time as mercenaries. They needed all the coin they could get to see them have a good life back in England.

The dead bodies had a sobering effect on the captives. They sat sullenly staring at the two dead warriors. Occasionally they would glare, not at us, but at the three soldiers we had captured. They had paid, as we had but, in their case, it was to defend their town. They had not done their job. When we left there would be three men at arms marching on the road to find a new employer.

Stephen of Kent walked up to us with four of the new men from the old Grey Company. We had been guarding the gate for some hours. "You are to escort the captives back to the town square and we will relieve you. There is food."

"Thank you. On your feet!" The captives rose and we pushed them down the road.

My spear was attached to my saddle from which hung my shield and helmet. We walked our horses. We could hear the shouts and laughter from the other companies. Not all were as well disciplined as we were. Sir John would punish those who broke his strict rules. The square was more organised. I saw Captain Tom speaking with Sir John and Sir Hugh. There were disconsolate captives by the water trough. There were more than a hundred of them. Six archers had them covered with their bows. We could see a fire burning and there was a pot upon it. Owen the Welshman was stirring it. The smell of the food was enticing and we made to head towards it.

"Red Ralph, bring your men over."

Long John mumbled, "I could eat a horse with its skin on! Have we not done enough?"

"Peace, John. We are the Blue Company and not the ragged and ill-disciplined Red Company. We obey orders."

"These are the men, my lord. They are the best scouts I have."

Sir John looked at us and studied us. He pointed to me, "That one looks a little young."

"Will Strongstaff is the son of Harry of Lymm. He has shown himself to be resourceful. He defended the standard without a shield."

Apparently satisfied he nodded, "I want you to ride east tomorrow and find a French army or the Gascon rebels. The Prince needs to defeat both of them. Our purpose here is to stop the French from taking our towns. The Gascon rebels are handing them over to their new masters. It seems the French King does not tax as heavily as our Prince. Take nothing for granted. Be cautious. You have tomorrow to do this."

I could see both Sir Hugh and Captain Tom watching our faces. Scouts were normally paid extra. There had been no promise of pay. Red Ralph nodded, "And we will be recompensed, my lord, for loss of horses?"

Sir John's face creased into a smile, "You are true warriors I see. Aye." He pointed to his own horse which was being tended by his squire. It had been wounded in the charge through the gate. "I think the next time I charge a bridge I will do so on foot. And you will be rewarded when you find the French."

Red Ralph nodded, "Thank you, my lord."

We had to succeed or we would not be paid. We walked our horses to our company. I saw my father nursing a wine skin. The rest had taken their bowls and were eating.

Owen the Welshman said, "We have left you plenty Red Ralph. It is mutton stew fortified with wine and mushrooms."

Long John said, loudly so that all could hear his words, "Was that to make Harry of Lymm eat it?"

Everyone laughed and my father glowered at Long John. There would have been a time when he would have taken offence but now he sank back into his wine skin.

The stew was good. Captain Tom returned from his conference. "You will have your share of what we took from the town when you return."

We were too busy eating to answer him. What was unspoken was that if any of us died then our share would be divided amongst the rest of our band of brothers. That was the way it was. We would share the risks and share the rewards. Captain Tom sat with us while we ate. He had a jug of wine and he poured us each a beaker full. When we had eaten Red Ralph asked, "Where does Sir John think we might find the French?"

"Look for the rebels. Sir Robert Knolles has taken Saint-Savin, to the east of us. I would look further south and east. Lignac is thirty miles away. They should be between here and there."

"That is a long day's ride."

"And there is a fat purse awaiting you." He smiled, "I know that three of you will be seeking a home in England soon. You know what they say, make hay while the sun shines. You are all clever enough to avoid capture. Just beware of false Gascons who feign friendship."

With those sobering words we retired. In contrast to many of the men we had had just one beaker of wine. That was another reason why we had been selected. That and the fact that we could be trusted.

Once again, we left before dawn. We took the road to Saint-Savin. It was in Prince Edward's hands. We gave the passwords and crossed through the town and over the bridge. We were now in rebel land. To the north and east of us lay the forest of La Brenne. It was a natural obstacle to an army. Keeping that to our left we headed down the twisting road. In theory the people were all loyal Gascons, subjects of the Prince but their lords were in dispute and objected to his taxes. They would be as neutral as possible until the rebellion was over then they would shout and cheer for either Prince Edward or King Charles. They were pragmatic and practical people. We passed castles but they were in the distance. An army is hard to disguise. It has to spread out over a large area. Horses leave a clear and pungent trail. The road was clear of their mess and empty.

We stopped at noon in a small town called Liglet. We had watered our horses when we forded the river but they needed a rest and we needed food. There were just a dozen houses in the village. Captain Tom had chosen us rather than any other because he knew that we would not alienate those in the villages we passed. We would be paid for our service and so we dismounted and addressed the inhabitants. They had stayed indoors. We might be brigands or bandits. Caution was always the safest option. Red Ralph shouted, "We are of Blue Company and we serve Prince Edward. We would pay for food and wine."

His words were greeted by silence. Our helmets, shields and spears hung from our saddles. We were wrapped against the cold in our cloaks and that hid our swords. Eventually, a door opened and a greybeard emerged, "I am Jean of Liglet. I am the headman here. We have little enough food for it is winter."

Peter the Priest spoke. He had a gentle way about him and could often disarm those who were suspicious of us, "And we have coin. I know that you will have a surplus for this is rich farmland and you look to have too many grey hairs to be someone who does not plan."

The farmer smiled, "And you are wise. We have some cheese and oat bread. The wine is a little rough."

Peter smiled, "Then it will be like Christ's last supper." We all made the sign of the cross. "It will suffice."

The bread would not have suited knights or squires but we did not mind for it was filling and wholesome. The cheese was freshly made while we had drunk far worse wine. As we ate and the villagers' suspicions allayed more came out. We knew to smile and humour them for we could find out valuable information. We discovered the local lord of the manor had called on his tenants and headed south east. We were told this without prompting. Perhaps they did not recognise its value. There was a muster and it was in the direction we were headed.

Rested and refreshed we left. Dick Long Sword glanced over his shoulder as we rode down the road in case one of the villagers left by horse. We had not seen any animals but that did not mean they had none hidden. No one left the village and we continued south and east. We were two miles shy of Lignac and approaching a crossroads which was surrounded by trees when Goldcrest whinnied and pricked her ears. I reined in and said, "There is danger ahead."

We all drew our swords and dropped our left hands to our shields. Red Ralph said, "Ride on!"

As we neared the trees I heard the sound of horse and men. Four men at arms stepped out from our right. They smiled. They had open palms and, like us, wore no helmets. Their leader spoke in Gascon. "You may sheathe your swords friends. We are not your enemies. Are you from Sir John's column?"

No password had been given and we knew that the only other scouts would be from Sir Robert at Saint-Savin. When we had ridden through the captain of the guard had asked to report back if there was danger. These men were not from Saint-Savin. Red Ralph was our leader and we trusted him but his attention was on the four men before us. I made as though I was going to sheathe my sword but I glanced to our left. The trees were thicker there but I saw a swishing tail. There were men hiding there. This was an ambush. Knowing that there were men there I looked more carefully. I saw a hand. It held a weapon. I caught Peter's eye and nodded at the trees. He had sheathed his sword and he leaned forward to stroke his horse's head. It allowed him to view the wood.

The Gascon sergeant had moved forward and was speaking with Red Ralph. He reached up to stroke Red Ralph's horse with his left hand. I saw his right-hand slide down. "A fine horse. Would you consider selling…"

He got no further for Peter shouted, "Ambush!"

My sword was still out and I dug my heels into Goldcrest to ride at the wood. Peter had reached down for his mace. We took our ambushers by surprise. Behind me, I heard a cry as Red Ralph slew the leader. Those three could deal with the others. I just managed to lift my shield when the sword came from the bush to slash at me. It was a hurried blow and slid down my shield. Goldcrest knocked the warrior to the ground. Ahead of me, Peter's mace smashed into the face of a Gascon, pounding it to a pulp. One was attempting to mount his horse and I rode after him. He had one foot in his stirrup when I swung my sword at his back. It grated against bone for the man wore no mail. A spear lunged up at me from my right. I swear I did not see it but I must have sensed it for I drew back my head. It rasped against the metal plates on my jerkin. I struck out blindly to my right side. I connected with something and I wheeled Goldcrest around.

I saw the man who had tried to spear me. He had a greybeard; that meant he was a veteran. My sword had torn through his tunic and wounded him but it was little more than a nick. He would not be worried by the blood seeping inside his tunic. Peter was still fighting the last of the ambushers and I could hear the fight behind us. I would have to fight this veteran alone and hope that the practice had been worthwhile. He was a big man and despite his wound held his spear overhand. I saw that he was well balanced and his feet were apart. He was ready to respond no matter which way I went.

He feinted at me. I know not why I did it but I feigned fear. I whipped Goldcrest's head around as though I intended to flee. I let my horse take one step and then dug my heels in and turned my horse to face the man. I took him completely by surprise. He had his arm pulled back to throw the spear at my back. It was the right move to make for I would not be able to protect myself and at a distance of three paces, he could not miss. Goldcrest could not stop herself. The spear came over her head as she bowled into him. The tip caught on the mail I had sewn on my shoulders. I had used more stitches than were necessary and they proved vital. The shield was torn from his grip as my horse's mouth struck his head. He fell beneath her hooves. I heard something crunch. Ready for another trick I whirled my horse around but he lay on the ground. I saw that the other Gascons were all dead or dying. Long John had been wounded and Peter the Priest was attending to him.

I dismounted and knelt by the greybeard. Red Ralph joined me. The greybeard opened his eyes. He smiled and a trickle of blood oozed from the side of his mouth. He spoke in English although it was accented. "You are a clever one. Fancy me falling for that trick."

Red Ralph knelt next to us, "John of Stafford! What are you doing fighting for the Gascons?"

"The same as you, coin. This was to be my last war and then home to Cannock. Is this your lad?"

"No, he is of our company though."

"He is a handy man in a fight. He reminds me of Young Jack. His horse has done for me. I pray you, Ralph, for old times sake, give me the warrior's death. I am in pain and I have born enough suffering already in my life." Ralph drew his dagger and hesitated. There was an unspoken question. The veteran closed and then opened his eyes. "I owe the Gascons nothing. There are two armies coming for you. Louis I, Duke of Anjou, is heading for Guyenne by way of La Reole and Bergerac, the other, under John, Duke of Berry is marching towards Limousin and Quercy. There they will unite and besiege the Prince in Angoulême. We rode with the Duke of Berry. I am too old to be a scout." He winced. "Quickly old friend."

Red Ralph nodded and slit his friend's throat. "He was a good man. He could have been a captain but when his son, Jack, died at Poitiers all life went from him." He looked at me. "Take his arms and coin. You defeated him and he would want that." He stood. "As he was a friend we will bury him."

I did so but I was not happy about it. I felt as though I knew the old man. It was like taking from our own company. This war set brother against brother and friend against friend.

It was obvious that Long John was hurt. Red Ralph wanted to send Peter the Priest back to the Prince as an escort. John would have none of it. "I will take four horses back with me and take it slowly. I would be no use in a fight but I can tell Sir Hugh what we have learned, in case…"

He did not need to finish his sentence. In case we did not return. He left while we buried John of Stafford beneath an elm at the crossroads. He was far from home and he was alone. I would not end my days the same way.

As we headed south and east, we were still making for Lignac. The men we had killed had been scouts. As Peter said, if they had to use old men like John of Stafford, then it was not the best army. They would be the closest to us. "Seeing old John like that makes me determined to get home. This is my last campaign. The money I get for this will be enough even if the Prince does not pay what he owes us. The purses we took back there were full."

Peter nodded, "Aye, you are right. When first we came here we knew for whom we fought. We were paid but we fought for England. Now we fight Englishmen and it does not sit well."

Poor Dick Long Sword was silent. If the two left and I was given a position by the Prince then it would mean he was almost alone. It was more than company. When you fought with someone who was a brother in arms you were more confident. You knew that someone watched your back. The prospect of watching over the two princes suddenly seemed an attractive prospect.

We led the captured horses which also carried the scouts' supplies, armour and weapons. As soon as we were within a mile of Lignac we knew where at least one army was camped. We saw their tents. We had done that which we needed to. Red Ralph wondered if we should go closer. "Perhaps Sir John might pay more if we were to give him accurate numbers."

Peter said, "You seek a good pay day, Ralph. It is unnecessary. We will be paid enough for the information we bring. Will here has good eyes. How many banners can you see?"

Using Peter as a prop I stood on the saddle and rested my hand upon his helmet. I knew the difference between bannerets, which belonged to bachelor knights and the banners of lords who led other knights. The banners of the Dukes and Counts were easy to spot. "There are six banners of Dukes and counts." I then used the time-tested method of counting. I counted my right hand twice and then held up my thumb. Another right hand twice and my forefinger. "One hundred and eighty knights who lead other knights." The bachelor knights were harder for their swallow-tailed banners were less easy to see. I slid down to the saddle, "As near as I can estimate there are more than two hundred and fifty bannerets."

Peter nodded. "There will be ten times as many mercenaries, perhaps more, as there are knights. We are talking an army the size of ours and a second one linking up. We need to get back, Ralph. The Prince needs to send more men from Angoulême and Cognac."

Red Ralph was convinced but, perhaps as a result of my standing on the horse, we heard the thunder of hooves. We had been seen and we had to flee back home. The spare horses slowed us slightly but if our pursuers closed with us we could change to the fresher horses and out run them. For that reason, we rode at an easier gait than the rebels who chased us. We soon passed the crossroads. The bodies which we had left lying where they fell might arrest the attention of those chasing us. At the very least they would slow to make certain that it was not an ambush.

We still had many miles to go. I kept turning around until Peter said, "All that will gain you will be a stiff neck. You will hear them when they close. This is the right pace."

By the time we reached the village where we had eaten, we could hear their hooves. Red Ralph said, "When we reach the river we change horses. We are half way home."

It was a risk and we all knew it. When the Gascons saw us stop they would speed up. All it took was a careless dismount or a skittish horse and we would be captured or killed. The horse I led had belonged to John of Stafford. I hoped it was a good animal. I had not had time to get to know the beast.

Our horses all smelled the water and they hurried accordingly. I threw myself from my saddle as Goldcrest began to drink. As the other horse began to drink I threw myself in the saddle. I was the first one mounted. I grabbed Goldcrest's reins and turned to look. The men who were pursuing us were spread out. Three of them had outstripped the rest. Just then Dick slipped as he tried to mount the new horse. The horse wandered five paces away. It was a disaster. Drawing my sword, I let Goldcrest's reins trail in the river and I charged the three men. I was not being reckless. None had drawn their weapons and they would have to slow when they neared the river. I hoped to slow them even more and give Dick the chance to mount. One of the rebels was more eager than the others and he began to draw his sword. As my new horse clambered up the bank I stood in my stirrups, it helped me to ascend and I slashed my sword over the horse's head. The Gascon pulled back too hard and his horse slipped on the muddy bank and fell. I whipped my horse's head around and galloped back into the river. I managed to sheathe my sword and grab Goldcrest's reins before the next men had negotiated the fallen horse and rider. Dick was mounted and we scrambled up the bank.

We kept our heads down and rode harder than we had before. As I glanced east I saw that night would soon be upon us. If we could survive until dark then we had a chance for the Gascons would not risk an ambush. After a mile of harder riding Red Ralph shouted, "We can slow down. They have dropped back."

As someone who knew horses I understood why. They had been riding harder than we had. They had speeded up when we slowed and tried to keep up with us. Their horses would be exhausted. By the time night fell Red Ralph called a halt and we listened. They had given up on the chase. The horses were weary. We swapped horses again and headed north at a walk.

Dick said, "I am sorry I slipped. You should have left me. It was my error."

Peter smiled, his teeth white in the twilight, "We are one company. If one falls we all fall. Besides we have a madman with us. Each time I think he has matured and ripened he emulates his father!"

I felt myself blushing. Luckily it was dark and I would not be seen, "It was calculated. They had no weapons drawn and I thought to surprise them. It worked against John of Stafford."

Red Ralph said, "Perhaps you are lucky. I have met such men but I have to warn you that luck comes at a price. One day it will run out. Do not be in such a hurry to use all of your luck up at once."

We reached Saint-Savin after the gates had been closed and we were taken to Sir Robert. After we had reported to him he said, "You have done well. Your fellow arrived earlier. Sir John will know some of it. Stay here the night and report back in the morning. We need the Prince and his men! The Free Companies cannot do this alone."

Chapter 11

Our news brought us the pay day which Red Ralph had hoped. As much as he might want to return to England he would not do so while we were needed. We sold our horses and spare equipment. More men had arrived. The promise of plunder was attractive and we were paid well. Sir John went on the defensive. We would wait for the Prince and his men to arrive. The weather turned even colder and the tents proved remarkably thin. Alone, out of the companies, the Blue Company was prepared for winter. The French and Gascon rebels grew bolder. They attacked Saint-Savin and drove out Sir Robert who fell back to Poitiers. With more French and Gascons heading for our position, Sir John had no choice. We had to join the retreat to Poitiers.

Prince Edward was still ill but he was heading north on a litter. None of us expected him any time soon. When Sir Hugh and the captains were summoned just before the New Year we wondered if this was the end of the campaign. Our gains had been wiped out and the Prince was still ill. None of us expected to fight. We thought that the message would come back that we were suing for peace. We did not know Sir John.

Captain Tom said, "We are to ride south. The Viscount is going to cross the bridge at Lussac-les-Châteaux and attack the French and the rebels from the south. Sir Robert will attack from the north. We will surprise them and regain that which we have lost. When the Prince arrives in a week or so we will begin the campaign to recapture that which we have lost."

I was not certain. I was inexperienced but even I knew that attacking a defended bridge was never a good idea. As we left the camp to march south we found we were riding on icy ground. It did not bode well as horses slipped and slid. We had less than eighteen miles to travel yet it took us until what passed for noon. Although the skies were cloudy the ground was still slippery. Mindful of his last charge across a defended bridge Sir John decided that he and his household knights, along with the Blue Company would force the defenders at the bridge. The attack would be on foot. It seemed a good idea for although the bridge was packed our knights were all mailed. If they could force the bridge then the Blue Company could move quickly and secure the crossing for the rest of the army.

Although it was freezing cold Red Ralph and Peter advised me not to wear my cloak. "It will encumber you. You will be hot enough once you swing your sword. I have seen men catch their cloak when they meant to thrust at an enemy. Better a little cold than a cold life below ground!"

They knew best and I obeyed them. We dismounted in the woods to the west of the bridge. We could not disguise our attack but we could worry them with the numbers. I saw that Sir John had not only a cloak but also a long surcoat which reached to his feet. The knights with him were similarly attired. Perhaps they enjoyed their comfort.

We left the woods and formed up. Sir John was flanked by nine knights. There were thirty knights in all. We were in the second rank. Our archers sent showers of arrows over our heads. The men on the bridge held up their shields. The Gascon rebels and the French could not use their crossbows for there was a hump in the centre of the bridge. They could not see us. Captain Tom had us bang our shields with the hilts of our swords. It helped us to march in time and intimidated the enemy. Keeping our feet would be as hard as fighting. I saw one knight, as we approached the bridge, suddenly lose his footing and slither off the road, down the bank and into the river. His squire ran to help him out of the water. As soon as the squire cleared the parapet of the bridge a handful of bolts were sent in his direction. Three of them hit and he slid into the icy river to join his floundering master. The weight of his mail dragged the unfortunate knight below the water. It was not an auspicious beginning.

The deaths seemed to inspire Sir John. He stepped forward with his knights and as one they struck the enemy line. It reeled and recoiled. I saw that some of the French knights, I recognised the livery of Sir Bagnac, were using lances. I wondered why for they were unwieldy. Then I saw that they were using them to support their swordsmen at the front. They were thrusting them over their comrades' heads and between them. While men on both sides fell Sir John and those around him seemed to bear a charmed life. He had metal plates on his fore arms and legs although he still wore an open face helmet rather than one with a visor. The coif around his neck overlapped his breastplate. The deaths and the wounds suffered by those before us meant that I was soon in the line behind the knights supporting Sir John, I heard him cursing the French for all that he was worth. I had my sword above my shield.

Ralph had been quite right. The presence of men around me and the efforts we had made thus far meant I was far from cold.

The knight next to Sir John was suddenly felled by a two-handed axe and one of Sir John's squires, his nephew, stepped into the space vacated by the knight. I found myself behind one Sir John Chandos. I was aware of his surcoat and cloak trailing along the ground and so I gave him space. He brought his sword across the neck of the axeman who had killed his nephew and as he stepped forward to engage the next man, Sir Bagnac, he slipped and fell to the ground. As he lay, prostrate, a lance was thrust at him. Sir John had an open-faced helmet and the wooden lance pierced him just below the eye. His second squire tried to step in to protect his body but a lance was rammed into his middle.

I had no choice. I could not let our leader be butchered. I stepped before his body. Red Ralph and Peter were nowhere near me. They were behind knights. I heard them shouting in frustration as they fought through the knights to get to my side. I would have to defend Sir John alone.

I placed my left leg before me and held my shield away from my body. Holding my sword above the shield I waited for the attack which would come to finish off Sir John. The squire who had used the lance to impale Sir John pulled it back for a second strike. He had no shield but he wore good mail and he had metal plates on his shoulders and arms. I stabbed downwards. My sword went through both of his legs. He squealed. It sounded like a pig being butchered and he crumbled to the bridge. Eager hands pulled him to safety as a lance was rammed at me. It hit my shield square on and I barely managed to keep my feet. As much as I wanted to swing my sword and keep them at bay the fact that they had lances meant they could strike at me with impunity.

I heard Captain Tom shout, "Captain Jack! Archers!"

As I fended off another lance a sword was swung from on high. I was slow to raise my shield and I only partially blocked the blow. It hit the mail protecting my shoulders. I lunged at the man and my blade went under his arm and into his body. His falling body dragged my sword down and a second sword hit my helmet. I felt myself falling.

I heard Sir Edward Twyford, Sir John's uncle shout, "Pull Sir John to safety!"

I kept my feet as long as I could but my knees hit the wood of the bridge. Now that Sir John had been pulled clear I could swing and I did so. My sword hacked into the knee of my nearest attacker. Another swung his axe at my shield. My new shield held but my left arm was so numb that I was not sure I would be able to lift it again. I rose to one knee and saw a bearded, grinning face. The Frenchman shouted something unintelligible and, as I stood, I launched myself at him. My helmet hit him under the chin and the warrior next to him in the arm but I ended up stranded on the bridge. I felt like a fish which had just been caught. Even as I tried to stand I knew that I would not be able to do so before I was butchered.

Just at that moment, I heard a primaeval scream from behind and my father leapt over the men behind me. Even as he stood a spear was rammed into his leg. He swung his sword and it tore across the spearman's throat. He punched with his shield and slashed with his sword. A sword sliced his bicep. He did not stop. He was cursing and swearing. I could smell the wine on him. He was like a man possessed. He would die unless someone helped him. I rose. I could feel blood dripping down my left arm. I had been wounded. A squire swung an axe towards my father's unguarded back. I dropped my shield and used my left hand to bring down my sword and hack through the squire's helmet and skull. I stood with my back to my father. I saw Red Ralph, Captain Tom and the others as they fought their way towards us. I was vaguely aware that we were three quarters of the way across the bridge. We had almost succeeded.

My left arm still felt numb but I drew my dagger. I could use that. As I blocked a sword strike I used my right hand to pull back the knight's shield and I rammed my dagger into the eye hole of his helmet. He screamed and fell backwards clutching his face. As he fell Peter the Priest drew closer to me. I could still hear my father shouting and screaming. I was aware that the ground was slippery beneath my feet. I glanced down and saw that it was not ice. It was blood. I heard a grunt from behind me and a weight came on my back. Red Ralph threw himself, along with Long John at my left while Dick and Peter did the same to my right. I was clear to turn. As I did so my father's body slid to the ground.

Captain Tom appeared and stepped before me, "You have done enough, Will. See to your father."

I rammed my sword into the wood of the bridge. I was oblivious to all that was going on around me. My father's eyes were closed. He had lost the fingers of his right hand and he had so many cuts that I could not see how he had lasted as long as he had. Then he opened his eyes and did something I had not seen before my mother left. He smiled, "I have done one thing for my son at any rate. I am proud of you, boy. I just wanted you to be tough. This is a hard life we lead. You will be a gentleman. Make something bet…."

His eyes glazed over. He was dead. I knew he was dead and yet it could not be so. I had much to tell him. "You cannot die! I need you! Come back! Do not die!"

All around me men were fighting and dying. Had any Gascon chosen they could have ended my life easily but God was watching over me. I do not know how long I waited there with his body but eventually, I felt hands around my shoulders and I was lifted up by Red Ralph. Peter the Priest knelt and began to mumble Latin.

Captain Tom said, "He is like the prodigal son. He has returned and redeemed himself. See, Will Strongstaff, he is smiling. He is at peace. He has atoned. Do not be sad. He wished this. He wanted to save you."

Red Ralph nodded, "Aye, none else could have done what he did. Your act was brave enough but your father…" he shook his head. "I know not how he survived for he took cut after cut."

Peter stood and saw the blood on my tunic, "And you are hurt too. Come let me heal you."

I shook myself free, "First we bury my father! Then, and only then, will I let you touch me!" I was unreasonable, I was petulant and I was angry.

Peter nodded, "Aye although where we find some ground we can dig I know not!"

By the time we had found the churchyard and dug the grave, it was almost dawn. We laid him, with sword and shield and wrapped in his cloak, in the hard, icy French soil. Peter spoke over the grave and sent my father on his way. My mother had been right. He had been possessed by demons and it was only the threat to his only son which had driven them from him. As he tended me Peter spoke quietly to me, "You cannot undo the past. You should not berate yourself for you could have done nothing to change your father. What he did was deliberate and his choice of death was chosen too. What father would not give his life for his child? I have no children but if I had then I would do exactly as Harry of Lymm did. And I would not expect my child to grieve for me. Your father has that which he wanted."

I thought about his words, "You are right. At the end he gave me a command. Am I bound to obey it?"

"That depends. What was the command?" Peter sounded worried.

"He told me to better myself and become a gentleman."

Peter looked relieved, "Then that is what you should do."

We walked back to our horses. I did not know who had won the battle and I did not care. When we reached them Captain Tom said, "Sir John is dead. We are being sent to Guyenne. The Prince will need to be told." He smiled at me, "You gained great honour and your father will now be remembered as a hero and not the drunken bully he was, albeit briefly. Sir Edward has said that you are to be given anything you wish for your brave act."

"What I wish I cannot have."

Captain Tom nodded, "Aye well the others are collecting your treasure. We have a long ride ahead of us. I think that I will join Ralph and Peter and return home. I believe it is time for me to sheathe my sword!"

By the time we reached the Prince he had heard the details of the battle. Although distraught he still found the time to seek me out. "I must be a good judge of character Will son of Harry. I saw, in you, a good model for my sons to emulate. I have been regaled by stories of the heroes on the bridge, father and son fighting together. When summer comes I will take my wife and my sons to England. I will hold you to your promise. You will help me to protect my sons. You will stand before their young bodies the way you did for my old friend, John."

We spent barely a week at Guyenne for the Prince received news from Limoges. The Bishop of Limoges, whom Prince Edward had considered a friend had surrendered the city to the French. He was determined to recapture it and we set off to take the town which was just forty-five miles from the bridge where my father and Sir John had died.

My wounds were not completely healed. I felt weak. It was not just the wounds. I found myself brooding about my father and his death. He had died to save me and that was humbling. I had only known his fists but having spoken to my mother and seen his death I wondered if I ever knew the man. I was silent as we rode south. It was warmer than it had been, as we headed towards the city. I had gained a good thick fur edged cloak from one of the knights I had slain. Sir Edward had given me a good horse which he had taken and so I was able to travel with all my newly found treasures. They seemed less important now.

Red Ralph, Old Tom and Peter were also silent. Their thoughts may have been on my father for he had been a shield brother but I did not know for certain. From the words they did speak I knew that this siege would be their last one. When the new grass came they would leave for England. Captain Tom had lost too many comrades in Gascony and France. He wanted to grow old with people and not watch them die. Eight more of our company had died in the battle for the bridge. A battle which had not been won despite our losses and the fact that we had taken our objective.

The icy weather had given way to wet, damp weather. The roads became slick and slippery. Wagons became stuck. Prince Edward chafed at the delay for he was still ill and rode in a litter. We all knew that was not a good thing. Red Ralph also worried about the lack of siege machines. I knew little of sieges. The Free Companies raided. They rode to war and avoided, whenever possible, walls. We would have walls and ditches to assail. We had neither trebuchet nor rams. Dick wondered if we might build them when we reached the town. Peter knew sieges and he had shaken his head and told him that would merely add to the time we were stuck at a siege. The ones in the town would be hungry but so would we. As Limoges was in Prince Edward's land we could hardly raid the very people we were trying to protect. We would also be on short rations. It was not a happy time. We also had, thanks to deaths and sickness less than three and a half thousand men. Our company was the only Free Company with the Prince. Long John took that as a good thing. It would mean more loot for us.

When we reached the town, we surrounded it and the Prince was taken to the gates to parley. Despite a chilling wind he braved the elements and spoke to the inhabitants. "The Bishop of Limoges, Jean de Cros, has betrayed me. He has led you all down a dangerous path. I am here to give you the opportunity to open your gates and admit your lawful lord. Do so and only the Constable and the Bishop will be punished. If you do not then the consequences will be dire for you will have to endure my fury and anger. What say you?" In answer the standard of the Prince, the quartered lions and fleur de lys, was torn in two and thrown into the ditch. The Prince shouted, "So be it. I have given you fair warning."

While we made our camp Captain Tom was summoned to a council of war. I was now curious about this siege. "Peter, how will we fight?"

"It will be a different war. We will make ladders and, under the protection of Captain Jack and his archers we will advance across open ground. Here the crossbows will work well. They have hoardings which will protect them and make it hard for our archers to clear the walls. There will be both oil and water which is heated up. That will be poured down. Perhaps they have a store of pig fat too." He tapped the kettle helmet which lay next to him. "This helmet not only protects from the sun it affords some protection from oil and water. If we manage to reach the top of the walls then we have to fight men who are above us. Each man who makes the walls will have to fight two or three men. The first ones over normally die."

I was appalled at the prospect. "Is there no other way?"

"Aye, we could mine. That takes time. It is not a quick process. It means we have to endure the siege works for longer."

Red Ralph nodded. "If we succeed then the men who enter Limoges will be angry men. They will take it out on those within: men women and children will suffer. I do no like sieges. Perhaps I should have left for England already."

Peter shook his head, "You know that you will only leave when the Prince leaves and he will not leave until Limoges falls."

When Captain Tom returned it was with the news that we were to build ladders but also begin to dig a mine beneath the walls. I listened as he explained what we would do. Many of our men had never mined before. "We will divide into three groups. I will lead one, Red Ralph a second and Owen the Welshman the third."

Long John bantered, "At last a proper use for a Welshman!" Everyone laughed for the Welsh were known as good miners.

"We will work through the night and the day. Most of the company will provide protection with pavise and shield. We will take it in turns to dig for it is hard work. Others will provide the wood for the mine. If we are lucky then after a week or so we should be far enough beneath the walls to set them alight and bring down the wall."

One man shouted, "Then why do we need ladders?"

"The men at arms of Sir Walter Hewitt will make an attack on the gatehouse so that the defence is split." As much as I did not relish the thought of digging a mine it seemed preferable to assaulting the walls.

Peter the Priest asked, "Who defends the walls?"

"There are Englishmen within as well as rebel Gascons. Sir John Villemur, Hugh de la Roche and Roger Beaufont all are within the walls."

That was another sobering thought. All of us felt that any Englishman was worth three Frenchmen. The defenders would fight as hard as we did.

The next morning all was assembled for the attack. Captain Tom led a third of our men towards the walls. Captain Jack and his archers sent arrows towards the walls but the hoardings made their arrows ineffective. During the night we had made thirty pavises. Huge man-sized shields they were held before the advancing men. The shields of the others protected the top. The pavises were thick and heavy. They would be propped into position while the diggers dug. I watched them march. Short Stephen was the first to fall. He was on the right and his shield was not held closely enough to his body or perhaps he slipped, either way it was a fatal error for a bolt struck him in the neck. Captain Jack urged his archers to greater efforts but there was no target for them. They stopped close by the wall. Stones were thrown from above. Spears were hurled as gaps appeared in the shields and men fell. We could see little save that the shields grew tighter. They endured this for some hours. The defenders either ran out of stones or tired for the hail diminished. At the gate, Sir Walter Hewitt's men had suffered too and they had withdrawn.

Peter pointed to smoke rising from the walls. "They are heating either oil or water." He and Red Ralph exchanged a worryingly serious glance. We would replace the captain at noon.

Red Ralph had a horn and when he saw the thin, cloudy sun reach its zenith he sounded it. The human shields moved back more slowly than they had advanced. When they were out of the range of the crossbows we saw why. Ten men were dead or wounded. We saw the black hole that was the entrance to the mine. The Captain shook his head, "That was hard. At least they had neither oil nor water."

Peter pointed at the smoke, "They have it ready for us, Captain."

Red Ralph said, "Standing here and worrying about a fiery death will not get the job done. Will, you are still weak from the battle at the bridge. You cannot dig. You will use your own shield. Your height will help protect the diggers. Wet your cloak before we go to the walls."

"I can do as the others do, Red Ralph. I need no cosseting."

"And I need men who have strength to both dig and hold the pavise! They are heavy!"

He was right and I obeyed. I soaked my cloak. It felt incredibly heavy and as I walked back to the shields I left a slimy trail of water. I would not need my sword and I lifted my shield up with two hands. Once we were in position Red Ralph called out the chant and we began to march.

'Death to the French and long live the King
We are the Blues so hear us sing.
Death to the French and long live the King
We are the Blues so hear us sing.'

It was not particularly witty but it helped us march and when we fought alongside other companies it identified who we were. We were the only Free Company. Captain Tom and his men had brought back the dead and wounded. The only obstacles on the ground were the bolts and arrows. They did not hinder us. I was two men behind Peter who was carrying a pavise. A bolt cracked into the pavise. I saw the tip. Peter said, "This sinner thanks you, Lord for saving me from the bolt!" That was the first of many. Bolts smacked and snapped into shields and pavise. One glanced off my shield and hurtled behind us. It would join the other wasted bolts and arrows. When night fell Captain Jack and his men would retrieve both bolts and arrows. The bolts' tips could be used to tip arrows.

We reached the wall without loss. We had seen the fate of Short Stephen and heeded the danger. Red Ralph shouted, "Down pavise! Diggers!"

Now that we were closer I saw that Captain Tom and his men had managed to dig a hole the length and height of a man. Dick and John bent down and began to use the mattocks to scrape out the soil. Others used their feet to shift it to the side and spread it out. We would not begin to shore it up until the next day at the earliest. We had twenty paces to excavate. We needed to be under the corner of these two walls before we fired it and, hopefully, brought the corner tower and two walls down.

The defenders began to throw stones down upon us. Red Ralph, who was at the front said, "They will try to break through the shields and then send down either oil or water."

Forewarned is forearmed. I had my soaked, old cloak on and the hood covered my helmet. I had two hands and arms under my shield. Suddenly the defenders threw a large rock down. It struck my shield so hard that I heard it crack. I had made this one of alternating layers of wood, some horizontal and some vertical. It had taken time but now it proved its worth for the shield held.

I heard a shout from the walls, "Ware!"

They were about to pour oil, pig fat or water on us. I could not smell either oil or fat and knew that it would be water. The others had told me of the dangers of water. It could find its way through any tiny gap. There was a cry from above us and then a body fell. It landed on the shields of Red Ralph and Peter. The defender's legs must have fallen on my shield. I felt the weight.

Peter shouted, "Do not move the body. Leave it. It will protect us from the water!" The others had worked out that it was water and not fat or oil.

The voice from above shouted, "Let go!"

The archer who had slain the man operating the cauldron had saved us. They could not move the cauldron and he had fallen on the very spot the water would fall. We heard the hiss and then the splash as it was poured upon us. Some of those not protected by the body shouted and cried out. It was more in shock rather than real pain. The water had first splashed on the body before pouring through the gaps in our shields. The men would be scalded, perhaps even burned a little but we had endured worse.

Red Ralph shouted, "Change diggers!" There would be a delay before the next batch of whatever substance they had could be poured upon us. Fresh diggers could make great inroads. As Long John and Dick Long Sword took up their shields two more diggers began to scrape and hack soil from the mine. My arms ached but I knew that if I lowered them then I might be seriously injured. I endured the pain. Red Ralph was correct. My wound meant I could neither fight nor dig properly. I was reduced to being a shield bearer!

When the horn sounded for us to retire we had changed diggers four times. Three men had burns which would need a healer and two men had been struck in the foot by bolts but none had died. As we moved backwards, chanting, I heard Dick Long Sword say, "Will Strongstaff's luck still holds!"

'Death to the French and long live the King
We are the Blues so hear us sing.
Death to the French and long live the King
We are the Blues so hear us sing.'

After two renditions we were out of range and Red Ralph told us to lower our shields. Owen the Welshman and his men would take over. They had the luxury of twilight. Captain Tom and his men would be even better off for they would have the night. When next we toiled, we would have some dark and then dawn. It would be a long day.

Peter saw me examining my shield. He nodded towards some pine trees. "Make some pine tar. It will seal it. You can use my shield tomorrow for I will be a digger again."

I had seen others make pine tar. I would try myself. I had bothered my shield brothers enough. I had had the easier day. I had just had to stand holding a shield. It was dark and the others had made food when I had finished. It had taken time to collect and heat the tar. I had used the helmet from the man who had fallen on our shields. It had been badly dented and would be of no use as protective head gear and little use as a pot. After taking off the front leather covering I had poured the liquid tar over the whole of the shield. The resin found its way through the cracks and gaps until it was stopped by the leather at the back. I left it to set.

Peter the Priest was worried about me, "Sit down Will. You should have taken more rest. You were badly wounded at the bridge."

"But I live. It will do me no harm and besides, I need a shield."

"If you are to become the Princes' guard you will not. At least not until they ride to war and that will not be for five years or more."

I saw that Long John had taken the mail from the man who had fallen. Long John was a big warrior and the one who had fallen, whilst not as tall, was as wide. Long John now had a mail hauberk over his leather mail. He looked pleased with himself. The others did not resent his treasure. It was the fortunes of war. When we breached, and Red Ralph had no doubt that we would breach, then there would be treasure galore. Prince Edward had warned the defenders what would happen if they did not surrender and they had ignored him. He would take out the losses he would incur in the taking of the walls with the blood of those who defended them.

I could barely keep my eyes open as I ate and I fell asleep as soon as I had eaten the last mouthful. I knew that part of it was my body's need to recover. The scars were now just angry but the bones which had been broken were slow to heal.

The next three days saw a monotonous repetition of the first day. The only thing which changed was the time of day. When we dug at night it was strange as the men on the walls could not see us but they threw stones, blindly, anyway. They were trying to hurt the miners. We could not see the diggers who were now getting close to the corner of the tower. Then came the day when I had to go into the mine. I had to prop the walls. My task was a simple one I had to crawl into the dark, confined space carrying wood which I would use to shore up the sides and the walls. Others were in the mine with me. That did not help! I did not enjoy the experience. I had to crawl into the dark space holding the wooden slats. Although safe from stones, arrows and bolts I felt as though I was drowning in the dark. I could not explain the feeling. I found it hard to breathe. What was worse was that I had to make certain that the wood was secured. It was not easy. I would put the two side beams in and hold one with my foot and rest my back against the other while I jammed the roof beam over them. If it was not secure then we could have a cave-in and all the work we had done would be wasted. When I crept back out of the tomb I felt joy.

On the fourth day as we were about to go back to the siege a rider rode in. He rode hard and threw himself from the saddle outside of the Prince's tent. We all stopped to watch for this was unusual. When we heard a shout from the tent then we wondered what the news was.

Sir Hugh strode over to us. "You men of the Blue Company, to the mines. You have work to do!"

We formed ranks and prepared to move but all of us were curious about the messenger. It was not simple curiosity. Bad news could mean that we might not get paid. Uncertainty was an insidious enemy.

Those of us in the middle had faggots to carry. Although the tunnel was not quite finished, Owen the Welshman would make the final preparations, we would gradually fill the tunnel with the kindling and wood. It would mean I had to enter the tomb once more and this time I would have to go deeper within it. The only saving grace was the fact that it was daylight. There might be a glimmer of light from the end and Peter and Red Ralph, who were digging, would have a tallow candle.

The stones were no longer hurled. They must have used all of their fat and oil in the attacks on the second day when Captain Tom's men had been assaulted by burning fat and oil. There had been no further use of oil and fat. We had lost eight men that day. Two died almost instantly and the others took a long day to die. They were in agony and it made me ever fearful of fire. The talk around the camp was that they hoped our mine would fail and we would simply leave. They did not know the Black Prince. He had been insulted twice. Once when he had been betrayed by his friend, the Bishop and then when a personal plea had fallen on deaf ears. The Prince was a proud man and did not bear insults and slights well. His authority had been questioned!

They used their crossbows to try to hit our legs and feet. The wounds men suffered were painful but not fatal. My boots, which I had taken from a warrior at the bridge were better protection than most men. One bolt had hit my boot but, even though it had penetrated the hide, it had missed my flesh. My luck had held again. I could now see why men wore greaves to protect their legs. We dropped our faggots. There was little soil to be shifted now. The land upon which we stood was now higher than when we had first attacked. I no longer needed to use two hands to support the shield. One was ample.

We had been standing there for the better part of an hour, I knew the time for I counted! Peter came out. "We are ready for the faggots. Follow me and I will show you where to place them."

As we moved forward the men on the outside slid in and put their shields under ours. We dropped to all fours and picked up the two bundles of faggots. We crawled between the legs of the men holding the shields. The tunnel looked dark and foreboding. As luck would have it I was behind Peter. He spoke reassuringly to me, "It will not collapse. The builders have made it sound. You placed the beams in the right place did you not?"

"Aye but it feels like we are descending into hell! I expect to meet Lucifer!"

Someone behind me laughed, "That will be John Falstaff. He has a red nose he could use as a candle!"

Somehow it helped and we pushed forward. There was less light than I had expected for the tunnel was filled with men such as I. I had my helmet on and it was fortunate for I scraped my head on the wooden beams more than once. The faggots caught on the shuttering we had used and all seemed to take an age. I saw a dim light after what seemed like we had travelled miles yet I knew it could not be more than twenty or so paces.

Red Ralph waited for us. He would determine where the faggots were to be placed. There had to be space for air to flow and ensure that the fire burned. We did not want it to burn too strongly. There was an optimum time. Others knew such things. Ralph took my faggot and nodded. I tried to turn but Davy Doncaster was behind me and I had to press into the side to pass him and his faggot. I had to negotiate the rest of the men. What was worse was that I would have to return with more faggots.

By the time we had finished the mine and tunnel were lined on both sides with faggots. Owen and his shift would finish the job and then ignite it. He would do so at night. The effect would be more spectacular and it would be safer for him and those lighting the fire. When I finally emerged, I swore I would never go below ground again. It was early afternoon when we washed off the dirt from the mine and thought about food.

Captain Tom came over and he had a serious look on his face. "The Prince has had bad news. His eldest son, Edward has been taken ill. They have sent for healers and a priest. It does not bode well for the boy. The Prince has raged all the while you were below ground. I fear this will not end well for the people of Limoges."

Peter shook his head, "But it is not their fault."

"In our Prince's eyes it is. Had they not refused his offer then he would be with his son."

"And why does he not return to be at his son's side?"

"Because Will, that would be a victory for the rebels. He is a father but he is the future King of England first."

It seemed that as much as he wanted his children protecting he valued his crown more.

The Prince roused himself from his sick bed and came over to join us as Owen the Welshman prepared his pots of fire to be taken down the tunnel. This would be the most dangerous and, possibly, the most spectacular, part of the siege. While he and his men prepared the pots, the Prince was seated on a folding chair waved me over. "I hear you have earned a good name, Will Strongstaff."

I nodded, "I like the name, my lord and I earned it honestly."

"And your father is dead."

"My father is dead."

"He was a good warrior. In his latter years… well, we do not speak ill of the dead. You have finished with the Blue Company when

Limoges falls. I will take you back to Guyenne. I have two sons who will need your protection."

"I was sorry to hear of your son's illness, my lord."

He nodded, "I have prayed to God and sworn to take the cross and Crusade if he is spared. God will listen to me for I have a true heart!"

I caught the sad look on Peter the Priest's face. He knew better.

Owen the Welshman bowed, "We are ready, my lord."

"Then burn the bastards!"

His voice was filled with venom and each word was spat out. I realised that I had been dismissed and I edged back to Red Ralph and Peter the Priest. Red Ralph smiled, "So all that you need to do is to survive scaling a wall, fight men who have nothing to lose and you will have a job which will make you a gentleman."

I laughed, "Aye, that is about the size of it."

We then turned our attention to the wall. The last shift was marching towards the entrance just as all the other shifts had. The defenders would not see the eight pots of coals which they carried. There was a desultory shower of arrows and crossbow bolts which rattled and cracked off the shields. They reached the pavise which we had left propped in position and we saw the pots and their carriers disappear with a length of rope down the mine.

"Why the rope?"

"If Owen lets the fire loose while they are down the mine then they will be burned. He will tie them together so that when he pulls on the rope they each topple over and spill their coals. They will begin to burn."

"And if they do not?"

"Then Captain Tom and his men will repeat this tomorrow morning. They will have to wait until then to make certain that it is not a slow burn."

The miners were inside for a long time and then they emerged. Owen must have been unlucky for he slipped as he left the mine and a bolt hit him in the leg before he could reach the safety of the pavise. Captain Jack pulled back on his bow. I wondered what his target would be. He sent an arrow through the embrasure. It was a prodigious arrow in such poor light for it entered and there was a cry. We did not see the result but we all knew that the crossbowman had been hit. Owen would send a jug of ale to the archer.

A hand was raised from the shields and Prince Edward nodded. His standard bearer blew three blasts on his horn. Owen pulled hard on the rope. I did not see anything at first and I wondered if it had failed and then a tongue of flame leapt from the mouth of the mine. It was as though a sleeping dragon had woken! Owen and his men cheered. The cheer was taken up by everyone else.

As the cheering died down I looked and saw, as darkness fell, a trail of black smoke rising from the mouth of the dragon. "Could the defenders have stopped this, Ralph?"

Peter answered me, "They could have sortied and fought us but they would have lost or they could have dug a counter mine. Perhaps they did not have the skill but they are doomed now. Tomorrow we will fight. I will get some rest. I would advise you to do the same."

The rest left but, like the Prince, I was mesmerized and wanted to see the tower fall. After what seemed an age the Prince waved a hand and his men lifted him, "Will Strongstaff, you can wait but you will see nothing. The fire will need the night to work. Rest. I will go to pray for my son and tomorrow we will take Limoges."

I was left alone save for the men of Captain Tom's shift. I went to the fire and lay down. I wondered what the morrow would bring.

I was woken, not by the sound of the falling tower but a heartfelt cry from the Prince's tent. I rose immediately and saw Captain Tom making the sign of the cross. He looked at me sadly, "A rider came in to camp not long ago. From the cry I fear it is not good news, neither for the Prince nor the town."

Peter and the others rose. It was not yet dawn. He stretched, "As we are awake what say we eat and prepare for war."

I pointed to the tower and wall. Smoke still came from the ground and was wreathed around them. "Either the tower and wall will fall and we will attack or our lord and master will order us to take to ladders and scale the walls. He will need something to ease his pain and assuage the guilt he feels."

"Guilt?"

"Aye," said Captain Tom, "a man who loses a child feels guilty that he has not done enough for his son. That will be Prince Edward."

He was right for even as we prepared our food the horns sounded for a council of war. As dawn broke we saw that the walls still stood. Smoke still billowed from the mine but the tower and walls were clear. We were armed for war. My shield had had time to set and I hefted it. We had not used our swords but I had still sharpened mine each day.

Old Tom returned, "Form your lines. He will not try to relight the fire. Sir Hugh nearly lost his head for suggesting it. We fetch the ladders and do this the hard way! This will be bloody. He has said no prisoners but he does not mean it. The death of his son has driven sense from his head. Let the Blue Company act well this day. I rely upon you."

We had to wait for the Prince to arm. He came slowly for he had not yet recovered from his illness. I saw Sir Robert and some of the other lords trying to restrain him but he was like my father when he had had too much drink. He was intoxicated with anger. He might die in the attack but no one would stop him.

The sun broke from behind us. I stared at the tower. We had spent all that time digging beneath the ground and it had been for nothing. My nightmares had been in vain! Just then I saw a line which had not been there before. It did not follow the line of mortar but seemed to zig zag up the tower's side. I willed it to grow and it did. Not only did it grow, it widened. I looked around. No one else had seen it. Their attention was on their weapons and the ground they would have to cross. Our ranks were remarkably silent. The sounds were of creaking, squeaking mail and armour.

"The tower is going!"

My voice seemed inordinately loud and everyone, including the Prince, looked at me. I pointed. My finger was trembling. I felt like a magician for even as I pointed the crack suddenly spread and one side of the tower seemed to break away. As it did so the tunnel suddenly collapsed. Smoke and debris gushed out and the tower, along with twenty paces of wall on either side collapsed. We all turned to look at the Prince. He shouted, "Attack! Kill every man you find!" And the horn sounded three times. We ran!

My leg still ached and I could not run as fast as I once had. The result was that I kept pace with Red Ralph and Peter. We did not run with swords in our hands for that would invite disaster but we did hold our shields above our heads. Without the metal armour of the knights we ran faster and it was the Blue Company which reached the jumble of stones which had been the tower and the walls. We clambered over them. The falling masonry had cleared the walls of defenders. Others were trying to get at us but there was no walkway. The fighting platform had gone.

As I climbed over the huge stones I saw a forlorn arm sticking out of the stones. It appeared to be waving. Stepping across the stones I drew my sword. Peter and Ralph were with me. I felt safe. A horn sounded from inside the town and I could see armed men running towards us.

"We hold here until more men join us." Red Ralph had a good eye for war. We had height for we stood on the debris of the wall. When the defenders reached us we would have the advantage. They could go nowhere. Men ringed the town. Dick and John joined us as did Captain Tom and the rest of our company. We were fewer now than we had been but we were a band of brothers. "Two ranks. Wait for my command."

I saw that Dick had slung his shield and held his longsword in two hands before him. He made circles with it. I had watched him do this before. It helped him to get into the rhythm of death as he called it. It was he struck the first blow and drew first blood. His sword struck the helmet of the knight who charged towards us. It knocked his head to the side and he fell heavily, his head striking a large piece of masonry. His helmet flew off and I saw blood puddling near to his mouth.

It was the knights who charged us first. Perhaps they had all been at breakfast in the Great Hall or it may have been that the men at arms, crossbowmen and archers were on the other walls. One ran at me and he swung his sword at my legs. Had he connected then I would have been dead. I jumped and his sword scraped along the stone. The edge would be dulled. I swung my own sword at his head but he moved it out of the way. He stepped on to the body of the dead knight and brought his sword around at my right. This would be a test of my repaired shield and the wound in my left arm. He hit them hard but I had endured worse from Red Ralph. I then raised my right leg and pushed against his shield. He tumbled backwards and fell to the earth. His squire, eager to earn the praise of his lord ran at me. I brought my sword from behind me and, as he lunged at my crotch sliced my sword through his helmet and into his skull. It was a poorly made helmet. His eyes glazed over and he fell at my feet. The enraged knight ran at me. It was not the right way to fight me for I was calmness personified. He lunged at my middle and I blocked the blow with my shield. He tried to backhand me but I blocked that with my sword. He had an open face bascinet and I could see that he was tiring.

Captain Tom shouted, "Now! We have reinforcements! Blue Company, charge!"

As the others leapt from the stones to fall upon the defenders of Limoges I waited for one last strike from the knight. He lunged upwards and, as he did so I jumped to his right and brought my shield around to hit him in the shoulder. He began to lose his footing for his squire's blood and brains had spread. His arms spread as he sought to keep his feet and I rammed my sword under his right arm. There was no metal plate there and my sword slid through the mail and up into his armpit, then his shoulder and finally his neck and skull. He was dead.

Although he had good armour and there was a temptation to take it I was honour bound to follow the rest of the company. I ran after them. The battle for Limoges was not over but we had won. We had breached their wall and broken the hearts of the defenders. The survivors of the battle of the breach were fleeing. In a normal battle we would be seeking surrender and the ransom which would come from that. The Prince's command had changed all that. The defenders fought to the death.

I saw a handful of men at arms suddenly burst from a building. Long John and the others had just passed the door and had not seen it. They would be attacked in the rear. I shouted, "Blues! Ware the rear!" I had a good voice and it carried. Two of the men at arms turned and, seeing me alone, ran towards me. Long John and the others turned around. I heard the clash of steel on steel. I ignored it. I had two men to fight.

Rather than slowing or even standing, I did that which they did not expect. I ran at the two of them. Even as I ran I evaluated their strengths and weaknesses. There were two of them. Both had sallets upon their heads and a coif over their padded arming doublets. They had shields and swords but they had neither greaves nor metal plates upon their arms. Both were shorter than I was. I pulled my shield tightly to my chest and tucked my head behind it so that only my eyes were above the edge. I held the sword behind me and I screamed as I ran. I had seen my father do this and, when I had been the horse holder, I had seen the terror on the faces of the men he faced. I saw it now on the countenances of the two men at arms. They made the most fatal of errors. They hesitated. Then the one to my left swung his sword in a long sweep. Had I been still it would have hurt but I was moving and he badly mistimed it. The hilt and his hand hit my shield. The other could not swing as he wished for his companion was there and he brought his sword overhand towards my head. My speed was such that I hit between the two of them. The sword struck the mail on my shoulder while my sword, which had swung from behind me, hacked into his thigh. I was through them and I whirled around.

The wounded one put his hand to his thigh. I leapt at the other, swinging my sword as I did so. He brought up his shield but the swing had so much power that even though he blocked the blow he reeled. The wounded man might recover and I had no time to think and deliberate. Instinct took over. I punched with my shield. The blow sent shivers through my arm but I hit him square in the face and he fell backwards. I hacked through the fingers of his right hand as he tumbled backwards. The sword fell. I whipped around and had my sword at the throat of the second man at arms.

"Drop your sword if you wish to live!" he hesitated. "One push from this, brother, and all your cares are over. I am giving you a life. Take it." Resignation filled his face and he did so. "Take your friend and run. This will not be the place for hired swords."

He nodded and then asked, "Why do you do this? We would have killed you had we had the chance."

I shrugged, "I know not. Now go!"

He went to his friend and, limping, helped him towards the fallen tower.

As I turned I saw that I was alone but I could hear fighting towards the town square. Long John and the others had killed the rest of the men at arms. I took it as a compliment that they had not waited for me. They knew that I would be able to handle the two of them. They had more confidence in my skills than I did. I turned up a narrow passageway between houses. There were more butchered bodies there. I came into a small square behind some houses. It was obviously a communal space. There was a table and some chairs and a small handcart. I saw that not only men had been killed but also women and the old. One boy, perhaps eight summers old, lay dead. This was not the work of the Blue Company. These were men who had obeyed the Prince.

I was about to leave when I heard a noise from my left. I went towards the door of the house there. I could hear breathing. Holding my sword in my shield hand I bent down to pick up the broken haft of a spear. I thrust it in the door and an axe smashed down upon it. Dropping the haft I grabbed the arm which held the spear and pulled the warrior from the door. He was not expecting that nor the blow in the face from my shield. He fell to the ground unconscious. I raised my sword and a woman prostrated herself over the man, "I pray you let my husband live. He has a wound in his leg." She was English.

I lowered my sword. Four young children cowered. Two of them were sobbing. "He could have killed me!"

"But he did not and perhaps God warned you but whatever the reason if you take his life what will become of us?"

I knew what that fate would be. I had seen too many orphans who had suffered when their father had died. Had it not been for Old Tom and the others then that would have been my fate.

"If you wish to live then do as I say. Wrap your man as though he is dead. Put that which you wish beneath him and take your children out of the gate. When the guards stop you say that you wish to bury your husband." I reached into my purse and took out a handful of coins. "Here, get as far away as you can."

She took the coins and kissed my hand, "How can I ever repay you?"

"Let your children grow and take them back to England. It will be safer than here. Now go."

I turned and headed towards the square in the centre of Limoges. That was my last battle as a member of the Blue Company. In later years I would hear of the massacre of Limoges and while it was true that too many were killed it was not the thousands that the enemies of the Prince said. His brother, John of Gaunt, was the one who spread the lies. He had his own reasons. I was there and I knew the true numbers. Less than two hundred fell when we breached the walls. But for the Blue Company the number would have been higher.

Part Three- Prince Richard

Chapter 12

It took three days for order in the town to be restored. Ironically it was the hired swords of the Blue Company who restored it. The battle had been too much for the Prince who took to his bed. Sir Hugh and Sir Robert used us to keep the wild knights and squires under control. I had better armour after the battle. The knight I had killed on the walls had been the same build as I. His arming doublet was largely undamaged. I took that, his mail, his metal plates and his sword. He also had coins. Perhaps that was God compensating me for the kind act I had done. I also took his shield. It was well made. I left him his helmet as mine had served me well.

Sir Thomas Holand came to me at our camp on the third night. "Will Strongstaff you are commanded to wait upon the Prince. You will be returning with us to Bordeaux and thence to England."

Now that it was finally happening I could not quite believe it. "Now?"

The knight smiled, "You may say goodbye to your companions but we leave at dawn. Do not be tardy. You will ride by the Prince's litter. Until you reach Bordeaux you guard the Prince." He paused, "You will swear an oath before we leave." He turned and left.

My companions were watching me as I turned. I did not want to go and yet I knew that the company was at the end of its life. Red Ralph, Peter and Old Tom would return to England. Long John would probably join them but this was as close to a family as I had.

Red Ralph came and clasped my arm, "Do not be sad, Will. You have grown since you joined us. We all regard you as a son. We have tried to be as a father to you and we are proud. It is a wrench leaving, that I know and we will be sad when you are gone."

Peter nodded as he clasped my arm, "Aye, you are a good man, Will. You have honour and that supersedes all traits of birth and station. You have humour and you are a good companion. When I am retired in England I will think back to the days we scouted."

Old Tom was next, "They are right Will. We took you in because of your mother but we kept you because of you. This is your chance. Those of us who leave the company and manage to retire to England are rare."

"Aye," said Long John, "Dick and I will be hard on the heels of these three and yourself. When we have accrued but a little more coin we will go back and become fat sentries on some quiet castle's walls. We have done enough killing."

Dick was the last to say goodbye, "I am now the youngest again but I owe you a life. Warriors do not forget such things. I will repay you one day."

I nodded. Their words have given me the composure to speak. "I have Goldcrest. The other horses we captured and the spare mail I give to you. I will not need it. I have the mail and metal from the rebel knight." I held up a bulging purse. "I have coin here. I will leave Goldcrest at the Black Lion in Bordeaux. Sell her and take the money." I knew that there would be no room for my horse on the ship which took us to England. The berths would be reserved for nobler steeds than mine. "I know not if we shall meet again but I pray that we will. You say I was as a son well you are as uncles to me, favourite uncles all. Where do you go in England?"

Red Ralph said, "Middleham for me. I come from a village not far from there. It is quiet and I will be content."

"I will travel home with Ralph. York has a fine cathedral and I think I would like to spend my days there by the Ouse." Peter the Priest would always be close to a church.

"My home was in Lincoln. I shall return there. Why do you ask, Will?" Captain Tom cocked his head to one side.

"I daresay that the Prince will take Prince Richard with him when he is in England and they travel the land on a royal progress. I will watch out for you when I am there."

Long John laughed, "You will be too grand for us. Then you will be a gentleman in French finery. You will smell like a Spanish whore and look down your nose at us."

I laughed with him for we had often seen lords who tried to impress others with their richly made clothes and exotic perfumes. I shook my head, "I will still be Will son of Harry who served with the finest company in Gascony and I will not forget those to whom I owe everything."

Dick Long Sword shook his head, "God's blood but this is maudlin! Let us drink and say goodbye to someone I shall miss for I will now be the youngest amongst this congregation of greybeards! I will be wiping their beards and putting them to bed!"

For the first time in my life I drank too much. I remember little of that night save laughing a great deal and weeping a little. In the coming years the memories I had forgotten resurfaced in my dreams and, in the dark days ahead, gave me comfort.

I swore the oath before the Prince's priest in the cathedral of Limoges. I never, in my whole life, broke an oath and I swore to protect the Prince and his son. I kept that oath though it would cost me dear.

We slipped away quietly almost as though the Prince was trying to put the shame that was Limoges behind him. I saw little of the Prince as we rode south and the rest of his retinue shunned me. It was as though I was beneath them. All knew my story. They had heard of my father and my mother. The nobles' attitude I understood but not the servants. As I rode, behind the litter, alone, I reflected on my decision. I had had little choice in the matter. What I did remember of the conversation with my shield brothers, before I passed out, was that by the next year all would be in England. The treasure from Limoges had been greater than we had expected. I had kept my coin but they had all had an extra share from me. In addition, the Prince had kept his promise. He had paid the Blue Company, or those who remained, at any rate. When Tom left it would still be the Blue Company but its nature would change. Its glory would fade. I had left at the right time. We had been the ones who emerged from the disgrace of the slaughter of Limoges with some honour. I decided to ignore those around me. I had been a lonely little boy for many years until Red Ralph and the others had taken me under their wing. I could be that boy again. I was resourceful. I had a goal. I wished to be a gentleman. That took money, position and power. I had the start of my money. Bodyguard to Richard of Bordeaux would give me position. All that remained was power, and being as close as I would be to the King I would see how to get power.

I observed, as we rode, those who were close to the Prince. I watched his advisers as they jostled for his ear. Some I knew, for they had fought bravely at his side. It was the ones I did not know that interested me. They were the dangerous ones. They were the men to watch. I had to smile as we headed south for the pace of the column was half that of the Blue Company. These were soft men compared with the Blue Company. They needed frequent rests. I found the pace leisurely. Not a man spoke to me with courtesy until we reached Bordeaux! When they spoke, they barked.

I learned, quickly, that if I waited to be offered food, ale, water and wine then I would starve to death. I kept my water and wine skin filled whenever I could. The first camp was the testing time. The weather was clement and needed neither a tent nor a hovel. I laid out my old cloak upon which to sleep and then laid my new cloak and blanket upon it. I groomed and fed Goldcrest. I checked my weapons and then, with sword and dagger on my baldric I took my spoon, platter and beaker to seek food. I was not foolish enough to risk the ire of the lords by sharing their food and I headed for the camp of the men at arms and the servants. The food had not been foraged, the Prince had brought it from Limoges. The servants were there to cook it.

I saw that most men had taken their food and I went to the cauldron. It was a chicken stew. The breasts and legs had all been taken but I spied some wings and the meat which had fallen from the carcasses. I reached for the ladle. Behind me, a voice said, "That stew is not for the bastard son of a whore."

I laid down my bowl, beaker and spoon and I turned. It was a sergeant at arms. He wore the Prince's livery. He was a large man but he was running to fat. I had not seen him at the siege works. He had squatted on his honour whilst men had bled. I recognised the type. He was a bully. I said, "I know not your name. Before I give you a lesson in manners I would know whom I am to knock from his feet."

There was an audible gasp. It was obvious that he was never challenged, "You little jackanape! I am Godfrey of Hastings and I will show you that being the Prince's lickspittle will not win any friends here."

His words caused me some concern. He was supposed to be one of the Prince's guards and yet his words suggested that he had little time for the Prince. The fact that no one challenged his words made me suspicious. There was a rumour that the Prince had been poisoned in Spain and that was the reason for his illness. We had dismissed the notion as being ridiculous but now I saw that there were plots aplenty and the Prince's need for a bodyguard for his son was understandable.

The sergeant at arms pushed up his sleeves and bunched his fists as he lumbered towards me. He was much heavier than I was and I think he intended to batter me into the ground. As well as learning how to fight with weapons Red Ralph and Long John had shown me how to use my fists. They had shown me the best place to plant a punch. It was rarely in the face. As Red Ralph had told me the face was hard and you hurt your fist. Godfrey of Hastings came for my face. As he swung I ducked and hit a hard left into his ribs on one side and then an even harder one to the ribs on his right. I heard a rib crack. He reeled and gasped. I did not relent I stepped forward and hit him hard in the guts, not once but three times in rapid succession. He fell to the floor gasping for breath.

I knelt next to him and said, quietly, "I will take those gasps for an apology. Do not cross me again for I have killed many men in fair fights. You, I think, have sat on your fat arse and watched other men die!"

I stood and looked at each of the others in turn. They all averted their eyes. I went to the cauldron and filled my bowl. I tore off a piece of bread and then filled my beaker with wine. I walked back to my camp deliberately slowly. I wanted them to know that I was not afraid of them. However, I was hungry and needed the food. The day's riding had worked the drink from my body and I was starving. I sat with my back to a tree and watched them as I ate my food. I saw the sergeant at arms rise. He sat with two companions and their heads were together. This was not over. The humiliation was not forgotten and he would need vengeance.

I washed up my bowl and beaker and made water. I knew that this was not over. I remade my bed so that I was close to the hooves of my horse. She would protect my back. I knew that she would not step on me. I had slept close to her before. I now had three daggers: the stiletto and two others. I placed the stiletto close to my hand. Then I knelt and said my prayers. I first prayed for my mother and my half brothers and sister, then for my comrades and finally for the soul of my father. I hoped he was in heaven but he had not been shrived and he had been a bad man. I knew not where his soul rested. Then I lay down beneath my blanket.

I was tired but I knew how to sleep lightly. It was in the middle watch when the sergeant and his companion came for me. Goldcrest stirred but I had heard them already. They had to approach from my front. I opened my eyes and saw them. The sergeant was ever the coward. He allowed his companion to come ahead of him. They had cudgels in their hands. They intended to give me such a beating that, although I would still be alive, I would be of no use to the Prince. I had to time this right. I held the blanket in my left hand. When the other warrior was less than two paces from me I stood, whipped the blanket across the face of my would-be attacker and readied my dagger. His arms flailed at me. I rammed my knee between his legs and when he doubled over punched my knee into his face. He fell unconscious.

Godfrey of Hastings stood stock still as his companion fell. He had a cudgel. The only blow he could make was to my head. He had to end this quickly for a blow to the body would not stop me. He knew the reputation of the Blue Company. Even as he swung it I was ducking.

You cannot change the course of such a weapon once it is started. I dropped to my knee and tore my stiletto across the back of his leg tearing through the tendons of his right knee. He almost managed to scream but my left had covered his face as he fell to the ground. He lay whimpering. I walked over to the unconscious man and, lifting my boot, stamped hard on the hand which still gripped the cudgel. I heard his fingers break. They would be a reminder of the encounter.

I put my face close to Godfrey of Hastings. "You have served the Prince long enough. When I wake you will be gone. Hurry back to your master. If I see you on the morrow then the Prince will learn of your treachery. I know what you did in Spain!"

It was all guesswork and bluff but his widening eyes told me that I had hit the mark. He had betrayed the Prince. I wiped the blood from my blade on his doublet and then walked over to the camp of the rest of Godfrey of Hastings' men. I kicked the nearest one hard in the ribs. He sat up and said, angrily, "What the…?" When he saw me above him he cowered.

"Two of your companions managed to stumble across me in the dark. They tripped and fell. They are hurt, go and fetch them!"

He shook the others awake and they went to the two men. When they saw the blood, they stared at me but it was in fear. They picked up the one who was unconscious and took them back to their camp. I curled up and went to sleep. I was undisturbed.

I was woken the next morning by the sound of raised voices. I heard Sir James de Vere shouting, "My lord, three of your men have run in the night! They have taken horses and some of the treasure!"

The Prince emerged from his tent, "God's Blood but am I surrounded by men or mice?" He pointed to me, "Will Strongstaff. Until we reach Bordeaux you will sleep in the treasure wagon! You will guard it for me!"

I smiled and said, "Aye, my lord, it will be a pleasure!" I turned and looked at the ones who had not fled with Godfrey of Hastings. I winked. They all looked away.

I was glad when we reached Bordeaux. I had had enough time alone and I needed to speak pleasantly with folk. Men had steered clear of me as we rode back for they feared me. I was young yet I had shown skills and ability which put them to shame. I decided that I would grow a beard and not shave my face. It would make me look older. Had I looked fiercer then Godfrey of Hastings might not have risked my wrath. I wondered which master he had fled to.

The Prince waved to me as we entered the castle of Bordeaux. "We will not be staying here long. Get rid of your horse. You will not need it. I see that you have mail and armour, that is good. You will need little else. When we reach London, you shall have my son's livery. You have half a day to do that which you need." He paused, "There will be no women on board."

I knew what he meant, "Do not worry, my lord, I have no carnal desires. I will sell my horse and buy that which I need. I will return here."

I went to the Black Lion. The inn keeper was an old member of the Blue Company. He greeted me warmly, "Is the company back?"

"No, Bob, but they will be. I leave my horse and saddle here. Red Ralph and the others will share the proceeds. She is a good horse." I handed him a silver coin, "Look after her."

"Aye, of course. And you?"

"I am to be Richard of Bordeaux's bodyguard."

His face became serious, "Then beware. I have heard of plots and conspiracies. Prince Edward is unpopular now. Poitiers is forgotten and men just speak of the tax he imposed. His brother... well John of Gaunt has made no secret of the fact that he would be king if he could."

"But the Black Prince has done so much for England!"

"And men have short memories. The plague has decimated towns and villages in England. We have less coin from Aquitaine these days. There are rumours that the young Prince Edward was poisoned. You will have to watch that his brother does not share the same fate."

I left John feeling sad. Perhaps my decision was not the best one I could have made. This was not going to be an easy task. I could stop someone from using a blade against Richard of Bordeaux but how could I stop plots and poisonings? I was admitted by the guards as soon as I reached the castle. I had bought goods which John had told me would be expensive in England. I had a full purse and it was better to spend my money wisely.

I left my war gear in the guard room. When I found out where I was sleeping I would move it although if we were sailing soon then it would be as well to leave it where it was. I went to the ante chamber and a servant told Prince Edward that I had arrived. When I met Prince Richard he was barely four years old. The death of his elder brother had upset him. He looked nervous, what men call fey. I am certain that the problems which beset him in later life began there in Bordeaux. He hid behind his mother when his father introduced us. His mother, Joan, the Countess of Kent, was less than enamoured when she met me. I could almost smell the disdain.

"Is he a knight, my husband?"

Prince Edward laughed, "No for Will can do something a knight cannot, he can fight. He is not here to teach our son, he is here to give his life for him if needs be and he will do that. You do not have to like him, my dear, just suffer him." It was not the most glowing introduction but I was a sword for hire and I endured it. "Will Strongstaff take my son outside and get acquainted. We sail on the morning tide. From now on you will be his shadow when he walks abroad. When he is old enough you will teach him how to win a fight in a tavern."

The Countess looked shocked, "A fight in a tavern!"

Prince Edward laughed, "It is a hard world out there and Will is the best teacher. He brought himself up from the age of our son. A few days since he defeated two of the men who were hired to guard me and he has not a scratch on him." My surprise must have shown on my face. "Oh, I know more than you think, Will Strongstaff. I had my suspicions about my guards. You managed to flush them out and for that I will repay you. Continue to keep your eyes open and your wits about you and when you are twenty-one I shall make you a gentleman!"

I had less but a few years to wait! "Thank you, lord."

"Do not thank me yet for you will earn it. We have yet to negotiate the treacherous waters of the English court. That will be harder than making Godfrey of Hastings lame. Now go. I wish to speak with my wife."

I looked down at young Prince Richard. He looked remarkably thin and frail. I impulsively held my hand down and said, "Come, Master Richard. I know not this castle. You shall be my guide."

He took it and walked with me. I saw a smile on the face of the Black Prince. I had passed my first test. Would the rest be as easy?

As we stepped into the sunlight he said, "Did you really make a man lame?"

I nodded. I had few dealings with children but I would speak to him as Red Ralph and the others spoke to me, honestly and as though we were equals. I knew that they had never told me all but they had never lied to me nor deceived me. "Aye, I did."

"How?"

I took out my knife, "I used this to slash behind his knee."

"Did he die?"

"No."

"And did he deserve it?"

I stopped and looked at him. "He did and before you ask me another question I will tell you why. He and another tried to kill me in my sleep and he was one of your father's enemies."

He smiled, "Then I am pleased that he is lame and I thank you... what do I call you?"

"I am happy to be called Will for that is the name my mother gave me."

He nodded and then laughed, "My mother does not like you. She thinks that you smell. I saw her wrinkle her nose."

"She is right to do so. I need a bath for the smell in your nose is that of blood."

"You killed men."

"I killed men but not all. Some I spared." For some reason I did not want the child to think badly of me.

"And will you teach me how to kill?"

"I will teach you how to defend yourself, then how to fight and as for killing, no man can teach you that. When someone tries to kill you then you either kill him or die. There is no one way to do that. If you kill your foe then you have won and he has lost. I am here to protect you and to do that you need to become a warrior but, at the moment, you are both too young and too small." I stopped and bent down so that I could speak to him quietly, "in return I need help from you. I am unused to the ways of the court and gentry. If I am about to make a mistake then tell me. I would not wish to look foolish."

"But you could just kill them!"

"I could but that would get me in even more trouble."

"Then I will help you for I like you. You do not talk to me as though I am a baby. I do not like it when people treat me as a helpless babe. When my brother was alive I was ignored. Now I am not ignored but I do not forget the way I was treated."

"And one more thing. There are enemies who seek to do your father harm. If you see any danger to him then you must tell me."

"You mean I will be like a spy?"

"If you wish to think like that then aye."

"I shall like this. And where will you sleep?"

"Where all good bodyguards sleep; across your door. To get to you they must get by me and that will not be easy."

"You would die to save me?"

"If I had to but I would rather kill your enemies and live!"

"So would I." He reached up and took my hand. I had made a friend and I was alone no longer.

We spent an hour walking around the castle and I answered his never-ending questions. I got the impression that he was lonely and needed someone to talk to. I suited. After the silence of the journey from Limoges it was a relief to talk to someone even someone who was just four years old!

A servant, Peter, came to fetch us. I discovered that he had a nurse and she had a servant called Peter. The nurse was a fat, lazy woman and poor Peter did most of the work. Angelica had been Edward Angoulême's nurse and she had ignored Richard. Now she had to tend to him and she did not like it for he did not like her at all. Richard and I both liked Peter. He was old but he was a happy soul.

"Master Richard, you are sought!"

"I was safe, with my bodyguard."

"So I was told." He smiled at me, "I am Peter and you must be Will Strongstaff."

"I am. I am sorry we were so long but Prince Edward asked me to get to know the boy."

"It is not me who sent for him it is Mistress Angelica, his nurse."

Richard said, "She is like a fat dragon and she smells too. Except her smell is because she pisses herself."

Peter looked at the Prince, "Master Richard!"

"It is true! I heard the captain of the guard say so!"

I laughed, "There are times when such honesty is not welcome. I will keep your secret and I am certain that Peter will too!"

"Aye, Master Will for I value my skin too much and Mistress Angelica," he shuddered, "well, she is a force of nature."

As we headed indoors, I was happy. I had thought I had lost my friends and now I had two. A young boy and an old man. It was a strange world.

Chapter 13

I did not sleep well the first night. Partly it was because it was the first time I had slept across a door and secondly because I knew my life was changing and change is always hard. Richard loved the thought of an armed guard sleeping in his room. The next day Peter informed me that I would be eating in the kitchen with the other servants. I was not insulted although he obviously thought I should be. The food was good and plentiful. The cook smiled as I wolfed down three portions. I still thought like a hired sword who did not know where his next meal was coming from. I think the rest were intimidated by me. I was a warrior. I was rough and I was ready. The Countess had been right, I did need a bath but I was not sure when I would be able to take one. The Nurse, Angelica got to eat with the Black Prince. The nurse tasted all Prince Richard's food. I suspect that explained her size for she had layers of fat around her neck and chin. The arrangement suited me. I had not picked up my war gear and so, after bidding farewell to the cook, who planted a kiss on my lips, I went to the guard room.

"Which is our ship, my lord?" Sir Geoffrey of Challans was in the guard room. As one of the Prince's household knights he would know such things.

"***The Black Dragon.**'" He smiled. I liked Sir Geoffrey. He was of an age with Captain Tom. His scarred face bespoke good service on behalf of the Prince. "I am glad you are with us. You are a brave young cockerel and Prince Richard will need your protection."

I lowered my voice, "You know of danger, my lord?"

"When Prince Edward had two sons there was no worries but the Prince's illness and the death of his son has made the situation change." He saw me about to ask another question. "Will, you are a good lad and an honest one. Your name is known to the real warriors amongst the Prince's retinue. You have swum into murky waters. There are many men who will try to deceive you. Keep your own counsel. When I return to England I return to my estates in Leicester. I am well out of this nest of vipers. Battle is one thing; there you face your enemy and know that he tries to kill you. Here you face a friend and find a knife in your back. Why do you think that the Prince has kept abroad all these years? His life is safer amongst his enemies. You will earn your pay. I pray you live to see twenty-one."

With that cheery thought I hefted my war gear on my back and headed to the wharf. Our ship was the largest of the five which was tied up. They were all being loaded. I stood at the gangplank. "I am Prince Richard's bodyguard. I have been told this is my ship."

A man who looked almost rusty in colour and was as wide as he was tall stood on the deck. He waved to me, "Tom son of Tom, first mate, welcome aboard. This is the right ship. We will be crowded. I would stow your gear by the bows just forrard of the forecastle. There is an old piece of canvas there. It will keep your gear dry although I fear the salt air will permeate your mail. You will have to clean it when we land!"

"A good warrior cleans it every day anyway. How many days to reach England?"

"It is not like riding a horse, young man. It depends upon the wind. We could have a fast passage and complete it in less than seven days. It is more likely that it will take twice that time." He leaned in to me, "If you like wine and wish to eat well then I would buy food and wine before you board."

I shook my head, "I am not a great drinker."

"Aye well, wine or ale will be better than the piss that passes for water here." He shrugged, "It is up to you but I would buy a skin of ale!"

He seemed an honest man. I found the place he had said. My gear fitted well and I took the scrap of canvas and covered my war gear and blankets. The weight of my mail and helmet would hold it down. I slipped ashore and found a seller of ale. I bought a skin of ale. The man grinned at me. "You are a veteran despite your age. By the time the fleet sails this will be ten times the price it is now!"

When I reached the castle again the Prince and his family were bidding farewell to the castellan. I took my place behind Angelica and my young charge, Richard. I had arrived in plenty of time for it took a while and then we marched to the ship. The people cheered as we passed for the Black Prince was a popular ruler. We were not to know that he would never return. Although I was not worried about an assassination attempt in the port I kept my hand on my sword and my eyes flicked around and ahead. My hand was close to Prince Richard. He was small enough for me to scoop him up if danger threatened.

When we reached the gangplank, I stood back. I assumed that the high and the mighty would board first. The Countess herself took Richard in her arms and carried him aboard. He was her only surviving son. To her he was not an heir but a child. I warmed to her. The nobles boarded and then Angelica waddled her bulk up the sagging gangplank. I saw sailors almost willing it to break so that the barrel of a woman would fall into the harbour. She survived. I boarded and went to the bow and my war gear. I did not know what my duties would be aboard ship. I did not think he would need my services as a bodyguard and so I began to sort out my gear. I had to ensure that the mail and metal suffered from the salt air as little as possible. I wrapped them in the sheep skin I had bought and then placed them in the canvas bag. When we reached England, I would have to thoroughly clean it. I had managed to acquire good armour. I did not want to be careless with it.

There were only the most vital of servants on our ship and so we were soon ready to sail. We would, however, have to wait for the other ships to be loaded before we could head downstream to the sea. I sat on my war gear and began to count out my coins. When I had been in Spain I had one silver penny to my name and I had stolen that. Now I had a chest with a lock. It was not a big chest but it was more money than my father had ever possessed in his whole life. I would ensure that I did not waste it.

A shadow passed over me and I looked up. It was the Black Prince. I stood, "I am sorry I…"

He smiled do not apologise. You have done nothing wrong. Until we reach England you are a passenger. Although I think my son will seek you out. He is quite taken with you. I believe that God sent you to me. I sleep easier at night knowing that you are watching him. You did not need to sleep by his door."

"With respect, my lord, I did. I have been attacked at night. No one will get by me!"

"Good."

"One thing, my lord, do you wish me to train him in the arts of war or would you prefer a noble?"

He snorted, "A noble? Half are incompetent and the other half untrustworthy. Aye, train my son. Make him wise to the ways of war. You are young but Thomas of Lincoln told me that you were raw clay yet but you were the best of his warriors."

"Me, lord? What of Peter the Priest and Red Ralph?"

"They were good but they had peaked. You have years of growing yet. A gentleman will not be your sole target. You could be a knight but that would be some time in the future. Let us take one step at a time eh? Enjoy the voyage. For myself, I will be busy with my advisers. A warrior's life is better than that of a prince. The battles you fight mean little to those who are self-serving and seek only position and power. The life we had in Aquitaine was better but…"

He turned and left. I knew that his father was old. No man had ruled for longer. Prince Edward needed to return home to help his father run and rule the kingdom. I was happy that I was able to protect his son. It was one thing less for him to worry about.

Eventually, we cast off and set down the estuary for the sea. I know not what I expected but the flat grey calm was not it. I had seen choppier lakes. I was also taken aback when we did not turn north after we had left the river but continued west until the land was a thin grey line in the distance. Only then did we turn. Tom son of Tom came forrard with a young seaman who scurried out along the bow sprit to tighten the rope there. I learned that they were called sheets and stays. I had no idea why the two names nor the difference but I did learn that seamen use their own language and woe betide any who does not use it.

"First mate, why do we not keep the coast in sight?"

He smiled, "You are afraid we will drop off the edge of the world?"

Although I shook my head I gripped the cross I wore about my neck. It did not do to joke about such things, "No but I would have thought it safer. There may be pirates."

He nodded, "Oh aye, there are pirates but they would be foolish to attack a fleet such as ours. We stay here for there is deep water beneath our keel. Further north there are rocks and reefs which will tear the bottom from an unwary ship. If a storm comes up then we will head a little closer to a haven but the weather is set fair for the next few days. When we reach the Channel, it may change but we are safe until we pass Guernsey. You can enjoy the voyage."

I followed the two seamen aft. There were two cabins on board. One was just aft of where I had stowed my bags. I was already learning the terms for the crew made no allowances for landsmen. The second, much larger one, was at the stern. It was there that the royal family had their beds. It was cruel of me but I could not help smiling as I saw Angelica vomiting over the side. Peter, too, had a sly smile on his face. Prince Richard, being a child who found such things funny, was laughing out loud, much to the annoyance of his mother.

"Richard it is not seemly to laugh at the discomfort of another." She saw me, "Here is your barbarian, go with him. He can amuse you until it is time for bed!"

If she thought it a punishment for either of us she was wrong. He ran across the slightly pitching deck and grabbed my hand. "She is funny, Will. She makes the sound like a pig." He dragged me to the seaward side. "Will we see sea monsters?"

"I hope not for I have never fought one."

"Nor a dragon?"

"Nor a dragon."

"I should like to see a dragon. My father said that they were all killed by our ancestors."

I had heard of men who claimed to have a dragon's tooth as a good luck charm. The ones I had seen were certainly larger than any teeth I had ever seen but I was not convinced of the existence of such beasts. "If one comes close then I promise to slay it."

I did not have my sword strapped to my baldric. I had heeded Tom's advice and I had a sheepskin wrapped around my weapons. It had cost me in Bordeaux but if it stopped the sea air and water from rusting my weapons then it would be worth it.

The young prince saw that I had no sword hung about my waist. "How many swords do you have, Will?"

"I have three although one is a short sword."

"Why so many? A knight needs but one!"

"I have fought in battles where my shield was shattered. Then I had to fight with two swords."

"Have you fought in many battles? You look young."

"I am young but when I was your age I was campaigning with the Blue Company. I did not fight then. I held horses and tended the wounded but I watched war and when it came time for me to take up arms and to fight then I knew how."

He asked me about battles and time passed until Peter came along and found us at the bow where we were watching dolphins racing across the bows of the ship. "Master Richard your mother sent me for you. It is getting on to dark. It is time for food and then bed."

"Will I see you tomorrow, Will?"

I waved an arm around the ship, "And where would I hide? Of course, you shall."

He nodded, seemingly satisfied and took Peter's hand, "Then I will come with you."

"How is the nurse?"

Peter grinned, "As green as an unripe apple and bringing up white bile. This is a good voyage!" We both laughed.

That night I procured a pail of water from Tom son of Tom and, after dark, I stripped naked and, with the soap I had purchased in Bordeaux, I washed myself and my clothes. The scummy water slipped down the scuppers. When I was done I felt cleaner and I towelled myself dry with my old cloak. I laid the washed clothes out on the deck. I had spares and the sea breeze soon dried them. I used my dagger to shave my face and to trim my unruly hair. I would not incur the wrath of Richard's mother.

I liked the life aboard the ship for we had a routine which was simple and predictable. We ate, we walked, we talked. When that was done we slept and the motion of the ship was gentle enough to rock me to sleep. As a royal ship the captain had ensured plenty of food. It was all cold for we could not risk a fire. The salted pork was familiar as were the fruits, onions and cheeses but the bread was unlike anything I had ever seen. It was dry and hard. The crew called it tack or biscuit. Tom son of Tom gave me a tip that first night. "Put the biscuit in your bowl and pour on some ale. Put the dried pork and the cheese on the top. It is easier to digest that way." He was right. As the ale soaked in it softened it and made it palatable. The pork added flavour to it but by the time the voyage was over I yearned for hot fresh bread, even oat or barley bread.

We made good time. After eight days at sea, we spied the coast of Kent and then began the long voyage up the river to London. After the lonely and empty sea, the river seemed packed with traffic. Although we were amongst the largest ships many others plied the river. The royal standard meant that none actually rammed us but some came mightily close. It took a whole day to warp ourselves up to the White Tower for the wind was against us. As we sailed up the river we took some hours to reach the Prince's home and I had time to examine it. Men still called it the White Tower but the white had become dirty and grey yet it was an imposing building. The tower itself was enclosed in a double wall. As a warrior I knew that it could not be mined. Any man who attacked it would have to cross the moat and two walls before he could get close to the massive keep. It was like a castle within a castle. I did not know that King Edward had improved the castle. This was not the one built when the Normans first came. It had been improved and enlarged. There was just one gate and one entrance. The Lion Tower could not be forced. Only treachery would give an enemy access.

We passed the water gate where I thought we would land and, instead, tied up at a wharf. The Nurse was still unwell and so, after I had dumped my war gear on the wharf I was given the responsibility of holding Richard's hand. With a moat on one side and the river on the other, the lively young prince needed a firm hand.

"I will fetch your war gear, Master Will."

"Thank you, Peter." I needed all my wits to keep hold of Richard for he was eager to get into the castle proper. To keep him calm I lifted him up so that he could see more and I could keep a firmer grip upon him. It also helped me to see the defences better. "See Master Richard that there is a mighty gate house there." I pointed to the west where a huge barbican guarded one entrance. To reach the barbican an attacker would need to cross the moat and endure the attack from the moat tower and then assault a large half tower. If they succeeded then they would have to turn and enter a narrow passage to the barbican. After that, they would have another narrow passage and a second barbican. "That is the most impressive entrance to a castle I have ever seen. Peter the Priest told me that they have better defences in Constantinople and Jerusalem but I have seen none finer in France."

"And we have to go all the way around to enter?"

Tom son of Tom had just brought some chests from the ship and he said, "No my lord." He pointed to the right. I saw a drawbridge which led to the second barbican. "The First Mate told me; that is how you shall enter."

The drawbridge was narrow. I guessed it was wide enough for two men at a time. The middle section could be raised or lowered. I saw that work was still going on to enlarge the wharf. King Edward knew how to make a statement. So long as he held the castle then London was safe and so were his family.

Eventually, the Prince was ready and I followed them across the drawbridge and into the castle. The Prince had recovered a little from his illness during the voyage but the long walk from the river through seven gates and three wards showed that he had not yet fully recovered for he was sweaty and pale when we reached the royal accommodation. On the ship he had asked me if I wished to continue to sleep across his son's door for the tower would be the safest place in England. I had told him that I was not used to comfort and I would be happy to do so, for a while, at least. It meant that I was taken inside the keep to the chambers reserved for the royal family. King Edward was travelling the country, a royal progress and so the castle was relatively empty. When he returned he would live in Windsor, just up the river. I settled into my new home. I would spend the next few years in London and came to know both the castle and the city well.

I was given a tunic with the livery and sign of Prince Richard upon it. It was almost identical to his father's. It gave me anonymity in the castle for I became part of the furniture. It allowed me to hear and see things which were of great use. That was in the future. For the first few weeks, I was just finding my way around. When Prince Richard had time with his tutor then I would be allowed to leave the castle and explore London. I did so but I used the time to scout rather than to enjoy. I knew that my future depended upon the young prince prospering. London could be a dangerous place and I needed to find my way around it. My livery gave me some degree of security but it also marked me as the King's man. Not all those in London liked the royal family.

I liked the young Prince. He was lonely and I understood that. It helped me to sense when he needed for me to talk. Over the next two years, I became more confident in my role and he changed from a young boy to someone who could begin to become a warrior. His father, if not his nurse and his mother was keen for that to happen. As we lived either at the Tower or the Prince's manor at Berkhamstead we had plenty of space to practise. He was enthusiastic for he knew of his father's reputation and wished to emulate him. He worked tirelessly although I remembered that when I had been young I had never had time to be tired, there was too much to do.

The Prince remembered his promise and I was given better armour. I was still growing and the breastplate I had taken needed replacing. During the next two years, all my mail and armour were changed. Red Ralph and Peter the Priest would not have recognised me. The good food I enjoyed and the exercise meant I was both bigger, stronger and well-muscled. The Prince had a servant who shaved him and for a few coins a week he shaved me too. I enjoyed being clean shaven and well groomed. Many of the young ladies who visited the Countess cast me covetous glances. I was not a gentleman but they found me attractive. If I wanted women then they could be had for a few coppers in the many inns which lay close to the Tower. I had a circle of friends whom I met at one of them, *The Falconer's Glove*. Most were other warriors who served in the castle. If we lived at Berkhamstead then I had no such distractions. Life there was quiet. We went there increasingly for the Prince was still not a well man and he had lost a great deal of money during the last campaign. He had been honourable and paid off the men who had served him. In contrast to the Prince my life was good.

It was while we were at the tower that I met King Edward's second son, John of Gaunt. I had heard of him in France. He was, like his brother, a good warrior but he had a really violent temper. It flared whenever anyone questioned his parentage. His father, the King of England, had not been present at his birth and there was doubt. He knew he would never be King but it did not stop him plotting and planning against Prince Edward. They did not get on. The two played a game; it was a dangerous game for success would result in a throne. John of Gaunt brought his son with him. Henry Bolingbroke was the same age as Richard. When they came to the castle the two boys played together. I was the adult who watched them and ensured that neither were hurt. They got on but like all young boys there was also rivalry. Thanks to my lessons Richard was more skilled with weapons and despite Henry's greater size, Richard normally bested him. It was then that I began to teach Richard more than just how to fight. I taught him how to treat those that he defeated. They were the hardest lessons to teach for all boys like to crow when they win. I am not sure that I ever truly succeeded. Henry asked me for lessons too and, when he came to the castle, I taught them both. Henry appreciated my efforts and tried to give me coins for my trouble.

"No, Master Henry, I am paid well enough by Prince Edward. I am happy to teach you. You are all the same family after all."

Life began to change when the King and his son set sail for France to relieve the siege of Thouars. Bad weather meant that they did not manage to reach France and they returned to England. Plots and conspiracies began to emerge as rivals for the crown saw that both the King and his heir were in ill health. They were like wolves circling a wounded beast. As Prince Richard approached his eighth year I was called upon to earn my money.

Chapter 14

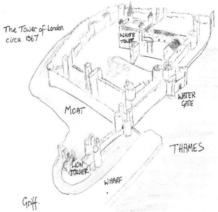

When the Prince returned from the abortive sea voyage, we were taken from London to live at his castle north of London. He was not in good health. The plague had struck London again and the air around Berkhamstead was considered healthier. Another reason for the decision was that Angelica, Prince Richard's nurse, died. I was not surprised for she was overweight and drank too much but the Countess feared that her death had been caused by the plague or one of its many variants. I was sad to leave London for I had many friends and enjoyed my life there but I was the Prince Richard's bodyguard and we left. Another reason for our departure was that the King, had not recovered from a recent illness. The King was now over sixty. He could not last too much longer. The problem was that his son appeared to be more ill than his father. Prince Richard might well be the next King of England. We could protect him better at Berkhamstead.

I now had a horse. It was not a warhorse for I would never need to go to war but it was a good palfrey. Even though his finances were not what they were Edward, the Black Prince was a generous man. Jet black, Star was a good horse. Prince Richard was envious. He had a large pony which was as clever a beast as I had ever seen but he was not as big or as powerful as Star. We rode from the castle each day. The nearby town of Berkhamstead owed its existence and prosperity to the castle and so we were welcomed by those in the town. At first that was as far as we rode. It was an easy ride down the hill and across the river. We rode mailed for the Prince was keen that his son was comfortable in mail. It pleased Richard who now had a short sword which was little longer than one of my daggers.

His father had been home for a month and he roused himself from his lethargy. He summoned his household knights, six of them lived in the castle with us, his foresters and his huntsmen. "It is time we hunted. My son has yet to kill his first beast." He looked at me, "Will Strongstaff, is he ready to ride on a hunt?"

I did not look at Master Richard but I could feel his eyes boring in to me and willing me to say yes. In all honesty, he was ready to ride on a hunt but not to kill. "My lord we can ride on a hunt but I would beg more time to give him the skills of using a spear from a horse before he has to hunt."

Prince Edward smiled, "You have grown into this role. That is good." He saw the disappointment on Richard's face. "We will make this a weekly event, my son. In the time between Will can train you. It will give you purpose."

He brightened, "Then I swear that it will take but a week for me to impress Will and I will hunt alongside you."

I wore my old leather jerkin for hunting. It had thongs and it still fitted although it was tighter for my chest had grown. It seemed like a lifetime ago when I had worn it to war. The Prince also had a good jerkin. I carried a hunting spear. I had never hunted but I knew how to use a spear from the back of a horse. The last two years in Gascony had seen me become quite proficient in the use of a lance and a spear. I knew how to kill a man. A deer would be as easy for it would not be trying to kill me.

The Prince liked Berkhamstead for the hunting park was enormous. As he had not used it for some time it teemed with game. I knew that the Prince would have preferred war but he was still unwell. His foresters and huntsmen knew where there was a large herd to be found. The next morning, we mounted and the Prince gave me a knowing nod as he mounted. Prince Richard was to be protected.

The huntsmen and the foresters were good. Leaving the chief huntsman to ride with the Black Prince the others loped off to beat the herd towards us. There were six lords with the Prince and their squires. Prince Richard and I rode behind them. He made to speak but I put my finger to my lips. I had already told him that this was preparation for war. You had to be silent. He nodded as he remembered my warning. This was the first time since Godfrey of Hastings had tried to hurt me that I had been in a position where I would have to be alert to real danger. Guarding Prince Richard had been the easiest thing I had ever done. I used my ears, eyes and nose as we rode through the verdant woodland. I held my reins and my spear in my left hand and my right was ready to either use my spear or grab the reins of Prince Richard's horse. The woods were silent. The birds and animals would not make a noise while the intruders passed through. The silence was broken by the beaters in the distance. The sound of their shouts and bangs was replaced by the thunder of hooves as the herd fled in panic.

Ahead of us, I watched as the hunters raised their spears. Each had three of them. They were not the fighting spear of a warrior. They were a throwing spear and the head was barbed. Any hit would slow the beast down and allow a second spear to finish it off. The sound of the deer grew louder. I hoped that no wild boars had been flushed along with the deer. For wild boar we needed boar spears and mail! When the deer appeared it was suddenly, like a dappled brown wave. I saw the Prince rise in his stirrups to thrust down his spear at the hart which led them. It was distinctive for its coat was not brown, it was almost white. It was a good strike but not a perfect one. The hart was not killed. It was just badly hurt. It turned its head to try to hit its attacker and the Prince wheeled his horse out of the way. I knew that his illness had slowed his reflexes for he did not thrust a second spear at the wounded beast. It almost proved fatal. His squire thrust his spear but managed to strike only the antlers and the animal was through our line and heading for Prince Richard. He was young and he froze. He saw the white hart before him and appeared incapable of action. I grabbed his horse's reins and rode so that Star and myself were between the hart and my charge. I braced myself for the collision but the hart managed to turn and head into the woods. Two of the lords turned their horses to pursue the wounded animal. I reined in behind a large oak tree.

"Are you all right, Master Richard?"

He was white. "It came so fast. It was a white hart! Why did it not die? My father's strike was a good one!"

"It was not perfect. It is like that when you fight an enemy. Unless you hit perfectly then he can fight on with many wounds." I did not say so to him but I was thinking of my father. The hart had done what he had. Even when he knew he was dying he fought on. "Now do you see why our lessons must continue?"

He nodded, "I thought you would be struck."

I laughed, "So did I but someone was watching out for me."

Prince Edward rode up. His face showed his relief, "Thank you, Will! I am getting sloppy. I should have made a killing strike. I am getting old."

"No, lord, it is your illness. When you are fully recovered..."

"Aye, whenever that day comes. Well Dick, did you enjoy your first hunt?"

"Are the animals dead?"

I pointed to an open patch of earth. Two does were already being gutted by the foresters. "They are Master Richard. It is like that in battle. There are battles going on all around you. Men are dying and yet you see nothing save the man you fight for if you lose concentration then you will die."

The hart was felled and we took the four animals back to Berkhamstead. The offal was given to the foresters. Nobles did not eat such fare. I thought that it was tastier than the choicer cuts which we would eat but then I had been brought up on the poorest of foods.

The first hunt had a chastening effect on the young prince. He was far more diligent than he had been. He paid more attention and he asked more questions of me. Over the next month or so we went out each week. Prince Edward improved and it made him happier. He had thought he was getting old. He was not, he was getting rusty and the hunt scoured the rust from him.

The fourth time we took spears out to hunt we gave Richard his own to carry. He had improved. The spear had been made for him and was much shorter than ours although it still had a metal head. It was too much to expect him to be able to hold reins and two spears. I had three. Mine were for protection and not for the hunt. If I had to use mine then it meant that the Prince was in danger. Each time we hunted we used a different part of the huge hunting park. It meant the land was different each time. I had not forgotten the lessons I had learned from Peter the Priest and I stored the paths we had crossed. Who knew when that sort of information would come in handy. As luck would have it we found ourselves close to where the hart had almost ended my life. I felt more comfortable for I knew where the bumps and hollows were.

The hunters made their noise and we heard the hooves. The foresters had told us that there were five herds in the park. Even if we had hunted this one before it would do the animals little good. This hunt was different in that we were behind Prince Edward. The squires were to our sides. That protected the young Prince even more. I had taught him to ride with his spear across the saddle. He was still young and carrying even a short spear would be tiring for him. The deer suddenly burst from the undergrowth. We had spoken before the hunt and the others would take all of the larger deer. Richard would target a fawn.

He had heeded his lessons for he kept his horse still and watched the woods. He raised his arm when he spied the first deer. I had a spear ready too. The others all hurled their spears at the harts and hinds. I watched for a fawn. One was following its mother which was taken by Sir John. The fawn ran on. I willed Richard to throw. He raised his spear but then allowed the fawn to escape.

His father saw what had happened and rode up, "What happened, my son? Why did you not strike?"

"I could not bring myself to kill it. There was still milk on its mouth!"

I shook my head, "It would have been kinder to kill it. There is no mother now. How will it feed? The animals who hunt in the woods will have it and that will be a slower death."

His father asked, "Could you have made the strike?"

In answer, he stood in his stirrups and hurled his spear at the carcass of the dead hind. It was a perfect strike. "I could. Thank you, Will. I have learned another lesson. I did not think that I was being cruel. I thought I was being kind. I am ever in your debt."

When we returned to the castle to celebrate, for it was clear that Richard knew how to hunt and he had not fled in fear, I was invited to dine with the others. His six household knights were as close to him as any and I felt honoured to be in the same company as they. I did, when I was seated at the end of the table next to some of the squires, as I had done when serving with the Blue Company. I would keep my mouth shut and my ears open. The conversation drifted to the constitutional problems facing the King and his family.

"Why, my lord, does your father have to convene a parliament and ask for money? Surely as King he is entitled to it. After all, if it were not for the King, yourself and the loyal nobles we would have no one to defend this land against our enemies." Sir John was almost the same age as the Prince and had stood with him at Poitiers.

I noticed, as he answered, that the Prince was looking a little unwell yet he spoke forcefully, "Because the barons forced my grandsire, John, into this position. I know that not all John did was good but we now have our hands tied. It is monstrous that we must go cap in hand for the money which we need."

Ralf, Lord Basset of Drayton was also a survivor of both Poitiers and Crécy. He was a very clever man. When he spoke then others listened. He glanced down the table at me before he spoke. The Black Prince said, "I trust Will Strongstaff as much as any other man around this table. Speak freely, my lord."

"I have heard rumours of factions who are already plotting to take the throne when your father dies. The rebels in Aquitaine and the French are paying for their supporters to gain positions of power in England." He paused and added, "They know of your illness, lord."

Prince Edward looked around the table, "I fear that my father will outlive me. I know not what pestilence I picked up in Spain."

"Or what poison."

Prince Edward nodded in Lord Basset's direction, "Or what poison. But I fear it has done for me. I have more blood in my water than piss!" I saw the look of horror on his son's face. "That is another reason we have summoned a Parliament. We will have the barons swear an oath of allegiance to Richard. We will make him heir to the throne." He smiled at me, "Now you see why Will Strongstaff is so important. When that news is leaked then my son will be in ever greater danger than he is now. The Parliament will be in a month's time. We will ride to the Tower in three weeks." He looked at Richard, "If you are going to make a kill while hunting then it should be soon. Once you are named as heir I fear your movements will, perforce, have to be restricted. We cannot risk the heir."

That night as he prepared for bed Richard was agitated. "Will, what will it mean that I am heir and not my father?"

"I confess that I know not. Your father must be ill for him to make this decision and I find that sad."

"I find it sad too. I wish it were not true but I am too young to be King!"

I smiled, "Neither your father nor your grandfather is dead. I learned, when I was in the Blue Company, that it is better to take each day as it comes. When you are King then you will have advisers. You have your mother."

"I have you."

"I am a low born man at arms. I cannot advise you."

"Yet my father holds you in high esteem as do I."

"Let us concentrate on other matters until we have to worry about taking the reins of the kingdom."

As I laid down behind the door, wrapped in my cloak I wondered how my life would change. I knew my role as a bodyguard but an adviser?

The next day I was summoned to the Prince's chamber. Richard was supposed to be with his tutor but he was with his father, a clerk and a priest. Had I done something wrong? The Black Prince smiled when he saw my fearful face, "Sit Will, you are not in trouble." I sat. He waved his hand at the priest and the clerk. "I promised you that when you reached the age of twenty-one then I would make you a gentleman."

"But I am not twenty-one!"

"I know but I fear that I may not live to see that day and I am a man of my word. I would not go to meet my maker with a promise not fulfilled." He took a parchment from the clerk. "This is the deed to a small farm just north of here at Stony Stratford. It is yours and with it the title of gentleman. With that goes the right to have a coat of arms. My clerk will advise on such matters." He paused.

"I know not how to thank you, lord."

"Firstly, you will continue to be my son's bodyguard. I do not release you from that duty and secondly, you will maintain the standards of behaviour which you showed in Gascony!"

I smiled, "Of course."

"There will be a letter which will be sent to the lord of the manor to which the farm belongs, the Earl of Northampton. You may wish to find someone to farm it for you or ask the lord of the manor to do so. You will have no time to make use of either the farm or those who live there. And now I bid you leave us. I must speak with my priest and Richard needs to return to his studies."

The clerk, Robert of Doncaster, rose and gestured for me to follow him. Richard accompanied us. I saw his tutor outside. Richard smiled at the tutor, "Will is now a gentleman too!" he skipped off happily to his lessons.

Alone with Robert I said, "I did not expect this so soon."

"The farm is a good one although no one has farmed it since Poitiers. It belonged to a bachelor who died on that battlefield. Dying he bequeathed it to the Prince. There will be an income but you would be expected to serve the lord of the manor once you have ended your service with Prince Richard." He saw my confusion, "Do not worry. Richard is young. You will be his bodyguard for many years to come! As for the coat of arms, the point is moot while you serve Prince Richard. However, the fact that you served in the Blue Company and your name is Strongstaff would suggest a staff on a blue background with perhaps a blue and red quartered shield to indicate your service to the Prince?" I nodded. "Good, then you may leave that with me." He held out his hand, "It will, I fear, incur a cost but you are now a gentleman and, as such, have obligations. I should also tell you that the village was emptied when the plague struck. The nearest manor is Stratford. It is a lonely farm from what I understand."

In an instant my life had changed. For good or for ill I was tied to Prince Richard. My survival depended upon his.

When we left to hunt the next week I had had seven days to reflect upon my elevation. I wondered what my father would think. He had asked me to strive for the position and yet I had found it easy. What greasy piece of road awaited me?

When we went hunting the following week I had an uneasy feeling. I put it down to my new status. My mind was filled with grandiose plans for the farm and the income it would generate. The lords who rode with us did not seem impressed with my new status but the other servants were overjoyed. I was one of them and I had made the next step. I gave them hope for such elevation. My sense of disquiet was nothing to do with that. It was the feeling I had had before a battle which went wrong. There was no logic to it. Richard was unconcerned about making a kill. He just wanted to impress his father. We had but two more hunts and then we would be heading for London. The exercise had served its purpose. I was wary as we headed through the woods. Richard had asked to ride behind the squires. His young son was growing. He was learning and I was pleased. Since he had learned he would be heir he had become a different student. He listened more and was desperate to become as skilled as I. We rode forty paces behind the squires. I knew that his father was happier when we were further from the action. The white hart had alarmed him.

The hunt followed the same pattern. We heard the sound of shouts and cries and we heard the hooves. Richard and I hefted our spears over our shoulders. If there was danger then I would be ready. Suddenly I heard a cry from ahead and one of the squires, Sir Ralf's, tumbled from his horse. There was an arrow sticking from him. Sir Ralf shouted, "Ambush!"

It had been some years since Limoges and that had been the last combat but I still had my instincts. Even as I drew my sword I turned around to look for an escape route or more enemies. My job was to save the Prince. I could not see enemies ahead but animals do not release arrows. I shouted, as I turned, "Ready your spear!" Richard had little more than a dagger but it would be better than nothing.

As I turned I saw four men on horses riding towards us. They were coming from behind. We were their intended target. They wore leather mail and helmets. These were soldiers. It was not just a band of brigands who had decided to take on nobles. This was an assassination attempt. The odds were too great. I turned to Richard. "Back your horse towards your father. You guard my back!" There was no point in his galloping toward his father, I knew not what danger lay there. I knew the odds here, four to one and a half!

He looked terrified but he nodded, "I will."

I drew my dagger; I had my spear already in my hand. and I pulled on my reins to walk Star backwards. Well trained, he obeyed. The four did not gallop towards us they walked their horses slowly. Why were they being wary? Odds of four to one were good odds. It was as I stared at them that I recognised at least two of them. One was Godfrey of Hastings and the other was Garth, the companion whose fingers I had broken. Surprisingly that made me feel better. Neither were as good on a horse as me and both were poorer warriors. It was the other two who might represent the threat. Then I saw that the two who followed Godfrey of Hastings rode slightly behind the other two.

I shouted, "You have crawled out from under your rock, Godfrey of Hastings. Do these two wood lice with you know it was I who hamstrung you?"

They still advanced and Godfrey shouted, "This time you will die, whoreson. This time there are four of us against one of you!"

Behind me, I heard Richard shout, "There are two! I may be a cub but I have teeth and claws."

I was proud of Richard. He had courage. I also kept my eyes on the four who advanced. The two new warriors watched Godfrey of Hastings. It would be he and Garth who initiated the fight. They were judging the moment when they attacked carefully. They would ride at either side of me and the two of them would strike at the same time. I said, quietly, "In a moment I will ride at them. You keep walking backwards. The two younger ones will come for you. When they do then turn and gallop for your father."

"But I watch your back."

"Obey me, Master Richard, and we both might survive."

"Yes Will."

The four of them were ten paces from me. There was the slightest glance between Godfrey and Garth but it was enough for me and I dug my heels into Star who leapt forward. I let go of the reins and continued to use my feet. Garth was on my left. He held his sword left handed. I would have to use my dagger against him. Even as we closed I calculated. He would not be skilled with his left hand and he would not be as strong. All that I had to do was deflect his blade with my dagger. Godfrey of Hastings had a sword like mine but he was not as skilled as me. I would risk a blow from Garth and try to end Godfrey's life. I hurled my spear. I wanted to distract them and then I would use my sword and dagger. Throwing from a moving horse at a moving target was never a good decision.

My horse was better and faster than theirs. I was approaching them quickly and I knew that Star would respond to my slightest touch. These killers had bought poor palfreys. The two younger ones rode rouncys. My spear made them both jink their horses away from it and that slowed them too. I held my two weapons to the side and behind me. I would have to block Garth's strike without looking. Peter the Priest had taught me how to do that. Godfrey of Hastings pointed his sword towards me. He would aim for my head and neck.

He shouted, as he urged his horse on, "David and James, get the boy. Kill him quickly!"

It was then I wondered about the ambush on the Prince and his knights. Had that been a lure to draw them further into the forest and allow Godfrey and the others to get the young prince? "Richard, begin to shout for help!" I cursed myself for not thinking of that before. Prince Edward would have heard nothing from us and assume that we were safe.

Godfrey finally got his horse going as did Garth. As Richard shouted, "Help! Ambush!" over and over I brought my sword across to strike just above Godfrey's horse's head. Even as Godfrey's sword struck my leather jerkin I sensed Garth to my left. I flicked up my dagger and heard the ring of metal on metal. My sword hacked across Godfrey's throat. His sword penetrated my leather jerkin and I felt the tip break my skin. Then his lifeless fingers dropped the sword and he fell backwards from his horse. I whipped Star's head around. Garth was trying to do the same. His horse was slower and I turned inside him. Ahead I saw the two young riders trying to catch Richard. In a perfect world, I would have tried to take Garth prisoner to find out who had paid him but the Prince's life was more important. As Garth tried to control his horse I stood in my stirrups and brought down my sword. I struck his mail coif. Even as my blade rang off the coif I heard his collar bone break. He screamed in agony and tumbled from his horse.

Galloping after Richard I saw his father and Sir Ralf emerge from the trees having heard his cries for help. They would not reach him in time. The two riders were just a horse's length behind him. Star's long legs were eating up the ground but I might be too late. I hoped he would remember our training. I had taught him some moves to avoid boars and deer. I shouted, "Richard, wild boar attack!"

He was a bright lad and he suddenly jerked his reins to the right. As his lively mount opened its legs it took the two men behind by surprise. I was already turning Star and I raised my sword. The two men who were chasing Richard were the same age as me but they did not have my experience. They turned as Star's hooves thundered. That allowed Richard to turn to the left and open up a slight gap. His father and Sir Ralf were now much closer. Richard rode towards them. He put his head close to his horse's mane to help his mount. I pulled back my arm as I neared the rearmost killer. Star's legs took me close enough to swing and I put all of my effort into the blow. His jerkin was short and I found the gap between jerkin and breeks. I hacked through his spine. It was a quick death. The other killer, realising that he was alone, veered off to the right and headed into the forest. It was tempting to go after him but Richard was my charge.

I heard Ralf shout, "One is escaping! On me!"

Prince Edward had reined in and was holding Richard's reins as I drew close to them. "I am sorry, my lord, your son was in danger."

The Black Prince shook his head, "And would have died had another not been guarding him. You took on odds of four to one." He sounded incredulous.

"My lord it was two of those who fled after Limoges. Godfrey of Hastings and Garth. I believe they were the ones who poisoned you in Spain."

Richard burst out, "Poisoned!"

Prince Edward looked at me and said, "I wondered at that but how did you know?"

"I did not, lord. There were rumours that you were poisoned amongst the company and when I suggested it to Godfrey he did not deny it."

"Then my interrogators will find out who put them up to this."

"Godfrey is dead but Garth may yet live." Keeping Richard between us we headed for the man at arms. Even before we reached him I could see that he was dead. His head was at an unnatural angle. He had broken his neck. I handed my reins to Richard and dismounted. I took the purse from his waist.

Richard said, "You would rob the dead?" He sounded shocked.

I smiled, "Aye, Master Richard, I would rob the dead but that is not why I take the purse. I look for coins."

I took out the gold coins I could see. They bore the head of the French King. I showed them to Prince Edward, who nodded, "Just so. That may be to throw us off the track, Will Strongstaff, for I have enemies in England." It was unspoken but I knew that he meant his brother. "Take the purse from the other and confirm." Godrey lay in a large pool of blood. He had a larger purse and there were more gold coins. I nodded. "Take the purses as reward for what you did. We need to get to London sooner rather than later. This will be my last hunt. I need to speak with my father. You will remain Richard's guard but we need good and loyal men to guard you both."

Sir Ralf rode in with the other men. They had bodies slung over horses. "I am sorry, sire, but we failed to take them alive. They all had heavy purses. They were paid."

Sir John de Vere said, "We were lucky. There were fifteen of them and some had bows."

Sir Ralf snorted, "Lucky? Tell that to Sir Geoffrey and the four squires who died."

Prince Edward said, quietly, "Not to mention the eight foresters and huntsmen who were killed or wounded. But Sir John is right. This was planned. They knew where we came and lay in ambush. They had observed us for they had four men to take Will and my son."

Sir Ralf clapped me on the back, "That was bravely and cleverly done. It is fortunate that Richard went the right way."

Richard said, "That was not luck, Sir Ralf. Will and I had practised that many times. I do not play at war; I train for war and I have a good teacher."

Sir Ralf smiled, "Aye, that you have!"

"Come we will return to my castle and I will have the bodies fetched. We have our last feast here. Now we begin to secure the crown for you, Richard. It now bears the blood of many brave men. We will not let it slip from our grasp now."

Chapter 15

Prince Edward sent a messenger to his father. We would all meet in London. The Parliament was due in a short time. Even as we headed down the London Road to travel the twenty odd miles to the Thames Prince Edward's health deteriorated even more. He was forced to take to the wagon we had brought. I rode next to Richard.

"You said my father was poisoned? When?"

"It was years ago, when we were in Spain."

"Then why is he not dead?"

"There are slow poisons and perhaps your father's body was stronger than the poison. I am no healer, I do not know. This disease began then and the doctors cannot find a cure. It is either poison or a curse from God."

"Then he will die." I hesitated. "Will Strongstaff, you once told me that shield brothers do not lie to each other. They tell the truth. We have now fought together. I count you as a shield brother. Do not treat me as a child. I am young in years but I know more of the ways of the world than others my age; the truth."

"Your father is dying. He would not have you named as heir otherwise. Once you are heir then you become an even bigger target. We will need to have you mailed whenever you walk abroad. I will have to taste your food. Once your father goes to Parliament then your life changes and you can never go back."

"I would not choose to be king. My brother was to be king and I was happy to be his younger brother. I would have been happy to have a life without a bloody crown! I enjoy training to be a warrior. If I am king then I cannot be a warrior, can I?"

"Your father and grandfather were both warriors. You could be."

That seemed to brighten and lighten his mood. The young are more resilient but I knew that I would have to watch him. When my mother had left us, I had often cried at night. They had been silent tears for my father would have beaten me for my weakness. I would be there for Richard if he needed to cry or to speak. I understood his pain.

The attack in the woods had had an effect on the Prince's household knights. They rode close to the wagon in which he travelled. There were armed guards around Richard's mother. Even Peter was armed although he was such a gentle soul that I doubted that he would be able to draw a weapon in anger. I was relieved when we reached the fortress that would be our home. This time we used the large entrance, the Lion Tower, but, as we were mounted we reached the White Tower quicker. The Prince was taken to his chamber where his doctors were able to examine him. Whatever they gave him seemed to help and he was able to walk about. He wasted no time in drawing up a will and in speaking with his father.

When the Parliament was called the Prince attended as did his father and, of course, Richard of Bordeaux. We were all dressed in our finest garments. The household knights of both the Prince and the King were in attendance. Even before the Parliament had begun to debate the money the King needed King Edward brought forward Prince Richard. I waited in the background, my hand on my sword. I doubted that any would risk an assassination attempt in the palace but this would their last opportunity before Prince Richard became heir. Once that happened then he was, to all intents and purposes, almost a king and regicide was not only a crime it was the most serious of sins.

The King presented his grandson. "I am here to ask all present to acknowledge that Richard of Bordeaux, the son of my son Edward of Woodstock, the Black Prince, will be the next King of England!"

There was silence. I am not certain what they expected. Then Prince Edward said, "This is not only the King's choice but mine also. Prince Richard!"

That swayed the nobles and they all acknowledged Richard as the heir. The Prince and his father ensured that all those present signed the document which was already prepared. That done Prince Richard and I returned, by boat, to the Tower. Ten good men at arms guarded us both. It was done. I would be bodyguard to the next King of England. My life would no longer be mine own. I could not take wife nor have a home. My home might not be the space behind the door but it would be wherever the King laid his head. I was a gentleman. I had position and a little power but Red Ralph and Peter the Priest, in Middleham and York, had more freedom than I.

When the King and his son returned he brought with him Anian, the Bishop of Bangor. Until Prince Edward died he was a constant at his bedside. The visit to the specially convened Parliament was the last one which Prince Edward took. From that day forth he did not stir from his chamber. Richard saw him every day, which meant I did too. The

Prince was remarkably organised. He had his clerk, the same one who had written the deed for me, Robert of Doncaster, make lists of all the gifts and bequests he wished to make. He did not trust lawyers and wanted the gifts made while he was still alive.

Some were large grants of lands and manors. Others were smaller, more personal ones, I was given one of his swords. It was not his best one, that went to Richard but it was the best sword I had ever had. The scabbard was magnificent and I felt humbled that the son of a mercenary should have a sword which might have been held by a King of England. A day or two before he died the Prince summoned Richard and myself. The Bishop and Robert of Doncaster, as well as Richard's mother were also in attendance.

"My son, you know that I have made many bequests."

"Aye, father."

"Then know that I would have you swear that you will not try to take back that which I have given once I am dead."

I saw Richard holding back the tears as he said, "I so swear!"

The Prince looked relieved and lay back on his pillow, "If you ask Will he may tell you what happens to oath breakers. They are cursed."

"I will not break my word!" Richard shouted it!

The Prince smiled, "I know. Will Strongstaff has given you the right values. I am content. Now leave me with the Bishop. I have much to say to God before I leave this earth."

He did not die that day but two days later on the eighth of June in the year of our lord thirteen seventy-six he died. He was but forty-six years old. It took some time to make the bronze effigy of him and it was September before he was buried in Canterbury Cathedral close by the tomb of Thomas Becket. It was another site for pilgrims. The words which were carved above the effigy were Prince Edward's own.

Such as thou art, sometime was I.
Such as I am, such shalt thou be.
I thought little on th'our of Death
So long as I enjoyed breath.
On earth I had great riches
Land, houses, great treasure, horses, money and gold.
But now a wretched captive am I,
Deep in the ground, lo here I lie.
My beauty great, is all quite gone,
My flesh is wasted to the bone

I confess that, like Prince Richard, I shed tears for the Black Prince. He had not always behaved well but his intentions had always been good. I would have to wait a long time for a warrior who was as good as he.

My charge and I now entered the murky waters of politics. The King was ill and John of Gaunt, Richard's uncle virtually ran the country. He and the nobles clashed many times. The Prince was too young to be involved in such matters and the King was too ill. John of Gaunt gained control of many lords during that time and his rule would come back to haunt young Richard.

I had other matters on my mind. I had to find ten men at arms who would be the guards for the heir to the throne. I had been charged with the task by Prince Edward before his death. There would be Sir Ralf and the other household knights but Prince Edward had known the value of men at arms who fought for coin. I had been given funds to hire, arm and pay for ten such men. Bearing in mind how Godfrey of Hastings had been suborned I was keen to hire good men whom I could trust.

I went, while Prince Richard was at his letters, to the inn I had used since coming to London. *The Falconer's Glove* was used by men at arms who returned to England. I let the landlord, Lame Llenlleog, know that I wished to hire good men and that I would be at his inn the same time each day. Conveniently it was around noon each day that the Prince was at his letters. I got to eat some of the beef and oyster pies for which *The Falconer's Glove* was renowned and some of their black ale brewed on the south bank.

The first day I went I found six men who wished to serve the Prince. After speaking with them and buying each one a beaker of ale I realised that none were suitable. I returned to the Tower feeling disappointed. The second day, in contrast, was the best of days for waiting for me was Dick Long Sword. He now sported a patch over one eye. When I first saw him, I thought he had been passing through but the landlord, Lame Llenlleog said, "Here is a keen one, Master Will. He has been here since first light. He is keen to serve the Prince."

I clasped his arm, "You would serve under me? I thought you would be a captain now."

He shook his head, "Those days are gone, Will and can never return. Long John became captain. He died last year in Poitou." He smiled, "He took ten Frenchmen with him and it is where I lost my eye! I returned to England for the Prince's funeral. I was outside. I saw you then. You have grown and you have prospered. Captain Tom said that you would."

I nodded, "Did you ever get back to La Roche-sur-Yon? Did you see my mother?"

He shook his head, "No but I heard that Sir Alan returned to England. Perhaps she is here."

"Perhaps." The ale arrived and I lifted my tankard. I came here so often that the landlord kept me a tankard over the bar. "Here's to the Blue Company."

"The Blue Company."

We did not speak for a moment and then I said, "Are you sure you would like to join me? The pay is good but you will not enjoy the freedom you did. You will not be able to marry."

"I was married. She was a pretty little Gascon. She died giving birth to our son. He died too. God was letting me know that I am not to be a father. There are whores and doxies. I am content." He smiled, "Besides, Will, I owe you a life. Like Peter the Priest and Old Tom I will have no children. I would be as a father to you. You protect the Prince and I will protect you both."

"Then you are my sergeant at arms. I would value your advice about the others we hire. I need ten. We look for another nine." I gave him a silver coin. "Here is your first day's pay."

"If you do not mind I will stay here for I like the inn and I can find others like me."

Two more men arrived before we had eaten. Dick pointed to one of them, "You are a poxy coward who ran away when we fought at Angers. Leave this inn now!" The man fled. Dick stared at the other. "Did you serve with him?"

He shook his head, "No, sir, I met him on the road from Southampton. I served with the garrison at Bordeaux."

I smiled for I could see that Dick had intimidated him, "Sit, friend, I am Will Strongstaff and I am the captain of the Prince's Guards. What is your name?"

"Roger of Chester."

"And tell me Roger, who was the sergeant at Bordeaux?"

"There were two or three, captain but the one I remember best was Walther of Southwark."

Dick nodded, "Aye then you speak truly for he knew Red Ralph."

I waved Llenlleog over with the ale. It gave me the opportunity to examine the man. Roger of Chester looked young. I was about to say so and then remembered that I was probably the same age. "Tell us what you have done and why you wish to join the Prince's Guards."

"After I left Bordeaux I served in Gascony. I was with Sir Geoffrey D'Urberville's men. When his lord died his son blamed us for his death and let us go. We had no pay." Before I could ask anything more he burst out, "It was not our fault, sir. He had an illness. He was bleeding from some disease within and he was wasting away. He forbade us to follow him and he rode into the heart of the enemy. His squire followed and they died. We obeyed our lord. Is that wrong?"

"No, it is not." It struck me that the son had conveniently saved himself coin by dismissing his father's men. He was honour bound to either employ them or pay them off. He had done neither.

Dick and I chatted to him. I could see that he was hungry and so I ordered food for us all. He fell upon the pie like a man who had not eaten for a week. I liked him but I was not as experienced as Dick. I waited until he nodded to me. "Well Roger, you are now one of the Prince's men." I gave him a coin. "Until we hire at least four more men I will not need you but you need to stay close."

He looked relieved, "Thank you, sir."

"I am not a knight. Call me Captain."

Over the next days, we managed to hire the rest. They all had different stories but one common thread ran through them. All had served with the Black Prince in Gascony. When he had given up those lands they had returned home. Some were like Roger of Chester and been forced to return home. Others like David Tallboy had tired of the life and returned to England which was their home. The Guards, as they called themselves were Robert son of Tom, Martin son of Martin, Harold Four Fingers, John, Hames' son, Edgar of Derby and Wilfred Loidis.

On Sunday after services in the chapel, I gathered them at the open Lion Tower. It was a symbolic place to meet. This was the main entrance to the Tower and was the first defence an enemy would find. They were the first defence of the Prince. He came with me as they were given their tunics and sworn in. Surprisingly the keeper of the royal purse had not objected to the expenditure. His existence was dependent upon Richard becoming King. If John of Gaunt had his way and he became ruler then all of those associated with his brother and father would be swept away. In those days many people believed that John of Gaunt would become King of England. Even the Prince's widow had warmed to me as she saw in me and my new guards, a sort of guarantee that her son would become King.

Once the men had taken their oath and been given their tunics which marked them as Prince Richard's men, they were given the passwords for the castle and then the Prince inspected them. He was now almost ten and, thanks to a healthy regime of good food and exercise he was growing well. He spoke to them all as he was introduced to them.

Prince Richard was eminently likeable. His cousin, Henry Bolingbroke was not.

Richard had decided to adopt the white hart as his badge. That hearkened back to the hunt in Berkhamsted. In later years it became the mark of all of Richard's men but on that first day, only eleven of us were given the honour of bearing the white hart. Prince Richard then returned to his tutor. His lessons were now even more important for he would be given the reins of state soon enough. Once he left us we marched to the armoury where they were issued helmets. They were all of the open bascinet type. They were given a mail hood and short hauberk. They were given greaves for their legs, a breast plate and plates for their arms. None of them had been so well protected and when we went to their new barracks I told them why.

"You have been given armour and mail which a knight would envy. I confess that until I arrived here I did not enjoy such mail. There will be those who will try to harm the young Prince who one day will be king." They all knew of the attempt on his life at Berkhamstead. "Make no mistake, my friends, we are sworn to give our lives for Prince Richard. You have taken the coin and sworn the oath. There is no going back now. There will be three sections. We guard our charge day and night. We will not need all of these beds for at any one time there will be three of you on duty. I leave Dick to finalise the details and to answer any questions you may have."

When I returned to the Great Hall Countess Joan was waiting for me, "Will, I wish a word with you."

Until Prince Edward had died I had had little to do with Richard's mother. Since the funeral she had often spoken to me and even smiled when she did so. The scowls I had received in Bordeaux were a distant memory.

"Of course, my lady."

She waved to a servant who hovered nearby. He brought a jug of wine and two goblets. When he had poured the wine, he left. She raised her goblet, "My husband, the Black Prince and the next King of England, Richard."

"The Black Prince and the next King of England, Richard." I drank. It was good wine. You learned such things when you served in Gascony. I waited. She had not summoned me without a reason. She would tell me in her own time.

"My husband thought as much of you as any of his knights, you know."

"He elevated me and I am forever grateful."

"Had he lived then I believe you may have been knighted. Certainly, he felt he owed you much when you saved our son. I just wanted you to know that I misjudged you when first you came. You were young, crude and I could not see a purpose for you."

The Countess could not help her nature. She was a noble and looked down upon all who were not. She did not mean to insult me and I just smiled. There was little else that I could do.

"My husband's brother and son are in Castile where he is trying to win himself a kingdom. We have a short time to ensure that my son, when he becomes king, will have the support of powerful men." She leaned forward, "There is movement afoot in the land. It is led by rabble rousers who say that the King should answer to ordinary men for his actions. It is against God's law and the law of the land. We need to have lords who will crush such opposition. Richard will attain the throne when he is young. I will not have John of Gaunt as a regent."

This was politics and I did not understand it. I was a loyal servant and I listened.

"Ranulf de Gerlac is Earl of Chester. He is a powerful man. He, Sir Simon de Burley and the Earl of Oxford, Thomas de Vere will be coming to our home for a secret meeting."

"My lady, why do you tell me this? I am just a bodyguard."

"Because the meeting will be secret." She spoke to me as though I was slow. I had heard her say secret. "It will not be here. It will be at Berkhamsted. The only guards will be you and your men. I need to know if you can protect Richard and his guests. Can you ensure that none will disturb the meeting?"

"To answer honestly, no." She looked disappointed. "If you wish to know will I be able to make it hard for any to spy upon proceedings then aye, I can do that. May I ask you something, my lady?"

She stiffened, "Within reason."

"Do you trust these men?"

"Of course. What a stupid question!"

"Not so stupid my lady for if we are guarding the building then we cannot be guarding the Prince. There has been one attempt on his life. I barely thwarted it. I say again, are you positive that you can trust these men? Your son's life will depend upon your answer."

For the first time she hesitated and then she said, "I see what you mean. How can we ensure that there will be no treachery?"

"I must be in the room for the meeting."

"They will not like that."

"To be brutally honest, my lady, I care not. You have asked me if I can protect the Prince and I can but there are certain conditions which must be met."

"I do not like demands!"

"When Prince Edward was alive he made it quite clear that I was to protect the Prince against all enemies. I am a suspicious man. Unless I am present then I cannot guarantee the prince's safety and I will not allow him to be in danger. When he is King then he can command me to be absent. Until then I will watch him."

Her face was white with anger. "I could have you dismissed."

"You could not for all the world knows that I am his bodyguard. If I was dismissed then people might suspect your motives. It would also put your son in even greater danger. The man who tried to kill your son also tried to kill your husband in Spain. I am the one person that you can trust."

She swallowed off her wine, "I do not like this!"

"Nor do I but events have forced us into this position. You and I must work together to help the Prince become King."

"Very well. You can attend the meeting. Can your men be trusted to guard us without you there?"

"Of course. I would not have chosen them otherwise."

Chapter 16

The King was so ill that it was now simply a matter of time before he died. John of Gaunt had, effectively, seized control of the treasury. The last parliament had granted enough coin for him to be secure. He and those who supported him were tightening their grip on the crown. It was under a veil of secrecy that we left for Berkhamstead. Peter attended as the only servant. There was a garrison and servants at Berkhamstead and the Countess and I were confident of their loyalty and discretion. My fear was that we did not have enough men to defend the walls if someone tried to assassinate Richard a second time.

We rode cloaked but beneath our cloaks, we were mailed and armed. Although every man was dressed the same each was armed with their own weapons. Only a few of my men had taken swords from the armoury. Roger of Chester was one such for his weapon was a poor one. The Black Prince's blade hung from my baldric. I had yet to use it in anger. I hoped that this would not be the first occasion. I had Dick and David Tallboy ride ahead of us as a vanguard while Harold Four Fingers and Edgar of Derby were the rear guard. The Countess and the two ladies who accompanied us could both ride and they were cloaked as well. That would make our journey quicker. I hoped we could sneak out of London unseen. The hardest part was getting out of the castle itself. We left after the setting of the watch. That meant that all citizens were expected to be within the city walls. We risked being seen but I could not divine another way to leave London. We galloped through the Newgate and headed north west. People saw us but we did not hear the sound of hooves. We would outrun any message sent by foot.

We reached Berkhamstead by dawn. The Countess had sent a messenger to warn them of our imminent arrival and we were whisked within the gates before anyone could see us. I had chosen Edgar of Derby for the rear guard as he was a clever man who knew how to use his head. While the Prince, his mother and their servants cleaned up after the ride, we unsaddled the horses.

"Captain?"

"Aye, Edgar. Something troubles you?"

"Just an itch that I can't scratch. I think we were seen when we left London. There was a shadow north of the city walls and it moved. I went to investigate but all I found was a pile of horse shit and it was fresh. I didn't hear horses so if someone did follow us, he is good and that worries me."

I nodded, "I am pleased you have such good senses. I thought we had been lucky. Be on your guard. While we are here we keep to the same three shifts. The garrison is loyal but they are just that, a garrison. We have all fought in the Free Companies and we know the difference. Until we leave I must not leave the Prince's side. Dick commands until then. I have complete faith in him and in you but this will not be an easy posting for any of us!"

I did not worry the Countess nor Richard with what I had learned. The visitors were due the next day. That gave me the opportunity to get some rest. When Richard slept so did I. When I woke Richard was still asleep and so I checked on the sentries. Martin son of Martin was on duty at the gate. "Any danger?"

"Quiet as the grave, Captain. We saw people coming from the village to trade but the steward met them at the gate. They have no idea that the Prince is here."

"Let's hope we can keep it that way then."

That evening I ate with the Countess and Richard. If the Countess had had her way then they would have dined alone but Richard had come to depend upon me. I learned about the three nobles who would be joining us. They were all friends of the Black Prince although I had not seen them in either Spain or Gascony. All had served at Poitiers. That was the battle which had made the name of Edward the Black Prince. Those who had served with him became close to him. That counted in their favour.

Dick sent Wilfred Loidis to me with the news that six riders were approaching, "The sergeant said to tell you that they were cloaked and hooded. No sign of a crest."

I nodded. That could either be sensible or suspicious. "I will be with you soon." I turned to the Countess and Richard. "If you would stay here I will ensure that they are who they say they are."

As I passed the guard house I summoned the rest of my men. Some had only come off duty a couple of hours since but if this was not the expected guests then I would need them. Edgar's words had itched at the back of my neck all night. I reached the gatehouse and joined Dick. Four men stood by the gate and were ready to unbar it. Dick was chewing on a piece of dried venison. He had been on duty most of the night and was easing the hunger pangs. "There are only six of them, Will."

I nodded, "They look like the ones we expect but we will be careful eh?" The six reined in.

One shouted, "Let us in, we are expected."

"Let me see your faces, my lord. You do not need to give me your names but I need to see your faces."

They threw back their hoods. Two were as I had expected. They were older men. I vaguely recognised Sir Simon but the third looked to be a boy. He was little older than fourteen or so. He did not even have the semblance of a beard. I shouted down, "Admit them." Turning to Dick I said, "You and your men can rest. We will keep the gate barred. If this meeting goes well then we can leave in the night."

"Aye, I confess that I am ready for some food and a sleep. I thought we were expecting three older knights. Did they bring four squires?"

"I will soon find out."

By the time I reached the ward they had dismounted and three squires were tending the horses. "Show the squires to the stables and then have them fed." I gave a slight bow, "I am Will Strongstaff, Captain of the Prince's Guards."

The eldest of the three nodded, "Then take us to your master. You have kept us waiting long enough."

These men were used to power and to command. Would Richard turn into them once he became King?

I led them to the hall. The Countess beamed when she saw them. Then she frowned. "Where is the Earl of Oxford?"

The boy answered, "My father is dead, my lady. I am Robert de Vere. I am the new Earl of Oxford."

Prince Richard's face lit up and I understood why. He had rarely had someone of his own age around him. His cousin Henry Bolingbroke had been the last and now that he was a potential rival, along with his father, John of Gaunt, for the crown then he had no one of an age to speak to. Robert de Vere filled that gap. As they sat around the table I could not but help notice that Robert de Vere was the most confident young man I had ever seen. He was assured. He was not afraid to speak up before those who were older. I could see that Prince Richard was impressed by him.

I stood behind the Prince's chair and I listened. Despite his youth, the influence of the Earl of Oxford meant that he commanded many knights as did the Earl of Chester. The three men could exert much power. It became obvious that this conspiracy had been some time in the planning. Robert de Vere's father had died suddenly, three weeks earlier. Our isolation in the Tower had kept the news from reaching us. At the back of my mind was the thought that the young Earl had deliberately kept that news from us. The knowledge which Robert de Vere demonstrated had shown that his father must have shared his plans with his son.

The talk stopped at noon when food was brought in. As there were servants present then all talk of the plans to seize power ceased. Prince Richard and Robert de Vere sat and drank together. They spoke as though the rest of us did not exist. I confess that I felt slightly disappointed. Normally Richard, at such times, would have sought my opinion and my advice. He seemed not to need me. A voice in my head, it sounded like Peter the Priest's, laughed and told me that I was just a hired sword. I might be a gentleman now but a King would be more likely to confide in an Earl.

The plans were set by late afternoon and the Earl of Chester and Sir Simon took their leave. To me, they were good plans and well thought out. They planned to secure the crown before John of Gaunt could move. They had the support of the Archbishop of Canterbury. This was a powerful conspiracy and had been some time in the planning. Could this have been planned before Prince Edward had died? The cynical side of me wondered if they had hired Godfrey of Hastings to kill Prince Edward in Spain. A raw young Prince would be easier to manipulate than the Black Prince!

We would not see them again until the time came for them to help Prince Richard seize power. The Earl of Oxford said, "With your permission, my lady, I will travel back to London with you. Sir Simon and the Earl of Chester are heading north to gather more support amongst our allies. As we were requested I only brought my squire. The Prince's Guards will ensure that I am safe."

It seemed reasonable although for some reason I felt disquiet. Prince Richard was delighted, "Splendid. Do not worry Earl, I have the best of warriors around me."

The young Earl gave me a disdainful look, "I would have thought that a King of the realm would have knights around him. I would be one such knight, sire."

It was flattery for Richard was not yet King and therefore not entitled to the address but I could see that the Prince liked the idea. "What is wrong with having both? My father liked Will and he has saved my life already."

Robert de Vere looked at me as though for the first time. "Really? And yet he looks so young."

It was on the tip of my tongue to say something then I remembered that I was just a hired sword. I had grown used to the familiarity of speech with the Prince. I saw now that our relationship would have to change.

Prince Richard said, "Will has been a warrior longer than I have been alive. Do not worry, Earl, if enemies try to harm me they have to get through Will and his guards. They are all chosen men!"

The Countess seemed happy with the Earl and they dined together. I was not invited. I stood behind the Prince's chair and, to my dismay, the plans I had made were changed. "Will, we will not ride back like thieves in the night. We will leave on the morrow. I do not think there will be danger."

"Nor do I, Master Richard, but why change the plans? If we travel at night then we know we can return to London undetected."

"You let your bodyguard speak to you like this sire?"

Richard coloured, "Will, you overstep your mark. I have made my decision! Go and tell the men that we travel in the morning."

"As you wish." I turned to leave.

"And as we are safe this night I will not need you in my bedchamber. You may sleep in the guardhouse." He smiled, "It will be more comfortable to have a bed eh, Will?"

His smile was the old Richard and I nodded, "You are too kind, Master Richard."

Dick and the others were surprised when I joined them. After we had set the watch Dick and I spoke together. "Will, this was to be expected. You have been close to the Prince, I can see that but when he is King… remember in Gascony? The King kept knights around him. Tom and the other captains were only summoned when they were needed. Why even Sir Hugh was kept at a distance. We are there to serve a purpose."

"Perhaps but I swore an oath to his father."

"And his father is dead. I like this position but me and the lads know that once Richard becomes King then we become irrelevant. He will probably dismiss us and that is fine for we will all have made coin from it."

I was surprised, "Then why did you join me?"

"Sentiment, Will. You and I are the last of the Blue Company who still wield weapons. I have no son, at least none I know about, and you are the nearest to a son that I will have. The others thought the same. That was why we all took an oath to watch over you when your mother left. When the Prince took you to watch his son it did not change things."

I had not known that. In the same way that I was bound to Prince Richard so the others were bound to me. That night I did not sleep well as I wrestled with my conscience and the dilemma which I faced.

We left early the next morning. Prince Richard looked as happy as I had ever seen him. He and the Earl rode together their heads closeted like a pair of doves. I had not forgotten my duties and we had the same formation. The difference was that I rode ahead of Richard and the Earl. The fact that I was not speaking with Richard helped me to concentrate. The road south was Roman made. That meant it was straight and it had a good surface. It was more than a thousand years since the road had been built and there had been changes. Villages and towns had sprung up along the road. Trees had sprouted. Each of them represented danger of some description. Dick and David examined each copse, village and hamlet before waving us forward.

The Earl of Oxford tired of this, "It will take us forever to reach London at this rate."

I turned and looked at him, "With respect, my lord, I am responsible for the Prince's safety and we will do it this way."

I could see that he was used to getting his own way and he turned to Richard, "I think your mercenary is getting above himself. Order him to speed up, sire."

It was the wrong thing to say because Prince Richard did not like to be ordered around. "Will knows his business and there is no hurry, my lord. We are having a pleasant conversation are we not?"

The Earl smiled, "Of course. I was thinking of the ladies enduring the sun."

A mile closer to London and our caution was justified. There were three huts ahead of us and a water trough. Our two scouts were more than a hundred paces from us and I slowed. I watched as Dick and David examined the huts. They waved us forward and then dismounted to water their horses. As I kicked Star forward David suddenly pitched into the water trough, an arrow in his back. There was no metal there to stop the arrow from penetrating. Even as Dick drew his sword an arrow struck his arm.

Edgar, at the rear, shouted, "Ambush!"

I turned and saw men behind galloping down the road towards us. At a glance, I estimated there to be ten or more. "Master Richard, you and the Earl guard the women. Martin and Harold go and help Edgar. The rest, with me."

I drew my sword and galloped towards Dick. He had his long sword out and was hacking through the neck of a horse whose rider had tried to spear him. David, although wounded, rose to his feet and drew his sword. As he did so a second rider speared Dick in the back. His mail stopped the head penetrating too deeply. His attacker was slain by David. I saw that there were five more men still to be despatched. "Roger of Chester go and help Edgar. We will deal with these."

Even as we raced to them Dick was hacking through the neck of the killer whose horse he had slain. David Tallboy lunged at the horse of one of the others. The horse fell but an arrow from the woods hit him. John son of James went to the aid of David and his sword sliced into the side of the killer. A second spear was thrust into Dick's side. He turned and flailed his sword at the spearman. He succeeded in hitting the rider's horse and as it veered I reached Dick and my sword took the rider's head. That was enough for the others and they fled. I shouted to the others. "Go to the aid of Edgar!"

I could hear the clash of steel at the rear. I was relieved to see that the Prince and the Earl were safe from attack. Dick and David lay in pools of blood but they had not died in vain. They had died hard and the ambush had failed. My vanguard and rear guard had served their purpose. I dismounted and went to David. His eyes were open and he was dead. I closed his eyes, "Go to God with honour intact. You kept your oath."

I turned and ran to Dick. He was in a pool of blood yet he still clung to life. He gave a rueful smile and said, "I am sorry Will, I am getting old. I should have seen those horsemen and the archers." He shook his head and a tendril of blood oozed from his mouth, "Red Ralph would have had me for missing the fresh horse dung."

"We will get you healed."

He gave a choking laugh, "Do not lie to a dying man. It is not our way. I have no other so give my war gear and money to the lads. They are good men. Roger of Chester should have my sword. He is a good man and his is a poor weapon. I am owed pay. Use it for my stone. I would like to be buried in a churchyard with a headstone."

"It will be done."

"If you see the others…" and then he was gone. Another of the Blue Company had died.

I cradled his head in my hands as I waited for the others to join me. When they did so I saw that Martin, son of Martin had been killed and his body was slung over his horse's saddle. I stood and said coldly to the Earl of Oxford, "And these men died so that we could get to London safely. These men died because my plans to ride at night were changed! Now do you see why I was cautious?"

He stared back at me, "I do not like your tone! I am the Earl of Oxford."

"And I care not for I am Will Strongstaff of the Blue Company and if you do not like it, my lord, then get off your horse and we will exchange blows. That way I will teach you a lesson which might make a man of you."

"Will!"

"Master Richard, three men who served you loyally have died today. A fourth whom I do not know would not bother me." I glared at all of them for none were worth the men I had lost.

I lifted Dick's body on to his horse and handed his sword to Roger. "Dick left this for you." He took it, nodded and kissed the hilt much as Captain Tom had done before a battle. "Fetch David's body and we will take them back to London. We will bury these brave men." I glared at the Earl of Oxford. "They are worth far more than some jumped up little lord who does not know his arse from his elbow!" I saw the servant Peter and my men smile. I knew I had made an enemy of Robert de Vere but I cared not.

The journey back for the last fourteen miles was in silence. Robert de Vere brooded about my lack of respect. Prince Richard was upset to have lost three men and I was thinking of the ambush. Edgar's instincts had been correct. We had been followed and there were men waiting for us. The killers all had coins in their purses. These bore the image of King Edward. That told us nothing save that men were desperate for Prince Richard to be killed. I did not wish King Edward dead but as he was ill then the land was ruled by John of Gaunt and that was not good.

Prince Richard invited the Earl of Oxford to stay with him at the Tower. For some reason that annoyed me. Once the Prince and his guest were safe and secure in the keep we took our three comrades to All Hallows church. For a handful of silver coins, the priest was happy to bury them. His words were meaningless for he did not know them but they were placed in the ground and it was done properly. When the priest had gone, no doubt to spend the coins we had given him, we gathered around the graves.

"We are come to mourn three oathsworn warriors. They did their duty and died doing so. Even though they died without being shrived I have no doubt that they will be in heaven for they died defending the next King of England." Even as I said the words I doubted them. An anointed King was one thing but Richard was just the heir. If I did not believe that they would be in heaven then what was the point of our defence of the Prince? The three would have died for nothing. "They are buried with their arms and their mail; they wear the Prince's livery for that is what they were, warriors. I swear that I will have a stone erected for each of them and I will pay for it from my own purse. Rest in peace, Dick Long Sword of the Blue Company, David Tallboy and Martin son of Martin. We will remember you."

Once back in the barracks I shared out the coins and war gear of the three men. Only Dick had asked me to do so but I knew the other two would have wished it had they had the opportunity to speak with me. I bought a jug of wine and we drank that. I was not hungry. I left them to return to the Tower and my appointed duty.

When I reached the Great Hall Richard and the Earl of Oxford were laughing and giggling. They seemed both embarrassed and annoyed at my intrusion. Prince Richard said, "It has been a hard day, Will. I will not need you in my room this night. The Earl's squire can sleep behind the door. Tomorrow you can return to your duties."

I was not happy but I obeyed. I would be keeping my oath for an enemy had to pass by the barracks to reach the Tower. The Prince would be safe.

As events turned out I had been chamberlain for the last time. King Edward had a stroke and died during the night. Prince Richard became King Richard the Second of England and my life changed once more.

Chapter 17

Events moved very quickly. I did not like the Earl of Oxford but he was quick thinking. Along with the Countess, they summoned the Archbishop to the Tower as well as the Earl of Arundel and the other lords who supported King Richard's cause. The Chancellor attended so that all was done properly and, while safe in the castle, he was proclaimed King. The Countess took charge and the Chancellor and Archbishop, Simon Sudbury, were instructed by her. All had been decided at the secret Berkhamstead meeting. As the King was just ten years old a council of nobles and churchmen was convened to advise him and to take charge of the finances of the country. In one fell swoop John of Gaunt and his son were marginalised. The King had died too soon for them and Richard had not been killed. I had no doubt that the men had been hired either by John of Gaunt or one of his supporters. They were playing for high stakes. They were playing for a throne.

I had listened to enough conversations to know that John of Gaunt was unpopular. King Richard was popular but that was due mainly to his father. His father had died with his memory and reputation intact. He was the hero of Poitiers. What neither faction could predict was the way the people would react. The Black Death had decimated the land. Ironically it had empowered those with skills for they were in great demand. A ploughman now earned four times what he had earned before the plague had wreaked havoc. When they had been dependent upon their lords and masters they had no power. Now they knew that they could, if they chose, hold the country to ransom. I knew this, even if the lords and nobles did not. I heard the conversations when I drank in the inns. I drank cloaked so that no one knew I was from the Tower. I became uneasy. However, I had little opportunity to speak with King Richard. He had been proclaimed and so he had the title. I could rarely get close to him. Robert de Vere was constantly at his side. They were inseparable. The Countess seemed happy with this state of affairs. As he rarely left the Tower then he was safe. I had served my purpose.

I found myself spending more time with the Guards than with King Richard. I was only needed when he left the castle and he would not leave again until he went to his coronation. In many ways, I was happy about that for he was safe from killers my unease was because it allowed him to fall under the sway of the charismatic Robert de Vere.

For the coronation my men and I were called upon to ensure his safety. The crowds who gathered on the route to the cathedral all cheered but who knew if there was an assassin hidden amongst them. In the event all went off well. Once again Robert de Vere was instrumental in the ceremony. Since he had inherited his father's title he had gained power and influence and yet he was younger than I was.

One King Richard was crowned I was relegated to the back of all the rooms where he held his meetings. There were many of them. Over the next year, the council of the Archbishop, the Earl of Oxford and Sir Simon tightened their grip on the land. For three successive years, an exorbitant poll tax raked in great quantities of coin. All of them were spent on military ventures to regain lost land in France. They failed and their failure fuelled the growing animosity towards King Richard and his council.

I saw a personal change in King Richard. Since Robert de Vere had entered our world King Richard began to drift towards what would be termed an absolutist viewpoint. He was King and as King of England, he could not be wrong. The people were there to serve him and it was God's will that this happened. He was young when de Vere got his claws into him and it was de Vere who moulded him. Had his father been King of England then I believe events would have turned out differently. It suited the Countess for she had always feared the mob.

There was another change. A year after the coronation we rode to Windsor from the Tower. There was no cheering as we passed. There were sullen looks. I could see that it upset King Richard. He could not understand why they did not like him. De Vere was not with us that day and so I rode, once again, at the King's side. "What is wrong with the people, Will? Why do they not cheer as we pass?"

"It is the poll taxes, sire. What little money they have goes to your tax collectors."

"But we need that money to pay for the wars in France! Do they not wish for us to have the glory and the land?"

As luck would have it we were passing some beggars. I recognised them as old soldiers. I pointed at two, one had one leg and the other had been blinded in one eye and had a missing hand. "That is the glory for the people, sire. They see men coming back from the wars maimed. The ones who benefit are the lords with estates in France. They would rather they paid less taxes and then they could eat better."

I saw his face crease with puzzlement. In those days he had not been completely seduced by de Vere. He was still able to think for himself. "Then perhaps we should think hard about the taxes. Is there not another way?"

"I am a simple soldier, sire. Whilst it is true that we need employment for our warriors we have battles to fight closer to home. The Welsh and the Scots raid the marches. The ones who live there suffer great privations."

I knew that I had posed questions he had not thought of. For the next month or so the old Richard returned. It coincided with a period when Robert de Vere was busy with his estates. King Richard used some of his own funds to provide food for the poor. During that time the ordinary people of London became his supporters. All of that changed when Robert de Vere returned from his estates. He was now a powerful man. He had used his position as friend of the King to gain estates from those who were considered traitors. The rule of law was ignored for Robert de Vere was part of the King's council. The Archbishop of Canterbury, the head of the English church, was on the council. No one could speak up. I saw all of this from the inside but I was powerless to intervene. I was a hired sword.

During the months and years which followed his coronation as King Richard changed from a boy to a man, and the situation reverted to one where King Richard had no idea what the people thought. I confess that I thought of resigning. I was stopped by the memory of an oath I swore to Prince Edward. The memory of Dick and the other's deaths made me stay. However, the matter was taken out of my hands. At de Vere's prompting the King had punished, by whipping, some apprentices who came to beg for relief from the taxes which they had to pay. All that the King needed to have done was to listen to them. I made the mistake of asking the King why he had punished them. De Vere flew into a rage. He seemed to dominate the King in quite an unnatural way.

"This is intolerable, sire. You are questioned by someone who is little better than a hired thug! You are the King. Your decisions are inviable. You are not to be questioned by any. Dismiss the man! He is a thorn in your side and we need him not!"

I heard 'the we' and wondered at that.

King Richard said, "But Will has been at my side since my father was alive. He has saved my life on more than one occasion."

"But not lately! Send him back to his farm! Let him cool his heels for six months. Perhaps that will teach him manners, although I doubt it!"

All I wanted to do was to punch this arrogant noble but if I had done that then all of my bridges would have been burned.

King Richard smiled, "That might be the best. You have never even seen your farm, Will. That is an excellent suggestion, Sir Robert. Will, you are tired and have worked hard. Enjoy some time off. Make it so!"

I saw the smirk on the face of Robert de Vere. He had manipulated both me and the King to get his way. With me out of the picture, he could gain more power and become a de facto ruler of England. He was a very clever and dangerous man.

Roger of Chester was now sergeant at arms. He and the others were angry at the King's treatment of me but were angrier about de Vere. None liked him. Harold Four Fingers murmured, "I could slip a knife in his throat one night, captain. He would slip into the river and no one would ever hear of him."

I shook my head. "It is but six months. I am still your captain. You must protect the King despite himself."

I was now a rich man. I had spent little of the money I had earned over the years. I still had almost all the gold I had taken from my enemies and the assassins sent to kill the King. I bought a sumpter to carry my baggage and I headed north for Stony Stratford. Perhaps it would be good for me. It might not be good for England but I had fulfilled my oath.

It was true that I had never visited there but I had knowledge of the farm. There was a tenant there. The lord of the manor had been happy to find him for me and he sent my share of the profits regularly. I would visit with him and then, if all was well, I would travel to visit with Red Ralph and Peter the Priest. I knew roughly where they had gone to live. York and Middleham were close to each other. I would have gone to visit my mother but I was not sure that Sir Alan would make me welcome.

I was twenty-six years old and this was the first time that I had not had to work. I wondered about finding a wife. If the King no longer needed me then that might be an option. I had had whores, a man had needs, but so long as I was the King's bodyguard I could not marry. Was this a sign from God?

I enjoyed a leisurely journey north. I had no need to rush and I stayed in inns where I was made welcome for I had coin to spend. It was informative because I learned that the further north I went the less the people resented the King. It was London where the antipathy was the strongest. The city had always been self-serving. Its populace looked to profit from its position as capital of England.

The lord of the manor was now Sir Robert Armstead. He was not at home for he had gone to Rome. His wife had died and he made a pilgrimage for her soul. I rode to the manor and spoke to the reeve. I wore my livery beneath my cloak. I knew that it would afford me a little more respect. He told me the name of the farmer. He added that I might not wish to go as there had been pestilence in Stony Stratford. He had not visited for some time. There was a time when I might have been worried by such things but the last few years had made me more philosophical about such things. Forewarned I rode to the village and the farm I had never seen.

The reeve was organised and whilst he would not go with me he was quite happy to give me detailed directions. He told me that there was no church in the village. Stratford had the closest one and that there were just six farms around Stoney Stratford. I soon found the farm. As I reined in on the small rise above the farm I was able to view it and I was impressed. Prince Edward had given me a fine gift. It had a good position above the Great Ouse River. There were three sheep in the field and two milk cows but they were the only signs of life. Worryingly there was no smoke rising from the farmhouse. I nudged Star. The reeve had said there had been pestilence. Had it struck this village and this farm? On my ride north, I had passed whole villages where everyone had died in the last plague outbreak. Soon many farms and villages would be taken over again by nature.

I reined in at the yard. The water trough was full and I sniffed it. It smelled clean. I let the sumpter drink first and when it did not seem distressed allowed Star to drink. I threw my cloak over Star's back and headed towards the seemingly deserted farmhouse. It was as though it had been abandoned but the reeve had visited the farm three months earlier to collect the taxes and the farmer, Walter of Stratford had seemed to be doing well. He was prospering. What could have happened? I walked to the farmhouse and pushed the door open. I could smell death. The house was well built and I saw an internal wall. There was an entrance to a room on the left. I peered in. It was a room with a fire. There was a table and three chairs. I walked to the fire. The ashes were stone cold. I walked ahead and found where they cooked their food. There was another open fire and a cauldron hung on a tripod. There was green scum on the liquid in the cauldron and the fire was cold.

That left one room. It would be the sleeping chamber. I dreaded going there. I had never met this farmer who had earned me coin and made a success of the farm. I did not wish to meet him when he was dead. I pushed open the door. There was a bed and two bodies were laid out upon it. They were dead. Someone had folded their arms, crossed their feet and closed their eyes. Why had they not been buried? I was about to leave when I spied a pair of feet sticking from the end of the bed. I went over and saw a third body. This was a young woman. I would have put her age at less than twenty summers but it was hard to tell. She had laid out the man and the woman and then died herself. Perhaps I had been sent here to bury the three of them. I leaned over to pick her up and, as I did so, I felt her move. She was alive. I grabbed her and took her outside. I laid her close to the water trough.

The horses had been drinking the water from the trough and so I took a pail and ran to the river. I was no healer but I knew that water was needed. I ran back, slopping the water as I did so. I took a cloth from my saddlebag and washed her face. I know not why I did that but when I had done it I saw faint traces of colour come back to her cheeks. Taking my own beaker, I filled it with water and held it to her mouth. More dripped down her cheek than went into her mouth but I emptied two into it. She needed a healer.

I took my baggage from my sumpter and draped the body of the young woman across it. I knew the church at Stratford was just a mile or two west of me and I rode hard. It was late afternoon when I arrived at the church. The door was open and I picked the young woman from the horse and carried her into the church. The only light was from the door. There were no candles lit. I spied a shape at the altar.

"Father, I need your help. I have a young woman here. She is, I think, close to death."

The priest stood and stared at me. "Who are you?"

"Not that it should matter but I am Will Strongstaff, gentleman. I found this woman at the farm of my tenant, Walter of Stratford. He and his wife are dead."

He ran towards me. "Then this is Eleanor his daughter, poor child. Take her outside the light is better and I will bring my medicine although this pestilence has taken many already."

I picked her up and laid her outside to the west of the church where the last rays of the sun would warm her. I stood while the priest examined her. "She has not the pestilence. I think she just needs food and the care of someone to watch over her." He looked around. "I am a priest and she is a young woman. I cannot have her here."

"She needs care."

"Then you must give it to her. The medicine I have given here will help her to recover but you need to feed her."

"Me!"

"It is your farm is it not? You have a responsibility!" The priest was young and not afraid of the hulking great warrior who stood before him.

I was about to argue and then remembered de Vere. Was I demonstrating the same attitude as that arrogant young noble? "Very well but I am a warrior and not a healer you will need to tell me what to do."

He smiled, "Kindness is all that it will take, Will Strongstaff."

The priest, I learned he was Father Abelard, led my sumpter. It did not look right to have the girl draped over the horse's back but there was no other way to move her. As we walked he told me what I needed to do. You must burn her parents' bodies and the bedding."

"What about the bed?"

He shrugged, "In an ideal world you should burn that too but I have not heard of the pestilence being carried by wood. Perhaps vinegar might be used to wash it down. I will speak over their bodies first. They were good people. So many good people have been taken by this disease. It is a curse from God. The world is out of balance. The lords take too much tax and it must change."

This was one of the rabble-rousing rebels I had heard about. What was unusual was that he was so far from London. "Have you been a priest here for long, father?"

He shook his head, "I came here two years since. My bishop sent me when the plague took the other priest."

A few years ago, I would not have thought twice about the priest's comments but now I could draw the threads together and make a picture. I had lived at court and knew the way that powerful men worked. The priest had been a rebel and in London would have found like minded souls. By sending him to this plague-ridden backwater the Bishop was ensuring that he could do no further harm.

It did not take us long to reach the farm but darkness was falling. We carried the girl, Eleanor, into the room with the table and chairs. I used my cloak to make a bed for her on the table. Then I carried her parents outside. I had to have a cloth for my mouth. The smell was as bad as anything I could remember. While the priest said what he had to say I went for the bedding and the feather packed mattress. Father Abelard had not finished and so I gathered wood and kindling. I laid the bedding and mattress on the wood and, when the priest had finished, the two bodies. As I lit the wood the priest made the sign of the cross. I waited until the flames had caught before I returned indoors. I found some vinegar but the light was becoming bad. I had to light a tallow candle to allow me to begin to clean the wood. Father Abelard helped me.

"She can sleep on the table but you must watch her. She will wake. She will be weak. When she wakes feed her. She needs a little food each time but often." He handed me a small vial. "She needs to sleep as much as she can. A drop or two of this in milk will help her to sleep.

The cow will need milking. You have much to do, Will Strongstaff. I will visit again when time allows."

"What about food?"

"Broths and soups. There looks to be plenty of greens in the vegetable garden. I am guessing that Maud would have had a ham somewhere. They slaughtered a pig last year. You will discover them. I can see you were a warrior. Now you will learn to be a farmer and a healer!"

He left and I took the candle to see to the horses. There was no stable but there was a barn. There was hay and there was a water trough. I watered them and tethered them. I had much to do before I could sleep. I searched the house and found a chest with more bedding. I found clothes for the girl. I should have taken her clothing and burned it but I could not strip a young girl. It was not seemly. I would have the clothes ready for when she woke. I laid the blanket upon her and then went to light the fires. I used a brand from the funeral pyre which burned well. The smell of burning bodies did not worry me. I had endured worse after battles.

Once the fire was going I filled the cauldron with water and then sought greens and food for a broth. The priest was right. A ham hung in a larder just outside the kitchen. It was well made so that rodents and carrion could not gain access. I sliced off a piece of meat to eat. That way I could ensure that it was not tainted. It was not. I sliced some more and put it in the water. Then I hung the ham in the room where the girl lay. It was what they did in Spain with their hams. The smoke would keep the flies from the ham and the smoke would add flavour. I went to the vegetable garden. There was enough light for me to see well enough to pick greens, roots and wild onions. I washed them in the water trough and then put them in the cauldron. I found some dried beans and put them in too. I smiled. My father had prepared me for this. As a forager, I knew how to make the best of a little. I would leave the root vegetables whole. I would keep adding water and they would continue to add body to the liquor. That done I searched the cooking room until I found the jug of fermented apple juice. I knew that the farmer would have had something. I used my own beaker and went back to the room where the girl slept. I had much to think on.

I was tired but I was used to standing a watch. I fed the fire and listened to the girl breathing. The priest had added some of his potion to the last water she had drunk and she would sleep. I had to consider what to do with her. She was an orphan but the priest had told me that Eleanor had seen seventeen summers. She could find a man. She was pretty enough and if the disease had not harmed her then she could bear children. I had a responsibility; that was what Father Abelard had said. If so then this was the first time in my life for such a thing to happen. Until now I had been bound by oaths. Prince Edward had made me a gentleman and given me a farm. The priest was right and perhaps that was why the people were unhappy. The nobles took all and when times were hard gave nothing in return. It seemed to me that the greater the lord the less he cared. I took the chest with my coins in it and I buried it just outside the kitchen door. When we had campaigned in France and Spain the men of the company had done this with their money. I suspected that some of the coins still remained where they were buried. Men died.

I must have fallen asleep for when I woke the fire was dying and I was stiff from the chair. The girl still slept. I fed the fire and returned to the pot of potage. I added more water and the last of the apple juice from my beaker. I tasted the soup. It needed salt. I found the precious salt and added a little. I needed to make water and went outside. Dawn was about to break. When I had been a warrior in France then that had been a time of danger. Here it was a sign of hope for a new day.

I heard the cows lowing. They would be in pain and distressed. They would need milking. Rabbits would have come to suck on their teats but that would have merely alleviated the pain for a short time. I stepped outside and saw the remains of the fire. There were still a few burning timbers but the remains had been incinerated. I found the milking pail and went to the cows. I had learned to milk when I had been but five. Then I had sneaked into farms and fields to steal the milk which was often the only food I had. The cows were much relieved when I filled the pail and returned to the farm. They and the sheep would need to be moved to another field soon.

After making up the bed which had now dried and putting a cauldron of water on the fire to heat I ate some of the soup. It was good and then I heard a movement from the other room. I hurried in. The girl was just awaking. She opened her eyes and looked at the roof. She knew the room and then she felt my cloak. It was unfamiliar. Her eyes widened and she glanced down. She saw me and pulled the cloak tighter about her, "Who are you?" she croaked.

I smiled, "I am Will Strongstaff and this is my farm."

She nodded, "My father told me that you would come one day he..." she started and her eyes widened, "my parents?"

I walked to her and took her hand, "Are both with God. Father Abelard did all that was necessary. We burned their bodies."

She nodded. "Master, you should go. I will die soon!"

"No, you will not. Father Abelard says that you will recover but you are weak. Lie still and I will fetch you some soup. And my name is Will. I am not your master. This is your home until you choose to go somewhere else. If that is your choice."

As I left I wondered why I had said that. I had felt a stirring in my body when I had held her hand. This was not the same stirring as I had felt when I had visited whores and doxies. I was confused. I busied myself with the soup. I ladled liquid only into a wooden bowl. It was handmade. Perhaps the farmer had made it. I found a wooden spoon and took them back to her. She was sitting up.

I fed her and spoke at the same time. "I have cleaned the bed and put fresh bedding upon it. When you have eaten then go into the room and change your clothes. I will burn these."

"I need to bathe... Will."

I will heat some water. You are still weak."

She smiled, "I am stronger than you think. You are kind. Why?"

"Why am I kind? I am just doing that which any man would do for one in need of help."

She shook her head, "Not so, for I have seen little kindness outside of this farm." She had finished and I took the bowl and put it by the fire.

I held out my hand for her, "Come, let us get you changed. The water should be hot enough for you to bathe." Once again, as her fingers touched mine I felt my heart race. They gripped my hand when we entered the chamber where her parents had died. "If you wish me to move the bed then..."

She shook her head, "No, I must be strong. Before he died my father told me to go on and find a life."

I left her and went back to the other room. I filled a clay pot with the water. It was hot but not boiling and I put it in the room. "Shout when you are in the bed. I have some medicine to prepare. Father Abelard gave it to me."

The milk from the cows was still warm. I poured it into a beaker and dripped, as I had been instructed, just two drops of the medicine.

"I am ready." I entered the room and the discarded clothes lay by the bed. Eleanor looked tiny in the huge bed.

I handed her the beaker. "This is just milk with medicine to help you sleep. The priest said you needed rest and food. You have had food and now you rest."

"It is too soon to sleep. Tell me about yourself for I can see scars upon your face and hands. There is a tale here."

I told her all. Nothing was left out. The telling of the tale made me reflect upon my life so far. I had been lucky and, in many ways, so had the girl. Had de Vere not insisted upon my dismissal I would not have come to the farm and she would be dead.

"You are an important man then."

"I would not say that. A lucky man. Now I have done my part. Drink the milk and tell me a little about you."

She nodded and drank the milk down, "There is little to tell save that I will end my days as an old maid."

"That is foolish for you are as pretty a maid as I have ever seen."

"And you are kind but I am tainted."

"Tainted?"

"I was promised to be married. I thought that John son of William was a good man but he ran on the eve of our wedding. No other man would look at me after that for they thought there was something wrong with me."

"There are many men out there who would take you as their wife in a heartbeat. You have shown to me already that you have courage. Who else would stay and nurse dying parents knowing that they risked death themselves? You have me for six months. When you are ready to ride out into the world we will see if we cannot find a man for you."

She laughed and snuggled down into the bed, "You are a strange one, Will Strongstaff. I have never met a man quite like you." She closed her eyes and the smile stayed upon her face as she slept.

I found myself smiling too. I brought my bags from the stable and changed into clothes which would be better for working. I had much to do. I made myself a bed in the room with the fire. I moved the animals to a new field and put the two horses there. They could run and the grass was good. Star would become stronger. Then I took an axe and went to hew down more wood. By the time the sun showed me that it was noon I was sweating and hungry. I would need more food for we could not exist on just the ham. I had found no wheat. I wondered if there was a bread oven in Stoney Stratford or would I have to travel to Stratford. It was as I was cutting some more ham that I reflected that I had not even thought about King Richard and de Vere since I had arrived at the farm. Perhaps this was my future?

The girl woke and looked better already. She smiled at me. "I am starving."

"I will get you some more soup."

"And I will make water."

Our lives settled into a very comfortable pattern. She gradually recovered and I worked on the farm. We talked endlessly. I had given her the main points in my life but as I got to know her I revealed more about my mother and father. I told her of the King and the plots. I learned more about her. Her brothers had gone to war against the Welsh and both had been killed. That was when her father had farmed on the Welsh marches. He had come east for peace and had determined to make my farm a success.

"He hoped that he might make enough coin to buy the farm from you, Will." She shook her head. "We made a good start but then the plague came and took many of our neighbours. We could not sell our surplus and rats took much of it."

By the time Father Abelard returned to visit Eleanor was able to move around the farm. She was industrious and insisted upon helping me. When the priest confirmed that she was healed she said, "Then as this is your farm you shall have the bed and I will sleep in the other room on the floor."

I laughed, "You will not! I think I have spent less than a month of my life using a bed. The floor is fine."

The priest smiled, "I can see God's hand in all of this."

I frowned, "I do not understand."

He said, enigmatically, "That is because you are too close. If you stood where I did then you would understand."

He left us. I turned to look at Eleanor and saw in her eyes something I had only ever seen in my mother's affection for me. Over the next month we grew closer. That was partly because we both had to work hard to make the farm workable again. She showed me where the oats and barley were kept and we were able to make bread. It meant riding to Stratford to use the bread oven but we enjoyed the ride. The village of Stratford had recovered from the plague and I was able to use some of my hoard of coins to buy from them. It made me popular but I could see that Eleanor was not happy to be there. There were too many bad memories. It was where the man she was supposed to marry had lived.

We might have continued just bumbling along had not the storm come from nowhere. We had had a hot spell and the clouds had gathered in the west. The animals were jittery and so we brought them into the barn. The rain began as we hurried back towards the farmhouse. In the few steps it took us the rain began to bounce on the cobbles of the yard. It was as we entered the farmhouse that there was an enormous crack of thunder. It felt as though we had been struck by the bolt. Eleanor turned and threw her arms around me. I protectively held her. She was shaking. The thunder cracked and rolled. It made my ears hurt. She looked up at me and then, I know not why, I kissed her. I was not certain how she would react but she kissed me back and held me tightly. I have no idea when the thunder stopped but it did and we broke apart.

She smiled impishly at me, "It has taken you long enough to do that Will Strongstaff."

"You mean you wanted me to kiss you? Why did you say nothing?"

"Will, I have been hurt by a man before now. I needed to know that you wished this too." She took my hand and led me towards the bed. The rain still hammered on the ground outside. "Come let us seal this."

I stopped, "But your name..."

"Is besmirched already. The man who left me spread stories about me. They were not true but all believe them." She shrugged, "I might as well earn the reputation I enjoy!"

I shook my head, "No for we shall be wed."

She did not smile, "I hear a but in that proposal."

I held her close, "I am sworn to protect King Richard. I must return to London and ask to be released from the oath."

Her eyes saddened, "You would leave me like the other."

I shook my head, "No! Come with me if you will! I would not be parted from you."

"This is hasty. We will live here a while and I will let you think on this. I owe you all for you saved my life and without you, my life would be nothing. Whatever you decide then I will live with that."

The next month was strange. We carried on but instead of my sleeping on the floor I shared her bed. That was all we did, despite her urging, we cuddled and we slept but we did not couple. I could not disguise the fact that my body wished to take it further but I would make an honest woman of her.

She sat before me, a month to the day since we had kissed, "You are the most honourable man I have ever met, Will Strongstaff. I offer myself to you. You want me and yet your sense of honour prevents you from taking me. Best you return to London and ask the Prince if you can be released from your oath."

She was right. We rode, later that day to Stratford. We went first to Father Abelard and we told him what we had planned. He seemed pleased. "This is good Master Will. I will watch Eleanor and the farm until you return. Stony Stratford is part of my parish and the fact that yours is the only farm which remains means that I have let down those who died."

We then bought all that she would need. There was no market in Stratford but it was a prosperous village and they had a surplus. When I returned I would buy more animals for the farm. Once we returned I showed her where the chest of coins was buried. "This is yours. The road is dangerous and if aught happened to me then you would have coin."

She looked frightened, "You must return. If you do not then ..."

I kissed her, "I will return! I shall be back within ten days!"

I left her the next morning. I did not keep my word but that was not my fault. If anyone was at fault it was Wat Tyler, John Ball, Jack Straw and Robert de Vere!

Chapter 18

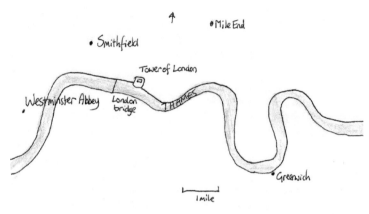

As I headed south I heard rumours of unrest and anger. I rode hard for the closer I came to London the more violent was the mood of the people. It appeared that Kent and Essex had risen and revolted against the taxes imposed by Robert de Vere and his council. It had begun on the estate of Sir Simon de Burley and some of his lands had been lost. This was not the work of the King I had left two months earlier. I now knew why the Earl of Oxford had wished me out of the way. I was a conscience Robert de Vere wished gone. The streets of London were threatening. I was armed and I had returned mailed. The closer to the tower I rode the more violent was the mood. At one point I was pelted with rotten fruit and vegetables. That was because I rode a horse and the poor did not ride! My cloak covered my livery else it might have been stones which were hurled. I saw two ships still tied to the wharf. When I reached the Lion Tower I was recognised and admitted.

"How long has this been going on Philip?"

The sergeant of the guard shook his head, "Too long Captain. It began three weeks since and has got worse each day. John of Gaunt's house has been burned down and there are gangs of peasants rampaging. They have demanded an end to serfdom. The King will be pleased to see you."

I wondered at that, "Is the Earl of Oxford here?"

The disdain showed on Philip's face, "No Captain. When the mood of the city became ugly he rode back to his manor. He said he was going to bring soldiers but he has yet to return. The Mayor of London is within. Those lords who remained in London had also taken shelter here."

I hurried through to the inner ward. I saw Edgar of Derby, "Take Star to the stable."

"Aye Captain, "You have returned just in time. The King was going to send Roger of Chester to summon you back. He fears for his crown!"

I could hear raised voices as I approached the Great Hall. Harold Four Fingers was on guard at the doors. He smiled, "The King will be glad to see you, Captain. He said no one was to be admitted. I think you are the exception."

I flung open the door and every face turned towards me. I recognised Sir Simon de Burley, William Walworth, the mayor of London and Michael de La Pole, the Chancellor but the other six men were nobles whom I did not know. The King's face broke into a smile, "Than God you have come! He has heard my prayers. Will, I need your counsel!"

Sir Simon said, "From a mercenary?"

The King had grown in the last few months. His face hardened, "Will has never let me down! Unlike others, he has always been at my side and I regret my decision to dismiss him. Have you heard the news?"

"I know that there is a rising in Kent and Essex, that is all."

"It is our worse nightmare, Will. Mobs are running riot and burning estates. They are slaughtering foreigners like the Flemish and even attacking churches. There are thousands of them. Many are old soldiers and they are armed. We have no army. Our best troops are in Gascony. The Earl of Oxford has gone for help. We need to hold on until he returns."

Just then the doors burst open and a bloody knight stood there, "Your majesty, the Archbishop of Canterbury and your Royal Chancellor, Robert Hales have been murdered by the mob at Greenwich. It is where they are gathered in great numbers. Six of their knights fell also. I brought the survivors, all eight of us here."

"They killed the Archbishop? They will burn in hell for that."

"They tried to negotiate with them but Wat Tyler drew a sword and struck the first blow. The roads are controlled by the rebels. I cannot see how aid can come to us."

The King looked at me, "Then what do we do, Will? You have the most experience of war. How do we defeat them?"

"We just have the garrison of the castle?"

"Less than two hundred men."

"Then we cannot defeat them by force of arms. We must talk."

"Talk?" Sir Simon almost spat the words out. "Did you not hear? They murdered the Archbishop!"

"The Archbishop is not the King. We still have the river and there are ships there. We could sail down the river to Greenwich. You could address them from the wharf there and if there was trouble then we could sail back here. The King must persuade them that he will listen to their demands."

"Madness!"

I turned to Sir Simon, "And the alternative, my lord, is to let the rebels grow in number. We either need to stop with soldiers or with words. Do you have the soldiers?" His silence was eloquent.

The King said, "Then we try Will's plan on the morrow. Now all of you leave me alone with my captain of Guards."

Once alone I considered broaching my resignation but this was not the time.

"I have missed you, Will. When Robert left for help I felt so alone. I am happier knowing that you are here."

I gave him a rueful smile. "There are just a handful of men on whom I can rely."

"I have confidence."

"I had better ensure that the men are ready, sire."

Roger of Chester confirmed what I had heard as I had headed south, "Captain this is almost a full-scale rebellion. There are thousands of men. Most are just opportunists who seek to wreak mischief and make money. There are a few with genuine grievances but not many. I have not seen as many armed men since I served in the Free Companies. Their ranks are swollen by old soldiers. They see a chance to get money they feel is owed to them."

"This will be a real test of our skills. I am loath to shed blood for once it is started then we will need a battle to end it. If we have to draw and use weapons then listen for my command."

"Aye Captain." He suddenly looked at me, "Why did you come back early, Captain? Did you hear of the trouble?"

I nodded and said, "Something like that." The last thing my men needed was uncertainty about their leader. I would keep my own counsel until this crisis was over.

That night I slept in the barracks with my men. It was not a conscious decision but the King had not asked for a chamberlain and I did not offer. Robert de Vere had driven a barrier between us. It would never be as it had been when he had been Prince and I had been bodyguard.

We left just after dawn and took the *'The Black Dragon.'*. Apart from my men we took twenty archers and ten men at arms. Unless we were guaranteed the safety of the King we would not go ashore. Also with us were Sir Simon de Burley, William Walworth, the mayor of London and Michael de La Pole. We had no churchmen. The death of the Archbishop of Canterbury had reduced all of them to quivering wrecks. Word must have spread about our progress for crowds ran down the roads which were close to the river. I began to fear for our safety long before we reached Greenwich. I had thought it a safer place to meet as it was on the south bank of the river. As we neared the landing place I knew that this was a mistake. The mob which was there was not ready to speak. They bayed and they chanted. I saw the leaders, or what I took to be the leaders; they rode horses.

Sir Simon said, "This was a pointless exercise. We have come for nothing."

I said, "Your Majesty, address the crowd. Tell them that you are willing to talk."

He shook his head, "If they reject me and laugh at me then I will have lost all power." He turned to the captain. "Captain, take us back to the tower. We will have to try something else."

The sight of the ship turning seemed to inflame the crowd even more but I saw that the leaders did not join in with the booing and the catcalls. They gathered their heads together. I knew then that they had realised that to win they had to force the King to accept their demands. If they killed him then John of Gaunt would take the throne and they appeared to hate him more than the King. It took many hours for us to reach the Tower and I came up with the plan during that time.

As we walked into the castle across the drawbridge I spoke quietly to the King, "Sire, let me go in the city and try to make contact with their leaders. I think they wish to speak with you."

"Will, that is a risk!"

"I have taken worse. I will go in disguise. If I do not think I can achieve that which we wish then I will return to the castle."

"You would go now?"

"I know where they are; Greenwich. I can take a wherry and cross the river. I will not use London Bridge for that will be guarded. I can slip ashore unseen and make my way to their camp. It is but four miles to

Greenwich. I can be there in less than two hours and back before nightfall."

"A wherry? You will be seen."

"No, Sire, I have a plan. The wherry is a common boat on the river. The bridge will be guarded. If I thought I would fail then I would not go. I would wait here for the Earl of Oxford." I did not think that the Earl would return until he was sure that we would win!

"Very well but I am not happy about this."

I went to the barracks and changed into old clothes. I still had the war gear I had worn when I had served with the Blue Company. The fact that it was ill fitting suited me for I looked like a down and out soldier. I left Prince Edward's blade and took my old short sword. I confided in Roger of Chester. Someone needed to know exactly what I was up to. Then I left. I did not go to the wharf. There would be men watching from south of the river. Instead, I went to The Falconer's Glove. Llenlleog was behind the bar and when I saw him he did as I had hoped. He was quick thinking and the hood over my head told him that I did not wish to be known. I gestured for him to come outside and speak with me. He nodded and shouted, "Myfanwy, come and serve while I talk to this man."

We went out to the back of the inn which led down to the river. Llenlleog had a wherry. He used it to fetch ale from the brewery he used. It was on the south bank where land was cheaper.

"This is a bad business Captain. You are in disguise and I did not use your name but if men find out that you are the King's bodyguard it will go ill for you."

"I need your help to cross the river. Will you take me on your wherry?"

"Of course, but what will you do? Are you running?"

"I am going to speak to their leaders. Do you know who they are?"

"Ball and Straw are the two fire breathing preachers. Straw is not his real name but the people call him that. The real leader is Walter Tyler. They call him Wat. His daughter was seduced, they say, by a poll tax collector and when he complained to the authorities he was beaten. He is the clever one. He knows how to organise. But this is madness, Captain."

"I have to try. I will return before the last watch is set. I will signal you. If I am not there then I have failed and you can look for my head on a spear."

"Why do you do this?"

"Because I promised the King's father that I would protect his son. If I do this then I have fulfilled the oath I took when his father hired me."

"I will help you then." He went back inside and I heard him shout, "Myfanwy, I am going for another barrel of the Golden Amber. I will not be long."

We descended to the wherry. We were fortunate that his brewery was half a mile to the east of us on the south bank. It would save me half a mile of walking. There was still, despite the disturbances, much traffic on the river. Those Londoners who were not trying to destroy the city were busy making money. Where there was disorder then there was no law. They could steal and loot knowing that none could gainsay them and the criminals could blame the thefts on the rebels. I learned this from Llenlleog as we tacked across the river. He tied up at the brewery and we parted without a word. I simply slipped off and disappeared into the throngs who were swarming through this part of Kent. It was no longer England. It was a lawless country.

I pulled my hat down over my ears. I thought to raise my cloak but it was high summer and that would attract attention. I was surrounded by raised voices. Many showed that the men who ranted were intoxicated. As I passed one inn two men stepped out and said, "Friend, come and join us. You look like an old soldier. We served in Gascony. Let us shake off the shackles of the King. What did he ever do for us?"

I could tell that they were both drunk. I smiled, "And that is what I intend to do. I am off to Greenwich. I have heard that is where Wat Tyler is gathering men. He will need men like us."

They thought about it and then one said, "A good idea but how about one more drink first?"

I shook my head, "When I have found Wat Tyler then I will drink."

"Farewell, brother, we will follow when we have had one more drink."

The two of them reminded me of my father. They were my father without the anger and the fight. They had been seduced by drink. They would not join the rebellion. I left them and headed further east along the road which ran alongside. There was almost a holiday atmosphere. There were shops to the south of the river although they were cheaper versions of those in the city. I saw that they had been broken open and the goods taken. This was wild lawlessness. This was not about the end of serfdom. This was a criminal act. The ones who had done this were taking advantage of the disorder. My mission was now even more vital.

The closer I came to Greenwich the more the crowds grew but my journey was easier for there were others like me. The clothes I wore smelled old and dirty. I had not worn them for years. I fitted in with the stinking mass of humanity who swarmed towards Greenwich. I knew I was close when I heard a cheer. One of the preachers was speaking.

Instead of trying to force my way through the middle of the mob I edged towards the side and insinuated myself between the crowd and the warehouses which lined the road. A wagon had been drawn up and there were four men standing upon it. One was ranting. Spittle flew from his mouth. He made wild gestures and leaned forward, his bulging eyes looking like he was either drunk or in a drug induced trance. Peter the Priest had told me of such preachers. He thought them dangerous.

"When Adam delved and Eve span, who was then the gentleman? From the beginning, all men by nature were created alike, and our bondage or servitude came in by the unjust oppression of naughty men. For if God would have had any bondmen from the beginning, he would have appointed who should be bond, and who free. And therefore, I exhort you to consider that now the time is come, appointed to us by God, in which ye may, if ye will, cast off the yoke of bondage, and recover liberty!"

His words were greeted with rapturous cheers and I joined in the applause, "Powerful words, friend, who is he?"

"Why he is John Ball! A powerful preacher and one of those who slew the treacherous Archbishop! Now quiet for Jack Straw now speaks."

The second preacher was smaller in stature and he did not use the same style as John Ball. His voice was not as powerful and men had to lean forward to hear his words. That helped me to move closer to the leaders. I kept moving forward and I lost the words of this preacher. The crowd moved away from the houses and I managed to get behind the wagon. I saw that there were armed men there. I recognised them as soldiers. They had mail hauberks and leather jerkins. I actually knew one. He might not remember me for he had left the Blue Company before the Spanish campaign. He had been a drinking companion of my father. He had left under a cloud. A man had been killed and his purse stolen. As my father had been one of his friends, suspicion fell on to my father. It took Captain Tom speaking up for my father to save him. John Wrawe was not a good soldier. He was not missed by the company but I might be able to use his friendship with my father. I moved towards them. The men were alert and when they saw my moves they grabbed their weapons.

I held up my hands and smiled, "John Wrawe, do you not recognise an old friend? It is I Will son of Harry; Harry of Lymm."

He frowned and narrowed his eyes. Then he recognised me, "You have grown! I am guessing your father is dead else he would have beaten you to death afore now!"

"He died defending Sir John Chandos at Lussac."

John Wrawe spread his arm and spoke to those around him, "See, it is what I said, we die for the nobility and they care not! This one is all right. His father was a wild man and if his son is half as good then we have a warrior here."

"Your word alone is not good enough. When they have finished speaking we will let our leaders decide. He may be a spy!" The man who spoke had a face like a ferret.

I laughed, "Then I am a piss poor one who walks up to the heart of the rebellion so openly!"

"Do not be cheeky or I will teach you a lesson."

My face became serious. "It will take a better man than you to do so. Do not take my youth for inexperience. I have killed men in battle. I am not a backstabber!"

I had hit the mark for he launched himself at me with a knife in his hand. I had been anticipating such a move from one of them and I was on the balls of my feet. I moved to the side and grabbed his hand. He had the knife in his left hand. That was a sure sign of a backstabber. I put my left leg across him and he flew over it. Keeping a tight hold of his hand I smashed him hard against the cobbles. The knife flew away and he struggled to get his breath. I lifted him up and said, "Just breathe!" He gasped. I smiled, "Next time make sure that you know the mettle of the men you try to fight." I picked up his knife. It had a long, narrow blade. I put it between a gap in the cobbles and, standing, kicked the hilt hard. The blade broke off half way down. I gave it to him. "Your next lesson is more expensive."

A voice behind me said, "Very impressive in one so young." I turned and looked into the face of Wat Tyler. He looked to be of an age with Red Ralph. "And why have you chosen to fight with one of my lieutenants?"

John Wrawe said, "He did not it was…"

"Let the young cockerel speak."

"He said he did not trust me and when I called him a backstabber he tried to gut me." I smiled, "He failed."

Wat Tyler stared at me and then laughed, "You have just met Poisonous Peter and have the measure of him already. You are a clever man." He turned to John Ball and Jack Straw, "What do you two think?"

John Ball shrugged and reached for the wine skin. Jack Straw said, "He may serve. We will have to shed blood before this rebellion succeeds. The Archbishop and the Chancellor were just the beginning. The hired swords are your business, Wat. If you want him then take him on."

Wat shook his head at the preacher's casual words. He put his arm around my shoulder and led me to the doorway of the house which was nearby, "Come, what is your name?"

"I am Will. My father was Harry of Lymm and he served with the Blue Company."

"And you are a warrior, I see." I nodded. We were now alone and away from the others. "So what does the Captain of the King's Guard want with me. Are you an assassin?"

I was afraid but I knew not to panic. "You recognised me from the ship."

"It is good that you do not try to deny it. Now before I have you executed what brings you here?"

"You are a clever man. You know that eventually armies will come from Europe. A revolt by the ordinary threatens every king and ruler. The Pope would call a crusade against you and you would fail."

He nodded. "You are clever. I can see that the King has not just appointed a mindless killer to command his bodyguard and you are brave for you have come here alone. What do you want?"

"The King would speak with you. He is young and not yet tainted by the likes of John of Gaunt."

"Yet he is under the rule of Robert de Vere."

"Who is not here."

"No, he is in Oxford." I saw him thinking about my offer. "We outnumber you. What would stop us taking the King?"

"Me and my men."

He laughed, "You have courage. You would die."

"And so would you. You do not wish death, at least not until you have achieved your aims. What can it hurt? Chose a place north of the river and we will meet you there tomorrow. As you say you outnumber us and the longer you wait the greater will be the opposition to you."

I could see that he was considering my words. "Where would you suggest for a meeting?"

I was winning. I rapidly ran through all the places that I could think of. "The hamlet at Mile End would seem suitable. It is close enough to the Tower for the King to feel safe and far enough for you to be satisfied that there is no trap."

He smiled, "You are not an innocent are you Will son of Harry? That would seem acceptable. You know that if I think it is a trap then it will go badly for you and your King?"

"And if it goes badly for my King then it will do your cause no good. We both know that John of Gaunt and his son Henry Bolingbroke are looking for a way to take the crown. It is in everyone's interests for this meeting to go ahead and to succeed."

He held out his arm, "Very well I will trust you."

I clasped his outstretched arm, "And I will trust you but know that I am sworn to protect my King and happy to sacrifice my life for him."

"And that is what this rebellion is all about, Will, son of Harry for men sacrifice for the King and he does little for us!"

I turned and saw that Poisonous Peter and the other men at arms were glaring at me. "I do not mind having to fight through your hired swords; they would not take me long but I fear it might cause you and your people problems if there was more bloodshed."

"Aye, you are right. Let him pass. He is a friend... for the present."

I breathed a sigh of relief as I reached the river once more. I kept looking behind in case I was being followed. Wat Tyler still held sway over his men and I was not followed. By the time I reached the river darkness was falling but it was not yet dark. I had brought a candle from the castle and I used my flint to light it. I covered and uncovered it three times. I counted to a hundred and repeated it. I counted it twelve times before I saw a light covered and uncovered three times. I sent the signal once more and then waited. It seemed to take an age for the wherry to reach me but eventually, it did and I stepped aboard.

Llenlleog grinned at me, "You must have the luck of the devil. I never thought to see you again."

"I confess I was uncertain too."

"And did you succeed?"

"Time alone will tell. I managed to speak to them and escape with my life."

The King must have been watching from the water gate for when I entered at the Lion Gate he came to greet me. I saw that Roger and Edgar were close by him. "Well?"

"I think it better, Sire, if we speak in private."

"Of course and I am pleased that you are safe. How on earth did you manage it?"

"I confess, Sire, that I am not certain myself."

I asked for Roger to stay with us when we were alone. He was vital to the plans for the next day. "The rebels have agreed to meet you at Mile End, Sire."

"To talk?"

"To talk."

"And I will be safe?"

"I believe so but, to be certain we will make certain that we can protect you by taking my men and the best of the rest of the garrison.

We can leave John Legge in command of the castle. He is a good sergeant."

"Are you certain of this?"

"I am certain that Wat Tyler wishes to talk with you beyond that I know nothing."

He nodded, "My cousin has taken refuge with us."

"Henry Bolingbroke?"

"The rebels have taken much of their land and destroyed many of my uncle's homes."

"We cannot risk him tomorrow then."

"But you risk the King?"

"No Sire. If you are alone then they will not harm you. But Henry is John of Gaunt's son."

I saw the King considering. "Very well but I want a good garrison leaving here. My sisters, not to mention my cousin are here. I would have them safe."

Henry wanted to come with us when we rose the next day and told him of our plans. The King persuaded him that he was safer in the Tower. There were just forty of us who left the castle. More than two hundred of the garrison remained. That day I saw that Richard was like his father. He had courage. We rode well-armed and all wearing mail. In the event that proved vital. There were crowds gathered outside the Lion Tower. They watched us sullenly as we rode by. The King smiled and waved. He and I did not wear our helmets. It was another sign of his courage.

As we neared the Mile End I saw that huge crowds had gathered. Wat Tyler knew how to strike a pose and he, along with Straw and Ball were atop the same wagon I had seen the previous day. I said quietly, "Remember lads, listen for my command. Keep your weapons sheathed until then."

We reined in just twenty paces from the rebels. They outnumbered us by more than fifty to one. Wat Tyler smiled, "Thank you, King Richard. I see that you are truly the son of the Black Prince. We are all brothers here. The fact that you come to talk is a good thing. I hope that we can come to an accord this day."

I saw that Ball and Straw did not share his good humour. As I looked around I saw that Poisonous Peter and the other hired swords were not to be seen. That worried me. Was there an ambush planned?

The King said, "And what are your demands?"

"They are simple. We would have an amnesty for all those who have rebelled and no law saved the law of Winchester."

"But that would mean every town and village ruled itself. It would be anarchy!"

Wat Tyler smiled, "Do you not have confidence in your people? These are the same men who fought at Poitiers and Crécy. You have to trust them to govern themselves well or are you afraid that there will be less money for you?"

"If I agree will you disperse the crowd and allow the documents to be drawn up? We cannot have the rule of law so disputed."

"Perhaps we need new laws but I agree that we must adhere to the laws which apply now. Later we can always have Parliament write new, more equitable laws."

The King looked unhappy but he said, "Very well. We shall meet you again two days hence. Here?"

Wat Tyler shook his head, "Smithfield and bring the Mayor next time and your lords. We would not have any dispute that the charters are not endorsed by the King."

"You do not trust me?"

"We trust you but Sir Simon de Burley we know to be a liar. Have him with you when you come. He will be safe but we want him to witness this momentous decision."

"Very well."

We turned to leave. The rebels cheered. They had won! I saw the King glowering. "I needed the Earl of Oxford! Where is he?" I could not answer but I suspected he was keeping away for fear of losing his life.

As we neared the Newgate and Fleet prisons we saw that other rebels had attacked them and opened the gates. The felons were fleeing. Worse, we could see smoke rising from within the city walls. The rebels had taken the city. I had been duped!

Chapter 19

King Richard acted quickly. "The Earl of Arundel has a home close by. He has men. We will seek his help."

I saw that the priories of both the Templars and the Hospitallers had been ransacked and attacked. I wondered where the armed men I had seen at Greenwich had gone. When we reached the house at Blackfriars I was relieved to see that the Earl, Robert Fitzalan had armed guards on the gates. They opened them when they recognised the King and my men.

"My lord, we need you and your men to restore order. I would have you take command of all the forces at our disposal."

"It would be an honour, Sire!" He and his men were already armed and it did not take long to mount them. We now had well over a hundred men for some of the Templars and Hospitallers, eager for vengeance, joined us. We thundered through the Newgate. The rebels had left it open. We did not stop for friend or foe. Many rebels were trampled to death beneath our horse's hooves and, I daresay, some innocents too. As we passed St. Martin Vintry I saw that the Flemish community who lived there had been butchered by a mob which was out of control.

As we approached the Aldgate I saw a bloody figure. It was Peter. He staggered from the doorway where he had been sheltering, "King Richard, the Tower has fallen! The rebels have it."

I looked to the Earl of Arundel, "We will retake it, Sire."

I put my hand down, "Come, Peter, Star shall bear us both." As we neared the Lion Tower I saw on the gates the heads of John Legge and William Appleton, the King's physician. King Richard's face became a mask of anger. He began to change in that moment.

The rebels were so intent on looting that they had forgotten to bar and guard the gates. All were open and we thundered through them towards the White Tower. The rebels were attacking women and butchering servants. This was not the work of rebels who sought equality. This was the work of self-serving thieves. I lowered Peter to the ground and, drawing my sword, rode towards the nearest rebels. I showed them no mercy. My sword and dagger fell with deadly accuracy. I did not know how they had defeated the garrison but had I been there then they would have failed. I felt responsible. I had arranged the meeting and men had paid for that with their lives.

When the outer and inner wards were clear I dismounted and ran into the Tower. We had left Henry Bolingbroke in the keep. If he died then everyone would blame King Richard. I ran upstairs and heard screams. Roger of Chester was with me. We entered a chamber and saw a servant girl. Three men held her down while a fourth was lowering his breeks. I saw that the man with his breeks down was Poisonous Peter. John Wrawe saw me and shouted, "Kill the spy!"

Poisonous Peter turned around and that was the last thing he saw. Prince Edward's sword ripped up from his middle and tore into his chest and his skull. I did not have my shield but I did not need it, I had my dagger. I stepped on the shoulder of the deceased Poisonous Peter and launched myself at the overweight Wrawe. He moved too slowly and barely blocked my sword strike. He was cunning and his hand went to his boot to pull the dagger that was there. My left hand punched him in the side of the head. As he staggered I brought my sword up backhand and across his throat. It carried on and was only stopped by his spine. I turned. Roger had slain one of the rebels. The other had an axe and was swinging it around towards Roger's unguarded back. In one move I pulled my own dagger and threw it at him. It only hit his leg but it made him turn and in turning allowed Roger to despatch him.

"I owe you a life, Captain!"

"You owe me nothing! I was too trusting!"

It took some time to clear every floor but we were methodical and killed every rebel. No prisoners were taken. They had violated the King's home. We found Henry Bolingbroke. John Ferrour, one of the guards had managed to hide him. The King's sisters had been humiliated by the rebels and I saw the anger on King Richard's face.

He whirled to face both the Earl and myself. "These are not civilised people. They are barbarians!"

"They are, Sire, but until the Earl of Oxford returns we do not have the men to defeat them."

He nodded, "I do not blame you, Will. I believe that Tyler meant what he said. These are animals. This is the mob. We will deliver what Tyler wants but when this is over I will hunt them all down and punish them for what they have done. Robert is right, all who question my authority should be crushed!"

A combination of factors had changed the King irrevocably. He was not the same youth who had been Prince. De Vere had corrupted him and the rebel attack had completed the transformation.

"Send for my clerk and we will have the document drawn up. I want the heads of the rebels displayed on the walls of the Lion Tower and their bodies thrown in the river. We have two days to prepare. Earl, I need one of your men to ride to Oxford and fetch the Earl of Oxford."

"Yes, Sire."

He turned to me, "And I need you and your men to fetch the Mayor of London and Sir Simon de Burley. They will both be targets for the rebels. Bring me every churchman who is loyal to me!"

It took until midnight but we succeeded. It was a much humbler Sir Simon who entered the castle. He had barely escaped the mob and was grateful to us for saving him.

That night I was in the barracks with my men. We were exhausted. Roger shook his head, "I am not certain I wish to do this longer, Captain. I thought I did but it is one thing to fight enemies of your country but this is Englishmen killing Englishmen."

"I know. The lines are not clear. I pray it will soon be over."

The rider did not arrive from Oxford by the time we left, two days later, to meet at Smithfield. Henry Bolingbroke refused to remain in the Tower and he came with us. We went first to Westminster Abbey where the King prayed. Then we headed to the meeting place. Smithfield was just a mile away and barely outside the walls. Most of the rebels had left the city to gather outside its walls. They were worried that we might sortie and they had no idea how few men we actually had. When we rode we had more than two hundred men and all of us were armed and mailed. We stopped outside St. Bartholomew's Priory and most of us dismounted.

Wat Tyler and his two preachers were there along with a huge mob. There were thousands of them and they were confident. They were baying at us and cat calling. Many were drunk but not their leaders. The King, the Earl, the Mayor and myself all walked forward. My handful of guards were close behind the King and I.

Wat Tyler smiled as he approached, "You have to know that the attack on your home was nothing to do with us. They were greedy men."

"Yet they attacked when we were meeting with you."

"You have my word, brother, that we knew nothing about it."

The King stared at the rebel. "I am not your brother! We are not even the same species and you are certainly no Englishman!" He had become a man almost overnight. I saw him fingering his sword.

"So, have you the document? Have you agreed to our terms?"

The King took the parchment from his belt, "I have and when I had it over then you and your mob will disperse."

Wat Tyler and his two preachers exchanged sly looks, "We require a further document. We want written assurances that no taxes will be raised unless a people's parliament agrees to it and that no one will be punished for anything they have done in this protest."

I could sense the growing anger in King Richard's tone, "People's parliament?"

"Every man should be given a vote. We wish serfdom to be abolished. We want the ending of the system whereby we have to bow and scrape the knee to a lord of the manor."

The King stepped forward. This was becoming dangerous. I nodded to Roger. We all gripped our swords but all eyes were on the King and Wat Tyler. "Now listen to me, you traitorous dog. You have reneged on one charter and I will not offer a second. You will order your men to disperse or you will be arrested."

He laughed, "You will arrest me with this handful of men? I think not!"

I stepped forward and had my sword at Tyler's throat before he even knew it. "You have lied to me, Wat Tyler, and men have died as a result. Do as the King asks or I will end your life here and save a trial which will be a waste of money."

The Mayor shouted, "Arrest this rebel!"

A number of things happened at once. Wat Tyler drew a sword as two men hurled themselves from the mob at me. I had to flick away their weapons with my sword. Roger and my men formed a defensive circle around the King and, as Wat Tyler swung his sword towards me, William Walworth pulled a dagger and stabbed Tyler in the side.

Tyler was merely hurt and he pushed the Mayor to the ground as he lurched towards Roger and the men guarding the King. I swung my sword in an arc and cut through his side. He fell dead.

The crowd then began to bay. I know that my men and myself were prepared to sell our lives dearly and we all expected to die. I saw that Ball and Straw disappeared. To my surprise, the King ran to his horse and, mounting it, galloped towards the rebels. He reared his horse, as I had taught him and he addressed the crowd. I saw the Mayor, he was shouting for the militia, who had been ordered to follow us, to form ranks. As Roger and I raced after the King I heard him address them, "I am your captain, follow me! No one moved. "My father was the Black Prince, Edward. Many of you here followed him at Poitiers others had fathers and brothers who did so. I am not afraid of Englishmen. Come away from here so that I may speak to you away from this unnecessary bloodshed."

"What about our grievances?"

"You heard me speaking with that man. I agreed to his demands. He made more. Is that fair?"

I saw men shaking their heads. The King seemed reasonable.

"I say again, I am your captain, follow me!"

To my amazement many hundreds did. The diehards did not. I turned to Roger, "We stay with the King."

We followed the King and the mob. He rode about half a mile and then stopped. He dismounted. I ran and reached his side. He lowered his coif and suddenly looked like a youth once more. "Friends all I ask is for you to give me time. I have only just begun the task of being King. I was a child when I took the crown. The attack on my home has left blood on that crown. I did not know your grievances and now I do but violence is not the way to achieve them. Many innocent people have died or lost their homes. That is not right, is it?"

I was so proud of him for he said all the right things. I saw men's faces. This was not Sir Simon de Burley speaking nor Robert de Vere, this was a young man who was learning how to rule.

One of the men said, "We will give you time, Sire, but we cannot have these constant poll taxes. We cannot afford them."

"Then we will stop them and I will find other ways to pay for the men to defend our land."

The spokesman nodded, "Then we will go home. Come on lads."

We waited until they had gone and then the King mounted. The Mayor and the rest of our men had now formed lines against the diehards. Seeing the King return, the mob began to disperse. It was slow at first and then became a flood.

The King smiled, "Thank you for following me, Will."

That afternoon as we rode back to the Tower I contemplated staying with the King but when we reached the Tower the Earl of Oxford had arrived. He brought with him five hundred men. Once we entered the inner ward then I was forgotten and he was closeted with Robert de Vere and the Earl of Arundel. Over the next few days, all the agreements which the King had made were revoked. The rebels around London were hunted down and the ring leaders hanged. The influence and power of the Earl of Oxford was clearly to be seen. As the King regained control of London so the rest of the country, which endured similar rebellions followed suit. The exception was Essex. Jack Straw and John Ball led them.

As we headed north east, with a well-armed and mailed army to destroy the last of the rebels I tried to reason with the King. "They are a broken force, Sire. When they see us, they will surrender."

Robert de Vere snorted, "You do not understand, do you? That is because you are merely a hired sword with no sense of family and honour. We have to destroy them. We have to crush them so that they will never contemplate such an action again. There will be no prisoners taken."

I turned to the King, "Is this true, Sire?"

"Will, this is necessary. When you have something bad in you then you cut it out. If your foot had the gangrene then you would cut it off before it could corrupt the rest of your body. It is painful but we must do this."

We found the last of the rebels at Billericay. They outnumbered us but they were not a match for our men. De Vere had found courage from somewhere for it was he who led the attack. Mailed horsemen against men who fought with old swords and pitchforks was not a battle. I was just grateful that my men and I were not asked to take part. I would have had to refuse. Ball and Straw were captured. I was pleased at that. They were taken away and we headed back to London.

As we neared the Tower the Earl of Oxford said, "The King is grateful to you, Will Strongstaff. You have helped to bring about the end of the revolt."

"I did my duty, my lord and was happy to protect the life of the King."

"Good. And you would do anything for your King?"

"That goes without saying, my lord."

He smiled, "Then you would be happy to relinquish your title of bodyguard to the King and retire to your farm and your men would also return to their former occupations?"

I was stunned. I had contemplated resignation but I was being forced from the King's side. I looked into the eyes of Robert de Vere and saw that he feared me. He needed me out of the way. I was the conscience which the King needed. He would become the pawn of de Vere. I had been outwitted.

"If that is the King's wish..." I turned to look at the King.

The King looked at me sadly, "It is Will. A new start would be for the best." He smiled, "I have gifts for you and your men to show my gratitude."

"Thank you, Sire, you have ever been a generous King."

My life as the King's bodyguard was over and I had handed him into the clutches of the most evil and venal man in the land.

Epilogue

Eleanor and I were married in Stratford in late August. The King had given me a large chest of gold and silver for my services. It was guilt money. The last of the Guards were also given good stipends. They came with me to my farm for we did not wish to go our separate ways just yet. They slept in my barn. It meant that there were others in the church when Father Abelard married Eleanor and I. They stayed two days more and then left. I had led a band of brothers for a short time but my life as a warrior appeared to be over. I would be a farmer from now on.

I was not sure that I was ready. What I did not know was that Fate, or perhaps God, had not finished with me yet. I would still be needed to protect the crown of England. I would have to go to war again but that was in the future. That was after the death of Robert de Vere, Earl of Oxford and Duke of Ireland. Until then I would sheathe my sword and plough my land.

Eleanor seemed to understand my mood. She had kept the farm going while I had been in London and she was the one, over the next year, who taught me how to be a farmer. I still practised each day with my sword and I rode three or four times a week so that Star would not forget me but, for a while, I ceased to be a warrior and became a farmer, a husband and then a father. My dream had been fulfilled. I had done that which I had promised my father and my shield brothers. I was a gentleman. Now that was not enough.

The End

Glossary

Chevauchée- a raid by mounted men

Hovel- a simple bivouac used when no tents were available

Mêlée- a medieval fight between knights

Sallet/bascinet- medieval helmets of the simplest type: round

with a neck protector

Historical Notes

I have changed the time scale to make my novel faster paced. Apologies to the purists but it is a work of fiction. The main events occurred in 1170. Sir John Chandos died at the bridge of Lussac. Edward of Angoulême died in Gascony and Prince Edward was so ill that he attended the siege of Limoges on a litter. He then returned to England with his son, Richard. The battle at the bridge of Lussac happened the way I wrote it and the events leading to the end of the Peasant's revolt were as written. King Richard, when the Mayor had stabbed Wat Tyler, led the mob away shouting, follow me, 'I am your captain'. They did. The improbable course of events is not fictitious. Robert de Vere did become close to the King. He was very young. His enemies and those of King Richard said that the two had a homosexual relationship. There is no evidence of that. John Ball's sermon was the one he preached.

This is the start of a series which will cover the kings of England up to Richard III. Like my other novels, you will see English history through the eyes of the men who made England the country it became: the warriors. Will Strongstaff will return. The next book in the series will be 'To Murder a King'.

Books used in the research:

- The Tower of London -Lapper and Parnell (Osprey)
- English Medieval Knight 1300-1400-Gravett
- The Castles of Edward 1 in Wales- Gravett
- Norman Stone Castles- Gravett
- The Armies of Crécy and Poitiers- Rothero
- The Armies of Agincourt- Rothero
- Henry V and the conquest of France- Knight and Turner

For the English maps, I have used the original Ordnance survey maps. Produced by the army in the 19th century they show England before modern developments and, in most cases, are pre-industrial revolution. Produced by Cassini they are a useful tool for a historian.

I also discovered a good website. http://orbis.stanford.edu/. This allows a reader to plot any two places in the Roman world and if you input the mode of transport you wish to use and the time of year it will calculate how long it would take you to travel the route. I have used it for all of my books up to the eighteenth century as the transportation system was roughly the same. The Romans would have been quicker!

Griff Hosker
June 2018

Other books by Griff Hosker

If you enjoyed reading this book, then why not read another one by the author?

Ancient History

The Sword of Cartimandua Series
(Germania and Britannia 50 A.D. – 128 A.D.)
Ulpius Felix- Roman Warrior (prequel)
The Sword of Cartimandua
The Horse Warriors
Invasion Caledonia
Roman Retreat
Revolt of the Red Witch
Druid's Gold
Trajan's Hunters
The Last Frontier
Hero of Rome
Roman Hawk
Roman Treachery
Roman Wall
Roman Courage

The Wolf Warrior series
(Britain in the late 6th Century)
Saxon Dawn
Saxon Revenge
Saxon England
Saxon Blood
Saxon Slayer
Saxon Slaughter
Saxon Bane
Saxon Fall: Rise of the Warlord
Saxon Throne

Saxon Sword

Medieval History

The Dragon Heart Series
Viking Slave
Viking Warrior
Viking Jarl
Viking Kingdom
Viking Wolf
Viking War
Viking Sword
Viking Wrath
Viking Raid
Viking Legend
Viking Vengeance
Viking Dragon
Viking Treasure
Viking Enemy
Viking Witch
Viking Blood
Viking Weregeld
Viking Storm
Viking Warband
Viking Shadow
Viking Legacy
Viking Clan
Viking Bravery

The Norman Genesis Series
Hrolf the Viking
Horseman
The Battle for a Home
Revenge of the Franks
The Land of the Northmen
Ragnvald Hrolfsson
Brothers in Blood
Lord of Rouen

Drekar in the Seine
Duke of Normandy
The Duke and the King

Danelaw
(England and Denmark in the 11th Century)
Dragon Sword
Oathsword
New World Series
Blood on the Blade
Across the Seas
The Savage Wilderness
The Bear and the Wolf
Erik The Navigator

The Vengeance Trail

The Reconquista Chronicles
Castilian Knight
El Campeador
The Lord of Valencia

The Aelfraed Series
(Britain and Byzantium 1050 A.D. - 1085 A.D.)
Housecarl
Outlaw
Varangian

**The Anarchy Series England
1120-1180**
English Knight
Knight of the Empress
Northern Knight
Baron of the North
Earl
King Henry's Champion
The King is Dead
Warlord of the North
Enemy at the Gate

The Fallen Crown
Warlord's War
Kingmaker
Henry II
Crusader
The Welsh Marches
Irish War
Poisonous Plots
The Princes' Revolt
Earl Marshal

**Border Knight
1182-1300**
Sword for Hire
Return of the Knight
Baron's War
Magna Carta
Welsh Wars
Henry III
The Bloody Border
Baron's Crusade
Sentinel of the North
War in the West
Debt of Honour

**Sir John Hawkwood Series
France and Italy 1339- 1387**
Crécy: The Age of the Archer
Man At Arms
The White Company

Lord Edward's Archer
Lord Edward's Archer
King in Waiting
An Archer's Crusade
Targets of Treachery

**Struggle for a Crown
1360- 1485**

Blood on the Crown
To Murder A King
The Throne
King Henry IV
The Road to Agincourt
St Crispin's Day
The Battle For France
The Last Knight

Tales from the Sword I
(Short stories from the Medieval period)

Conquistador
England and America in the 16th Century
Conquistador

Modern History

The Napoleonic Horseman Series
Chasseur à Cheval
Napoleon's Guard
British Light Dragoon
Soldier Spy
1808: The Road to Coruña
Talavera
The Lines of Torres Vedras
Bloody Badajoz
The Road to France
Waterloo

The Lucky Jack American Civil War series
Rebel Raiders
Confederate Rangers
The Road to Gettysburg

The British Ace Series
1914
1915 Fokker Scourge

1916 Angels over the Somme
1917 Eagles Fall
1918 We will remember them
From Arctic Snow to Desert Sand
Wings over Persia

Combined Operations series
1940-1945
Commando
Raider
Behind Enemy Lines
Dieppe
Toehold in Europe
Sword Beach
Breakout
The Battle for Antwerp
King Tiger
Beyond the Rhine
Korea
Korean Winter

Tales from the Sword II
(Short stories from the Modern period)

Other Books
Great Granny's Ghost (Aimed at 9-14-year-old young people)

For more information on all of the books then please visit the author's website at www.griffhosker.com where there is a link to contact him or visit his Facebook page: GriffHosker at Sword Books

Printed in Great Britain
by Amazon

76640921R00129